THE SHADOWS OF REGIA

BOOK 2

FERAL

BY

TENAYA JAYNE

COLD FIRE PUBLISHING, LLC

Copyright © 2018 Tenaya Jayne

Cover design by Cold Fire Book Covers

Edited by Michael Kennedy.

Cold Fire Publishing, LLC

ISBN 10: 0-9986741-4-1

ISBN13: 978-0-9986741-4-8

FERAL

To Amanda,

artist, heart-sister, best friend extraordinaire…

This one's for you.

CHARACTERS FROM THE LEGENDS OF REGIA

Forest

Half-elf, half shapeshifter. Skilled warrior, now the highest judge in Regia. Has the elven ability to become invisible at will. Can shapeshift her full appearance, except her eyes. Caries a sword of obsidian glass infused with lightning. Mated to Syrus. Daughter of Rahaxeris. Mother of Tesla and Maddox.

Syrus

The vampire prince. Mage and master of the Blood Kata. Has the power of lightning. Can heal almost all wounds and illnesses. Gave up the throne, in favor of making Regia a republic. He works in the Obsidian Mountain, training other masters in the Kata. Mated to Forest.

Shi

Dryad princess. Died when her race was poisoned and existed for thousands of years as a ghost in the Wolf's Wood. Close friend and adopted mother to Forest. Mated to the late vampire king, Leramiun.

Netriet

Vampire. Thief. Murderess. Sacrificial messenger. Tortured by the leader of the werewolves, resulting in the loss of her arm. Possessed by a dark entity. Used as a pawn by Baal, a priest of the *Rune-dy*. Given an illegal, alien robotic arm. Finally finds redemption in the love of her mate Merick. Mother of Melina.

Rahaxeris

Elf. Father of Forest. Former high priest of the *Rune-dy*. World jumper. Strong magical abilities, some unnatural. Loves his family but nothing else. Deadly. No scruples. No morality. On a constant quest for more knowledge and power.

Journey

Alien. Storyteller from the world of Illumistice. Has the power to look inside your heart and spin a *story* from your deepest desires. Can hypnotize you with just her voice. Gentle, and healing nature. Mated to Redge. Childless.

Shreve

Clone. Shapeshifter. Created by the wizards. Has Rahaxeris' DNA. Considered Forest's brother. Deadly fighter and weapons master. Lived as an outlaw. Redeemed through family love. His blood was the key ingredient in the blood lock that kept out the wizards before the war. Mated to Sabra. Father of Sophie.

Sabra

She-wolf. Became the leader of the pack through combat. Lost her sister to the insurgents. Mated to Shreve. Vicious in battle. Loves without restraint. Mother to her people, and Sophie.

Tesla

Daughter of Forest and Syrus. Half vampire. World jumper. Has the power of lightning in her hands. Can manipulate natural laws. Created her own mix of magic, science, and technology. Revered as a legend and the savior of Regia. Killed the wizard king. Mated to X.

X

Human. Necromancer. Cursed by a witch. Has the power to always know the truth. Helped Tesla save Regia from the wizards. The only human able to survive in Regia. Tesla's soul mate. Granted unnatural long life by the heart of the world. Works in Regia's government as an interrogator.

The Heart

Deity. Lives under the ground in the Wolf's Wood. No one had ever seen the Heart. All that can be seen is the manifestation. The manifestation is an immortal flame that burns in a circle of crystal trees. Speaks to few. Protected and served by the Dryads.

PROLOGUE

A hart I dreamed, high and golden: now is sped the shaft and spilled the blood. A wolf thou gavest me for woe's comfort, in my brethren's blood he bathed me red.

–J.R.R. Tolkien

You've heard the stories…You know the history…Even still, you are not prepared as you face the crystal trees. You know there are twenty of them but you take the time to count. Each as colorless as glass, just as cold, just as dead. The Verdant, that's what they were called. Twenty barren dryad princesses, set in a perfect circle around the Heart of Regia.

The Heart is not visible even though you strain your eyes to see it. It lives under the ground. You feel the pulse of it under your feet. Above it burns the manifestation. A fire that never dies, its white flames stretch up three times the height of a man. Its light dances, distorted and refracted through the crystal trees. The leaves clink and chime in the breeze, every note drips the emotion the Heart bids. You can always know how the Heart feels if you listen to the music of the crystal leaves.

Listen. The sound breathes along your skin and down your spine, raising shivers all over you. You've waited so long to approach the Heart of Regia, but the beauty overwhelms you to the point of pain. Measure your steps slowly and with reverent fear. Bow and press your palms to the soil. Exhale. Go on. This is your chance.

"I want to speak to you." You can barely hear your own voice.

White light slides along the ground toward you, illuminating roots under the surface like veins, before caressing your hands. Don't move, you'll break the connection.

Pressure and heat flow up as it enters you. Oh yeah, it's good. You like it.

Speak. Its guttural voice, neither male nor female, fills your head.

"There have been many years of peace since the war of the wizards…but now, is Regia truly safe?"

Sparks snap around the tops of the flames as the Heart laughs at your question. *Safety is an illusion. Regia is protected. That is all.*

"Tell me what you fear."

The past and that it will repeat itself. I have done what I can to guard against my chosen ones falling into the patterns of their ancestors…but they are confused. I watch their branches stretch to the sky. The first resurrected generation has reached adulthood. I love them...I fear losing them to their own vice...I suppose I am no different than most. I confess I love and so I fear losing what I love.

"I fear losing what I love as well...If I love nothing, then I will have no fear."

If you love nothing, you have no life. If you choose to truly love nothing, step into the flames and I will absorb you. It will be a mercy killing.

The light pulls tighter on your hands, jerking you forward. "No...please," you beg.

The Heart laughs again as the light releases you. You scramble to your feet and back away only to bump into something solid the next moment. You turn and your mouth gapes. Black iridescent eyes stare down at you from a striking face. His rough hands grip your shoulders.

"You should leave," the dryad's voice is quiet, but it carries the force of a threat. "The Heart belongs to us. Your presence and audacity is offensive. If you come to speak to the Heart again, I will kill you."

Cold dread runs its fingers down your back. You believe him and scramble through the trees and into the night.

ONE

If only the screaming inside her head would quiet down for a while, long enough for her to get through her sister's engagement party with grace. Sophie's feet were killing her and this damn dress made it hard to breathe, but she smiled serenely as if she was perfectly comfortable and enjoying herself.

The great hall in the heart of the wolves' mountain hummed with people. Hollowed from the rock like the inside of husk, the hall was dark except for the candlelight flickering down from the chandeliers overhead and candlesticks in the center of the tables. The warm light bounced on the wine-filled glasses and winked from the jewelry dripping from every ear and neck. Only the finest was acceptable tonight and everyone crammed into the space had dressed accordingly. Silk and satin, powder and braids, adorned and cinched the highest of wolf/shifter society that night.

Sophie was suffocating. The mixed smells of the food and different types of perfume people wore was beginning to turn her stomach. Then there was the accursed noise. String music played by a quartette, she assumed was supposed to sound elegant, was a cringe-worthy resonance mixed with the clattering plates, chewing, swallowing, laughing, and talking non-stop. All of it was a perfect recipe for pain, at least for her. The sensory overload made her skin ache and her head throb.

Seated at the long table with her family, Sophie's smile never faltered as people stared at her. Even if she didn't see them looking, she felt it. Their gazes, whether they held judgment, admiration, or anything in between pressed down on her like a physical weight, hot and scratchy like a fur coat on a summer day.

Her gaze traveled down the length of the long table and settled on her parents. Beloved and respected, Shreve and Sabra worked tirelessly for their community. Through the years, as pack leader, her mother had turned wolf culture on its misogynistic head. And her father, being a shapeshifter and not a werewolf, had brought the displaced shifters into wolf society, giving them a community they severely lacked before. Proud of her heritage, Sophie pushed down her desire to escape the party, not wanting to do anything that embarrassed her parents.

Her gaze moved to her sister, Lacey. It was her engagement party after all. Sophie tried to look for the slightest inclination that her sister's happiness was somehow false. She watched every little movement, every small touch and look between Lacey and her fiancé, Callen. She'd been doing this ever since they'd announced their intentions of mating.

Sophie looked back to her plate of untouched food and allowed herself a small sigh of relief. She might not like Callen all that much, but Lacey's smiles were genuine.

"It must be embarrassing. Being passed up by your younger sister," Aunt Myrna whispered loudly, leaning close, her corset groaning with the movement.

Sophie's hands clenched and unclenched on her skirt as she turned her attention to her Uncle's mate.

"Not at all," she kept her voice modulated. "I'm very happy for them."

Aunt Myrna waved her chubby hand dismissively. "Of course you would say so, even if you're not... Twenty-two," she tsked, shaking her head. "Almost an old maid. Your sister's engagement must cause you terrible jealousy."

Sophie could feel her eyes narrowing. She inhaled and forced her face back to its bland happy expression.

"I understand, sweetie. You can tell me the truth."

As if you fat, old gossip. "I'm very happy for my sister. Who gets mated first is hardly something to compete over."

Aunt Myrna smiled slyly and leaned closer. "It must be hard to be considered Princess-Wolf...I hear what people say about you. Everyone is so relieved you're *finally* in your own relationship. I guess you were just holding out. And what a catch, I must say." She winked dramatically. "If I was your age I'd be after that man, too. I hope you can convince him to mate with you. I'm rooting for you. There's plenty of other young women trying to turn Tristan's head, just so you know." She turned back to her third plate of food.

Sophie took a drink of wine and then allowed herself

another as a reward for coping with her aunt politely while her inner-self called her all kinds of bad names and smashed her puffy face into her plate. But her aunt's words burrowed into her mind and she glanced around the great hall to see if she could spot Tristan.

He was at a nearby table, laughing and talking with his friends. Abruptly, he looked up as if she'd called his name. He smiled and winked one of his bright blue eyes at her. Her cheeks heated and she took another sip of wine. They hadn't been together very long and she still felt off about it. Why did he want her? Aunt Myrna was right, he could have anyone. Sophie didn't like all the attention that gravitated around him. She'd done nothing to entice him, but he'd pursued her relentlessly until she caved.

He told her how beautiful she was, that he thought perhaps he was falling in love with her, and that he wanted her body. But their relationship was still very new and his moods shifted rapidly, always keeping her off balance. He wasn't the only guy to pursue her, but she'd always kept romance at arm's length. She couldn't let anyone that close. Intimacy was a terrifying prospect to a freak like her. No one could know about her *abnormality*. But Tristan was so adamant. He wore her down with his charm and persistence.

Sophie's attention shifted to Jordan as he got up from his seat at the other end of the table and walked over to her. He yawned and rubbed his eyes as he crawled up onto her lap. Her little brother rested his dark curly head on her shoulder and yawned again.

"I'm tired, Sophie. Can you take me home?"

"Sure, Jorgie." Her inner-self jumped into the air with glee at the excuse to leave the party.

He scooted off her lap as she stood, adjusted her dress slightly and picked him up.

"Ugh, you're getting too big for me to lift. Your feet almost hang to my knees."

She carried him down to the end of the table and leaned over her mother's shoulder. Sabra looked up at her concernedly then her expression smoothed and she smiled.

"He's beat. I'm going to put him down if that's okay."

"Thank you. Are you coming back after he's asleep?" Sabra asked.

"I'll try, mom. If he goes to sleep quickly."

"I won't," he whispered in her ear.

Sophie went to her sister and touched her on the shoulder as well. Lacey stood and kissed Sophie on the cheek.

"Is it okay? You won't be hurt if I leave?"

Lacey smiled and shook her head. "No. It's fine. I understand."

"You look gorgeous, in case I didn't tell you. Congratulations on your engagement."

"Thank you."

Callen nodded to Sophie but said nothing. She headed toward the back of the hall and almost made it to the exit.

"Sophie! Wait!" Tristan called.

She sighed and patted Jorgie's back. "Give me minute to get rid of him," she whispered in his ear and put him down. He walked to the archway and plunked down on the bottom stair.

Tristan bounded up to her. "Where are you going?"

"I need to put my brother to bed."

"You need to put *me* to bed," he countered with a smirk.

She looked down, her cheeks heating.

"Are you coming back?" he asked.

"I don't know. Maybe. Don't wait for me."

He kissed her hand, his black hair falling into his eyes. "But that's what I do. I wait for you. It's what I've done my whole life."

"Please," she rolled her eyes and tugged her hand out of his grasp.

He only moved forward and wrapped his arms around her, pulling her against him. "I'm going out with the boys in a while anyway. I'll see you tomorrow. Dream about me won't you? Kiss me goodnight. I need it. You make me so crazy."

She closed her eyes, trying to shake the weight of so many people looking at them. She hated this. If she did want to kiss him, she wanted it to be private. Nothing about this type of public display could ever be enjoyable to her. He seemed to relish it.

"I'm tired! I want my bear!" Jorgie whined loudly.

Sophie pushed out of Tristan's arms and picked her brother up again. "Goodnight." She said over her shoulder. "You're really not that tired are you?" she asked as they went up the long, snaking stairs toward the top of the mountain.

"No."

She tsked. "What does papa say about lies?"

"I had to rescue you," he argued.

"From Tristan?"

"From the party."

She kissed the side of his head. "You're my hero."

"I love you the best."

Her heart flooded as he clung around her neck. "I love you the best, too. Sometimes I feel like you're the only person who really sees me."

"What do you mean? You're not invisible. Or do you mean your true face?"

She chuckled. "I mean you *see* who I am. You understand me."

He nodded seriously and rested his head back on her shoulder. "I wish I could see your true face. Is it very different from your regular face?"

She smiled "It's somewhat different. My eyes are green, just like yours in my true face, instead of brown. My hair is still mostly the same, wavy and dark brown but I have this odd blonde streak that frames my face in my true form. Weird, huh?"

"Blonde streak sounds cool," he said emphatically making her laugh. "Why can't you show it to me?"

"Hasn't anyone told you?"

He shook his head.

She sighed, weighing her words. "There is only one person in Regia who can see my true face, my destined life mate. If I have one, that is. If they exist and I ever meet them, they will see my true face and I will never be able to hide it from them."

"Even if you shift?"

"Even if I shift. No matter what everyone else sees, my life mate will only see my true face. Understand?"

He nodded.

"What about you? What does your true face look like?"

"I don't know. I haven't seen it yet. I've tried. I stare at myself in the mirror when I'm alone but my reflection always stays the same," he whined.

"Ah well, maybe you're not old enough yet. You know you still have to go to bed when we get home? I told mom I was putting you to bed and I am a woman of my word, young man."

"Okay," he sighed.

"You're not going to argue?"

"No. I had to save you from the party. It was worth it." He kissed her cheek.

Darn, wonderful, sticky kid. She'd do anything for him.

She huffed it all the rest of the way and was thoroughly out of breath by the time she reached the huge double doors that led into their family home. Two guards stood stoically on either side. They nodded to her as she entered. She put Jorgie down and closed the doors behind her.

"Pajamas on now. I'll come tuck you in."

He charged to his room. She kicked off her shoes and closed her eyes, breathing deeply for the first time in hours. It would take her a while to decompress. She carried the party with her. The stress, the sensory overload, it clung to her skin like a thick grime. *It's over now. Let it go. Breathe. Nothing but that. Just breathe.*

She picked up her shoes and crossed the main room to the far wall and up the narrow stone stairs leading to her room. Her room was more of a loft, and it was the highest living space in the whole mountain. Anxiously she unzipped her dress and slid out of it.

She stood naked in the very center of her darkened room, the pain still dragging on her skin like jagged talons. Moonlight spilled through her window, on and off in an inconsistent dance as the clouds shifted over the sky, blown by the wind. Berating herself always made her anxiety worse, but that damn voice in her head wouldn't stop telling her what a disappointment, failure, and freak she was.

It's over. Let it go.

She still felt everyone looking at her. The expectations she didn't live up to was like a solid weight in their eyes. She couldn't be her mom. If only. Her sister was almost a copy of their mother. But Lacey wasn't the oldest. Sophie was. *Princess-Wolf*. That's what the pack called her despite the fact there was no royalty in their society. They wanted her to be a fighter.

Tension layered down the muscles of her neck as her arms began to shake. The pressure was building. A familiar desire pushing under the surface. *No. Not again. Don't do it.* She didn't listen to her own advice. She stepped forward and stuck her index finger in a band of aquamarine moonlight. The light rippled like liquid around her finger and stuck to it. She pulled her hand back, the moonlight color sticking to her fingertip like paint. It was cool and refreshing like a breeze. Other light, other colors felt different. She rubbed it between her thumb and finger. The color changed, turned darker, tinged metallic as something of her own spirit mixed into the light. Morbid relief sighed into her core but shame and fear flooded her at the same time.

Why can't I stop this?

She lifted her finger and wrote with the color. *Hate.* The word hung there as if she had finger-painted it on a pane of glass. As far as she knew no one else in all of Regia had this ability. That alone would have been enough for her to want to hide it. But that wasn't all. This *art* was far from innocuous. An invisible force lived under the surface of everything she painted. It whispered darkness and spoke the language of shadows.

The word hanging before her moved, the color pooling together in a circle. She should have grabbed it before it morphed, but the desire to see it change was stronger. It began twisting, the shape undulated, blob-like for a second then a shock went through it and it froze, razor-sharp spikes decorated the edges. It looked like a snowflake. She only knew one way to get rid of it. She had to reabsorb it.

Bracing herself, Sophie stepped forward into the art. It adhered to her chest, then it sank into her skin, cutting her as it went. She winced and bit down on her lips. The bleeding lines would heal quickly without leaving a scar. This was the worst part. Emotion bottled and pressurized inside her all the time. It had to come out sometimes. And yet when she tried to empty herself of the overflow, the relief was only momentary and then she had to take it back, swallow it. Sophie feared one day she'd just break open like a husk and the art inside her would bleed out like a plague.

She needed to finally work up the courage to tell her grandfather, Rahaxeris about this. He was the only one she could fathom even whispering the truth to. He was the only one she could think of that might be able to fix her *abnormality*.

TWO

The light of nightfall, deep bruise hues with the gilt edges of the setting sun, caught on the metal. The blood colored armor on the three soldiers approaching the aged tree clanged like music, only it wasn't the music deserved for this death. Beauty was withheld for execution. The light bent over the axes on their shoulders, glimmering like monstrous teeth.

The king pointed his finger at the Dryad man standing next to the tree. He nodded, his eyes holding the goodbye he didn't have time to say again to his people as they stood watching, transfixed in sorrow. It had to be. It was him or everyone. He turned and walked into the trunk, his corporal form absorbed under the bark.

Eli held his breath as the axes raised. Cold disgust and fear slid down his spine as his eyes focused on the blades. One…Two…Three…the metal bit into his father. Then again. And again. And again. Deeper and deeper they went. Brute force with a deadly edge. The phantom of his father's pain hacked into him as he watched. The soldiers were fast and precise but reality and his perception kept different time. The smell of death was sweet. Split wood and sap mixed with Fer's golden blood.

Unable to turn away, Eli watched until the end. His father's mighty tree fell and was carried to the flames of the Heart. Everyone dispersed. The Dryads all singing the song of death with their heads down. The vampires left the same way they came, walking in unison, with their axes on their shoulders.

He looked at Leramiun, the vampire king, feeling conflicted.

Eli blinked, the vision fading. It wasn't really his memory, even though he'd carried it his whole life. All the Dryads had memories of their parents. The Heart imbued them all with knowledge of the ugly past of the death of their race. Over ten thousand years they had been dead. Now the Dryads lived again and they were all the same age, and they were all orphans.

There were only two who were older: Shi and Ler. The love affair between the Dryad princess and the Vampire king had brought death to their race. And their love also urged the Heart to bring life back to the poisoned ground and allow life to bloom again in the dormant seeds deep underground. Eli was one of those seeds. Now he was a man and a dryad warrior.

He never met his father. Fer had been executed justly. In that past life, it had been Eli's adoptive father, Ler, who had been the vampire king that sentenced him to death. When the dryad race was resurrected, Ler had been resurrected as well, the Heart pouring his ghost into a dryad, no longer a vampire.

Past life, long over, still haunted, and cast shadows inside Eli's heart. It was justice. It was ancient history… It still stung.

Darkness surrounded him as he waited. He closed his eyes and leaned back against a tree trunk just as Lex came up beside him and socked him in the shoulder.

"Wake up." Lex smiled.

"I'm awake, jerk."

"You look glazed."

Eli blinked and rubbed his eyes. "Death memories…"

"Caught you off guard? I hate when that happens."

"Where's Rom and Sen?"

"They'll be here. Ara found out and wanted to come."

Eli swore. "How did she find out?"

"Rom. He's got it bad for her. Apparently, he talks a lot while *amorous*…And she's got this notion she can be a warrior or something like that. I don't see it. I think she just wants to mate a warrior."

"Well, she's got Rom then."

Lex smirked and shook his head. "She wants you, bro."

Eli frowned. "The hell? That's not happening. She's not for me."

"Apparently no one is. You're too picky."

"No. I don't have time for that shit and I never will."

"Don't let Ler or Shi hear you say that. You'll get the procreation lecture. *You are generation one. It's your duty to bring the next to life.*" Lex's snicker faded as he stared off into to distance. "You're lucky to be out so far away from the Heart. It's quiet out here on the fringe. I'm rooted right in the middle of everything and I'm treated like the prince."

"You'll get no envy or pity from me, Little X."

Lex groaned. "*Please* don't revive that title. I've only just broken Shi from calling me that. What possessed her and Ler to name me after X is beyond me. You have no idea how many times people ask me if I think I'm like him, or if I'll follow his example and save Regia from some great peril." He shook his head and rolled his eyes. "X is awesome, but what do I have in common with a human necromancer? Stupid."

Eli grinned. "I bet you'd take Tesla off his hands though."

"Yeah. Love it when she visits. She and I are so happy

in my dreams…Too bad our kind can't crossbreed the way the other races can."

"You don't really mean that." Eli's voice was sharp.

"No. You're right. I can appreciate beauty where I see it, but that's all. I'd rather cut off my hands than put them on a woman of another race. That type of disgusting love killed my parents."

"The shadow sand killed your parents."

"The sand wouldn't have been brought here if it weren't for Shi and Ler having no regard for the boundaries of reality."

"You speak pretty harshly of your family. At least Shi is your actual aunt. No one else of this generation can claim kin ties like that."

Lex's face hardened. "My death memories are not only of my mother and father. I died that day, too. My mother was pregnant with me when she died."

Eli pursed his lips and nodded but didn't comment. He'd wondered about Lex's death memories but had never asked. Everyone's were different. Almost all were of their parents dying on the day the Shadow Sand was brought in from the vampire lands, destroying their ecosystem and creating an instant and deadly addiction in the dryads. Eli had echoes of that day in his subconscious from his mother's death, but his strongest death memories were always of his father being executed.

Lex paced for a moment. "Shi and Ler are my adoptive parents, as much as they are to you...to all of us. I love them."

"Never thought you didn't. Memories of a past we didn't live through is sometimes...*conflicting*."

"The Heart doesn't want us to ruin everything like they did. So it makes us remember."

"I guess." Eli straightened up and bound his long dark blonde hair back, anxious for the fight coming his way. He could burn off the scratchy emotions churning inside him with a good brawl with the wolves. Rom and Sen arrived silently but Eli felt them coming. They slid through the darkening shadows, their corporal feet falling on the ground sending vibrations into the earth.

Lex elbowed Rom, knocking the smaller dryad off balance. "Took your time. Couldn't shake Ara?"

"At least I have a woman, which is more than I can say for you losers." Rom lifted his head smugly, drawing himself up to his full height, still four inches shorter than the rest of them.

"Lucky for you Eli doesn't want her, or you wouldn't have her anymore," Lex teased.

Sen snickered and Rom glared at Eli, who in turn

glared at Lex.

"Stop it, Shit-starter," Eli ordered. "The only fighting we're going to do is with those jerk wolves once they show up. You got a problem with me?" he asked Rom.

"You after Ara?"

"No."

"I've got no problem then."

"Good." Eli turned and snorted. "Hear that? I bet they think they're being stealthy."

The others all chuckled.

"Can literally hear them a mile away. I bet that's how far those wolves are," Lex said.

"Let's move further out," Eli said.

"How far?" Sen asked.

"As far as we can go."

The four of them headed toward the sound of the werewolves coming their way. At a quarter mile, Lex began to slow his pace.

"I can't go much further. The pull in my back is starting to hurt."

"Me too," Rom said.

"And me," Sen added.

Eli didn't feel it yet because his tree was on the outskirts of the forest. The other three were rooted close to the Heart. This was as far as the end of their invisible tether would allow. It was the worst thing about being a dryad. You were bound to your tree and could only go so far, a few miles at most.

"This is a good place. The ground is uneven. It will up the challenge," Eli said. "We need to train harder."

The four of them faced the werewolves as they came up the slope through the darkness. Callen, Ansel, Satran, and Tristan climbed over the boulders on the incline where they waited for them. This would be the fourth time the eight of them met like this. But this was the first time they had faced off in this location. Usually, they were further in, closer to the Wood.

There was only one rule, no weapons. Eli's eyes flashed as hot as the rage he felt when he caught sight of the axe strapped to Tristan's back. The four wolves stood in a defiant line facing the four dryads. Eli crossed his arms over his chest and glared at Tristan, demanding an explanation to the offensive weapon with only his expression.

Tristan smirked and then gave an unconvincing theatrical start and unhooked the axe, placing it on the ground. "How embarrassing. I'm sorry. I forgot I had that on."

"The hell you did!" Sen barked out. "You've got a nerve."

Eli gritted his teeth, wishing Sen had just ignored Tristan, but now he'd given him just what the prick wanted.

"I'm sorry," Tristan said again, his sappy apologetic tone in sharp contrast with the glint in his eyes. "I was doing some clearing near the Lair's edge today. Oh, forgive me, I know you don't like to hear about trees being cut down. You garden gnomes are so sensitive. It's a good thing I left my machete and pruning shears behind."

Lex laughed darkly. "Since we beat you so badly every time we meet like this, I guess you've decided to up your game with trash talk. I know that's not the only thing your pretty mouth is good for."

"Ooooooohh," Eli, Sen, and Rom all said together before laughing.

Tristan's nostrils flared, then his lips curved in a sneer. "Been thinking about my mouth, have you?"

"Maybe. It looks just like your mother's."

"At least I had a mother. All of you are nothing but walking, talking plants."

All four dryads chuckled at his weak insult.

"Perhaps it's your lack of understanding what we are that makes it so easy for us to hand your asses to you every time we fight," Rom interjected. "But you're short on understanding since you're nothing but a pack of mongrels. I doubt any of you know how to sit or fetch."

"We only let you win because we have such an unfair advantage in, well, everything else," Ansel chimed in. "I mean really, you're so geographically challenged, and if we wanted to rid the world of you, a little arson, and you're all dead."

The smile on Lex's face absorbed into a hard mask. He took a step forward and pointed at Ansel. "You're mine." His voice was deadly cold. "You and me go first."

Ansel frowned and looked unsure, glancing at Tristan. Tristan nodded and gave him a little shove forward. Eli, Rom, and Sen backed up as Ansel moved toward Lex.

Eli's gaze cut through the fight before it began. Ansel outweighed Lex but Lex had a longer reach. Lex was pissed off, so that would either make him fight better or make him sloppy. Eli wanted their fight to be fast so he could take on Tristan. He was going to teach him a stern lesson in manners. Bringing that axe hit a nerve with Eli.

Lex and Ansel stripped off their shirts, the moonlight illuminating the planes of their muscles. Ansel began circling, but Lex charged straight at him, tackling him to the ground. Dirt flew into the air as Lex pummeled him with his fists and Ansel tried to get away. If he didn't get out, this was going to be over in another couple seconds with the hammering he was getting in the face. He twisted around and brought his knee up into Lex's side, knocking him sideways long enough to get loose. Both of them were on their feet again.

A tremor went over Ansel's skin as he started to shift into beast form.

"No, you don't," Lex said dropping down and sweeping Ansel's legs out from under him.

He coughed as the wind was knocked from his lungs when he hit the ground. He stopped shifting. Callen, Satran, and Tristan all yelled out in anger, grumbling about unfairness.

Ansel got to his feet, his face bloody and starting to swell up from Lex's initial pummeling. He wiped the blood from his nose and held his hand up in surrender but just as Lex dropped his guard, Ansel surged forward and cracked him in the face with a head-butt. His head snapped back and he stumbled once but Lex remained on his feet.

The next moment they were grappling, clinched together, both trying to land body blows and break ribs. Ansel grabbed Lex in a bear hug and threw him in the direction of the boulder-covered slope. Everyone gasped but he didn't go over the edge. It looked like Lex slammed into an invisible wall. He'd reach the very end of his tether.

Ansel roared and charged at him.

"No! Stop!" Eli shouted.

Ansel plowed into Lex, trying to shove him over the edge. Lex caught him with an uppercut and sidestepped. Dazed, Ansel stumbled toward the edge. Lex reached out, grasping the air wildly but the invisible wall made it impossible for him to grab Ansel. He fell over the edge onto the rocks. Everyone rushed forward. It wasn't that far of a drop, but the second Eli looked down, he knew Ansel was dead. His head was broken open over the rock he landed on.

Shock held them all in silence for a few seconds. Lex seemed to deflate next to Eli, going down onto his hands and knees, his breathing raspy.

"I couldn't...I couldn't reach him."

Callen, Tristan, and Satran rushed to Ansel's body. Satran began crying, clasping Ansel to his chest. Eli hadn't noticed the family resemblance between them until that moment. Ansel and Satran were brothers.

Eli froze on the horrible thought of what happens now? It was an accident, but in the next seconds, what would it lead to? What was supposed to be harmless fun was now anything but.

Callen pointed up at Lex. "He pushed him!"

"No, he didn't!" Rom barked. "Ansel tripped."

Satran and Callen began shouting. Lex remained silent, his gaze still glued to Ansel's mangled body. Rage burning in their eyes, Satran and Callen climbed up the boulders. More were going to die, Eli realized. Where was Tristan? Just as he thought it, Tristan charged up beside them, his axe raised over his head.

"NO!" Eli shouted.

The moonlight slid along the axe as it came down in a killing strike to Lex. Eli held his breath as he stepped in between his friend and death, catching the blade with his forearm instead. The blade sliced down to the bone but it was dull or it would have cut Eli's arm off.

Tristan's eyes bugged as Eli jerked the axe out of his hands. He took advantage of everyone's momentary shock, reached down, pulled Lex to his feet and took a step back from the wolves. Rom and Sen followed his lead, backing away.

"This was an accident." Eli didn't even recognize his own voice as he said it. "See to your dead. Let's not turn this tragedy into something worse."

Blood surged out of the gaping wound on his arm. The pain was unimaginable, but he ignored it for the moment. They had to get out of there. The wolves stared at them as they left, but they didn't move to follow.

As soon as they were too far away for the wolves to see or hear them, Eli leaned back against a tree, panting.

Lex looked at his wound and swore. "Geez, you're bleeding a freakin' river. Sen, give me your shirt."

Sen took it off and handed it to Lex. He tore it into strips and tied them around Eli's split flesh.

"If we don't get him to the Heart soon, he's going to bleed to death," Rom said.

Eli's vision began to tremble and darken. His friends held him up and began carrying him. In spite of his head swimming and the pain, his grip on Tristan's axe never slackened. He needed it. He couldn't think why. He couldn't think at all, but nothing was going to make him let go of it.

Consciousness drifted in and out and he grew cold, colder than he had ever been.

"What happened?" Shi's panicked voice broke through the haze along with the sensation of her soft hands on his face.

The white flames of the manifestation overtook his vision as his wounded arm was placed in the fire. All he could see was white and heat filled his body down to his bones. The rushing quickly became overwhelming. The sensation its own warning that too much direct contact with the Heart was dangerous, potentially deadly. Outside of the dryads, only Tesla, X, and Journey could touch the Heart and come away unscathed. Lucidity returned slowly as the flames sewed his arm back together with strands of energy.

Why are you holding an axe, Eli? The Heart asked inside his mind.

"I need it. I don't know why. I just do. It's important."

Keep it safe then...You're physically healed now. Try to stay that way.

"I'll try."

He pulled his perfectly healed arm from the fire the wound now a straight scar. He turned, confronted by many worried sets of eyes. Lex, Sen, and Rom all stood off to the side as Shi and Ler came at him, Shi fussing, and Ler tossing questions at him in quick succession. Shi's pregnant belly bumped into his stomach as she hugged him.

"I'm fine," he reassured her. "But there's been a terrible accident I fear will lead to other problems."

He exhaled and began to tell them how Ansel died. He didn't get very far into his explanation when Ler stopped him and turned to Shi.

"I'll deal with this." He kissed her forehead and

smoothed her hair. "Go rest." He laid his hand on her stomach for a second.

Shi's worried, maternal gaze cut to Eli and then to the others. "Alright...Don't be too hard on them, Ler."

He kissed her again. She nodded and turned away, going to her tree and was absorbed into the trunk.

Ler crossed his arms. "Alright, give me the rest of it, *unedited*."

"Yes, sir." Eli's hands tightened on the axe handle and he was seized with a second of madness, imagining striking Ler with it. Confused and instantly contrite, he shook himself and continued to tell his adopted father the whole story. As his words hit the air, they seemed to circle back to him and cling painfully to his shoulders. "It's my fault...fighting like that was my idea, but I never meant it for anything but to help us train. I swear."

Ler sighed deeply and clapped Eli on the shoulder. "I know you would never mean anything like this to happen. And you saved Lex's life...Accidents happen. I would go to Sabra right now, offer our condolences to the family of the dead, but I cannot travel that far. None of us can. We will have to wait for them to come to us."

"What if this goes sideways? I don't trust them to be honest. Should we prepare for battle, father?" Lex asked.

Ler paced for a moment. "No, you're getting way ahead of yourself. And they outnumber us so greatly, conflict must be avoided. Sabra is a good and just leader, but she cannot see and control the whole pack. I know how she must feel." He pinched the bridge of his nose and in a second his mood shifted. His ire swelled and he gave the four of them a withering look. "I didn't live and die then exist for ten thousand years in agony as a ghost, and be resurrected as a dryad only to have a couple of idiots endanger my family with carelessness!" His rage seemed to settle on Eli and the axe in his hands. "Get rid of that thing!"

"But what if we need it as evidence? Tristan carved his name on the handle."

"I said get rid of it!" he shouted. "And get out of my sight, all of you!"

Tristan's eyes slid out of focus as he looked into the shadows of the forest where the dryads left. Ansel's death was an unexpected gift to him and his future plans. He would overthrow Sabra and become pack leader...but this little mishap of Ansel's brain slipping out of his skull would speed up Tristan's climb to power if he used it right.

He blinked, his vision clearing as he walked forward until he could see the boundary of the Wood in the distance. The Dryads messed things up. They lived too damn close to the Lair. The Wood used to be called The Wolf's Wood...under his rule, it would be called that again.

He turned and came back to Callen and Satran as they lifted Ansel and began to carry him back toward the mountain.

"I have an idea," Tristan said.

Three

"Sophie?"

"You startled me, Jorgie. What's wrong?"

He rubbed one eye and walked over to her, disheveled from sleep and dragging his stuffed bear. "I had a nightmare. Can I sleep with you?"

"Sure, kiddo."

He crawled up on her bed and snuggled down beside her. She tucked her blanket all the way around him, making sure his feet were all the way under. She pressed her face into his curly hair and inhaled.

"Do you want to talk about it?" she asked quietly.

He shook his head and hugged her tighter. She stroked the back of his dark, wavy hair over and over slowly until he dozed back off.

The peace he embodied caused her to relax and drift back to sleep.

"Sophie!" Lacey's urgent whisper jolted her.

She opened her eyes, taking stock of the moonlight. It was almost the dead middle of the night.

"What's wrong?" she asked, trying not to rouse her brother.

"I don't know exactly, but I think it's serious."

"Is there danger?"

"I don't know. Get up. Leave Jorgie here."

Lacey headed out of the room. Sophie heard it then, the urgent voices coming from the floor below. She shifted, trying to extract her arm from under her brother. He made a little whine in his throat. She kissed the side of his head and smoothed his hair again. He settled back into deep sleep.

Sophie belted her robe over her pajamas and headed down the narrow stone stairs from her bedroom to the main living space in their home at the top of the mountain. The scene hit her hard in the stomach. Tristan was there, his face bloodied like he'd been in a fight. Callen leaned against the wall, holding his ribs gingerly as if they were broken, his face was swollen and bloodied as well.

"How many were there?" Sabra asked Tristan.

"I don't know for sure. At least ten. They came out of the shadows and just attacked. We didn't know they were there. If we went over some boundary line, we didn't know it. They never said anything..." Tristan's voice broke. "All we did was try to defend

37

ourselves...and now Ansel's dead. He's dead!" he looked past her mother and locked his gaze on her. "Sophie..."

The plea in his voice tore at her heart. She came forward. He clasped her tightly against him. She held him back, trying to offer whatever comfort she could. He let go and took a step back from her, wiping the tears from his cheeks.

"I will go to the Dryads at first light and get to the bottom of this," Sabra said.

"Please don't go alone," Callen's voice was adamant. "It could be dangerous."

Sabra gave him a half smile. "Don't worry. And before we know all the facts, let's keep this to ourselves. Ansel's killers will answer for this, make no mistake. But the actions of one or a few doesn't mean we have a problem with the dryads. Give me your word, both of you, to remain silent and not stir up rumors."

"Yes, ma'am." They said together.

"But..." Callen began to argue. He fell silent at the flash in Sabra's eyes. She reached out and grabbed him by the throat, her hand elongating into a nightmarish beast claw.

"Don't question me. When have I ever backed down from spilling blood that needed spilling? Trust me. I will find out what happened." She let go of him, her hand shifting back to normal. "Go home. I'll meet with you again in the morning after I go see the dryads."

Callen nodded and left immediately. Tristan hesitated for a moment and pulled Sophie against him again for a second, then he left too. The heavy double doors shut behind them and Sabra slid the bolt through the handles.

"Where's papa?" Lacey asked.

"He's with Ansel's family." Sabra paced, her eyes tunneling.

The stress hung in the air like a bad smell. Sophie stood next to her sister and leaned her head on her shoulder. Lacey began trembling. Sophie stiffened and grasped her sister as she collapsed in a fit of tears. Sabra came over and Lacey shifted into their mother's arms.

Sophie backed up, her stomach twisting into a painful knot. The emotions coming from her sister surrounded her, sank through her skin, and made her heart feel swollen.

"He was my friend."

Sophie turned away and tried to disconnect herself from everything. She sank down on the couch and put her head in her hands.

"Go back to bed. Try to sleep," Sabra told Lacey.

Lacey hung her head and shuffled to her room and shut the door. Sabra came over and reached for Sophie's hand.

"What can I do for you?" her mother asked gently. "What are you feeling?"

Pain. Guilt. "I'm fine, mom. Don't worry about me. You've got enough on your plate."

"I wish I could help. I wish you would confide in me. I see you on the edge of opening up sometimes only to have you retreat the next second. It only makes me worry more because I don't know what's troubling you."

"I'm sorry. Please don't worry. Please. I'm fine. I promise."

"Just tell me one thing. Help me understand."

"I wish I was like you, mom. Everyone calls me *tame*. I guess I am. I'm not wild, or brave like a she-wolf should be."

Her mother frowned and squeezed her hand. "Have I ever made you feel like that?"

"No. Not you or papa, but—"

A knock sounded on the double doors.

"I'll get it," Sophie got up.

She unbolted the doors and opened one side.

Tristan stood there alone, looking at her intently. He'd changed his clothes and all the blood was gone from his face. His shoulders slumped and his dark hair hung into his bloodshot eyes.

"Tristan..."

His gaze beseeched her. "I'm sorry, Sophie. I just...I'm heartbroken. Please come with me for a little while. Lend me your company. I hurt so much."

She exhaled, the weight of his request burrowing into her shoulders. "Alright. Give me a moment to change out of my pajamas."

He nodded and she closed the door again.

She turned to her mother still sitting on the couch. "He needs me. I don't know how long I'll be gone, perhaps the rest of the night. Don't stay awake because of me...Jorgie is in my room, by the way."

"No problem honey. I won't worry about you."

She slunk into her room and changed her clothes silently so she didn't wake her brother. Clad in jeans, boots and a sweatshirt, she pulled her hair up into a ponytail and headed out. As soon as she came back out to where Tristan stood, he grabbed her hand and began pulling her swiftly away. They made their way all the way from the top, through the halls that snaked around and around down the heart of the mountain to the ground level exit without saying a word to each other.

"What are you doing?" a guard asked gruffly.

Tristan pulled her close to his side and smiled suggestively at the guy. "Just going for a little run in the moonlight, if you know what I mean."

The guard smirked and nodded for them to pass. Annoyance picked sharply at Sophie. She was pissed off Tristan would say that. It was embarrassing not to mention untrue, and if he was so heartbroken how did he manage to act like an ass?

He pulled her outside by the hand and led her around the back of the mountain where it was hard to walk. You had to climb over boulders and watch your footing on slopes covered in gravel.

"Where are we going?" she asked finally.

He stopped and turned to her then, pulling her close to him and kissing her mouth. When she tried to pull away he tightened his grip.

Exasperated, she pushed on him and turned her face to the side so she could breathe. "Stop it. Give me some space."

Sorrow swam in his eyes, diving deep, filling them up. Guilt poked at her. He let go and walked a few steps away. His shoulders slumped and he sat cross-legged on the ground. Maybe she didn't understand. He was hurting. She was supposed to help not make it worse.

Sighing, she sat next to him and rubbed her hand over his back. He put his head in his hands and his shoulders began shaking with tears.

"I'm sorry. What can I do to help? Do you want to talk about it?"

His head snapped up and he looked out toward the Wood. "It would be so easy to kill them all. That's what we should do before they have the chance to really grow in numbers."

Sophie recoiled from him. "Why would you say that? Kill them all? The Dryads are peaceful."

"*Peaceful?* We were jumped tonight for no reason. Ansel is dead! The rest of us barely escaped. They meant to kill all of us."

"Maybe there's some mistake. Maybe it was an accident and in the dark, it just seemed that way. I mean, why would they attack you for doing nothing? That doesn't make sense."

An odd expression of patience and contemplation came over his features.

She frowned. "What?"

He raised his eyebrows. "Nothing. Just listening.

You've obviously thought it through. Please continue."

"I...I haven't thought it through, I was just thinking that—"

"Ah! You haven't thought it through. Maybe you should before you open your mouth and try to tell me I don't know what I know."

Inside she reeled back from him. "Why are you being mean?"

"*I'm* mean? Me? I just lost one of my best friends. I asked you to come out to comfort me, but I guess that's asking too much. You're the mean one, Sophie."

She looked away. Was he right? Was she mean?

"I'm sorry," the words came out of her automatically.

"Are you?"

"Yes. You're grieving. I wanted to help lessen the pain, not make it worse."

"You can make it better. You can make it all better, baby." He grabbed her hand and pulled it over to his crotch.

She jerked her hand back. "No."

"See how mean you are? I don't even know why I bother with you. You're cold. And you piss me off on purpose."

"What? I do not!"

He grabbed her ponytail. "Oh really? I've told you before I like your hair down. You put it up just to deny me what I like."

Confused and infuriated, she stood up and began to walk away.

"Sophie, wait!"

She turned back. He rushed up to her and went down on his knees, wrapping his arms around her waist, and buried his face into her sweatshirt. "I love you. Please don't leave me. I know I don't treat you right. I don't know how. Please."

"I'm sorry," she said again. "I don't think I can continue in this relationship."

"No Sophie. I know you're the one for me. We should tell your parents of our intention to mate right away."

"Didn't you hear me?"

"It will be the biggest ceremony our people have seen in a thousand years. It will be perfect. I promise. And I'll make you happy. I swear I will."

She tried to wrench his arms off, but he didn't

budge. "Tristan stop! I never agreed to mate with you."

"Yes, you did."

"No. I didn't."

He chuckled and got to his feet. "I like when you play games with me."

A spark of fear lit her insides. Maybe if she could mollify him she could get away. "Just...Just give me some time to think about it. Okay? I'll answer you in a few days. I'm just not sure."

He smiled. "Okay. Of course. I know you'll say yes."

"I'm tired. I think I should go back home now. Will you let me leave?"

"You're not my prisoner. Of course, you can leave." He pulled her close and kissed her mouth. "I love you."

When she didn't answer he pinned her with his gaze. "I. Love. You," he said again forcefully. He stared directly into her eyes.

Everything inside her wanted to pull away. "I love you, too." Her voice was tiny. Why had she just lied like that? She didn't love him. Why did he stare at her and pressure her like that? What did she do now that she'd said it? How did she get away from him? Did she even know how she really felt about him? Did he see and understand something between them she didn't?

He kissed her again and let go. "I'll see you later."

"Okay. Goodnight."

She felt on the verge of tears as she walked away from him. What kind of a trap was she in? She could figure it out once she was home, with her family's support around her. That was it. She couldn't be alone with him, he was too confusing. Walking alone over the rocky terrain she focused on trying to hurry without falling.

Suddenly, Tristan grabbed her from behind. "It's later, baby." His mouth was against her ear.

Before she could struggle, he wrapped his hand around her wrist and stretched her arm straight up into the air as he lifted her off her feet. She kicked back at him but then he slid her hand into a crevice in the boulder next to her. The rock sliced into her skin as her body weight dragged her hand down till it was stuck. He let go and backed up. Sophie cried out in pain, hanging by her wrist. She could almost touch the ground with her feet if she stood on her toes.

He watched her struggle to gain some footing. Slipping and gaining no purchase she was pulled down harder. If he left her like this, the rock might slice her wrist just right and she'd bleed to death, the bones of her hand might shatter, or at the very least, her hand would never work right again.

"Oh, that must hurt. I could help you if you asked."

"Help! Please!" the pain was beyond anything she'd ever felt as her arm pulled out of socket.

Lazily he picked up a fist-sized rock and set it under one of her feet. She couldn't get her balance on it as it tottered under the ball of her foot.

"Oh dear, I don't think that will work very well." His voice was calmly amused.

"Please! Please!" she cried again, her mind muddied with the pain.

He wrapped his arms around her waist and lifted her up one stingy inch, enough to slightly ease the weight pulling her down, but not enough for her to free her hand. She fisted her free hand in his hair and pulled as hard as she could. He hissed and let go of her, dropping her back down hard.

"Listen to me!" he shouted over her cries. "If you want to get loose, you're going to have to hold on to me, not strike at me. If you try to hurt me again, I'll gag you and leave you here, where no one will find you until well after you've died. Understand?"

Desperate she nodded. "Yes! I understand!"

He leaned down and put a different rock under her feet, barely bigger than the last one and more wobbly.

"Wrap your arm around my shoulders," he instructed.

She did but she was just as stuck as before only now there was a small amount of relief in her arm and hand.

"That's some better, huh?"

"Get me down. If you leave me here, and I die, you'll be lucky if my father kills you before my mother has the chance."

"Shh...I have no intention of leaving you here. So don't force me to. Just relax and everything will be all right. Everything will fall perfectly into place, you'll see."

"Get me down! Now!"

"Not yet, baby. I have something to teach you. I'm going to show you how I can love you."

"You've got to be kidding," she growled as he unbuttoned her jeans and worked them down over her hips. Without any other choice, Sophie was forced to hold on to him as he raped her. She retreated down into herself until she was barely lucid. The feel of him as he pressed on her, the smell of his hair as it brushed her cheek, his breathing, and the sounds of his pleasure all blurred in her consciousness. When he was finished, he got her down, fixed her clothes, wrapped up her hand, all as she watched from the recesses of her mind.

He clapped his hands loudly in her face, she blinked

but otherwise didn't respond.

"Hmmm…" he pursed his lips, grabbed her dislocated arm and jerked it roughly. That woke her up. She cried out again as the bones ground together and popped back where they were supposed to be. She straightened up, trying to regain some fragment of her dignity.

"You're dead, Tristan. You know that don't you? I hope it was a good time. I hope it was worth your life."

He slapped her in the face and pinned her again to the boulder with his body, squeezing her injured wrist tightly with his hand.

"You don't understand at all. Listen to me. You're mine. You're not going to leave me, and you're not going to tell anyone what I did to you tonight."

"The hell I'm not."

"No, you're not because you're a coward. That's one of the things I love about you. I'm your master and I'm quite certain I just put a baby in you, which was the point. That's why I came back tonight. I knew you were in a fertile state. So you are going to mate with me, like it or not. You're stuck with me forever because I'm the father of your child." He eased back from her. "And when you go home you're not going to tell anyone because if something happens to me, bad things will happen to other members of your family. I've already made sure of that. Especially Jorgie...just let that sink in. If anything happens to me, a dark shadow is waiting to avenge me and this *person* already enjoys watching Jorgie. He thinks he's such a cute kid."

Tristan smiled his most charming smile and touched the tear running down her cheek. "Yes, Sophie. Take it all in. I know you'll protect Jorgie. You might not love me, but you love him and love sacrifices."

He turned and walked away from her. She watched him go, not moving as he vanished into the darkness. Alone, she leaned back against the rock, her heart beating painfully fast. Being raped was nothing compared to his threat to Jorgie. The thought alone of something bad happening to her brother caused her more pain than what radiated through her hand, up her shoulders, and between her legs.

Shaking, she tried to stop breathing so hard. Murderous rage layered on top of humiliation, guilt, and fear. The pressure built and pushed under her skin until she was sure she would shatter into a million jagged splinters. She had to move. She had to release this terrible urge inside.

Instead of running home, Sophie charged through the shadows, her destination unknown. She didn't see where she was going, she just ran, some instinct taking over her feet while her mind momentarily lost its shape. It had to come out, whatever it was. She had to purge it.

She continued to run until the darkness around her grew absolute. She stopped dead, the air around her moist and mineral. Sophie held her breath and just listened to the black space. The sounds of water dripping and running bounced around her. Unless she was very much mistaken she was in a cave. How deep had she gone before she stopped? She turned around, squinting for some faint light to show her the entrance.

Her pupils dilated, adjusting after a moment. The cave wasn't large, but there was a tunnel at the far end shrouded in a darkness so mature her eyes couldn't process it properly. A thin stream of water ran down the wall, pooled and snaked along the crevices in the ground toward the mouth of the cave. She spread her hands out and grabbed the shadows. They clung to her palms like mud. She smeared them on her face and arms. Here in this void, in this womb of hate, she would transform. Whatever was pushing under her skin to get out began to quake, rushing to the surface. A new pulse began. A different rhythm, a new heart formed beside her old one.

Her entire skeleton cracked, every bone down to the marrow, split apart like new cells. Only when these new bones started to push to break free of her skin did she begin to scream. Smoke poured from her mouth as ribbons of green light undulated from her eyes. Sophie put her hands on her chest, the color of her soul clinging to her hands. She reached inside and pulled out the thing trying to get out of her. Once she had a hold of a thread and tugged, it came straight out of her core in one gagging heave. Raw, unnatural life pulsed in her hands. Disgusted, she dropped the black mass to the ground. It pooled and rippled like a misshapen puddle. A figure rose up from it.

The silhouette stood in front of her like a terrifying reflection. It was *her*. The exact size and shape of her, like her own shadow cast on the wall. Then it breathed.

Sophie gasped and jumped back. The dark thing opened its glowing green eyes and smiled at her. It surged forward and grabbed her by the throat. She clawed at its hands, as it choked her.

"Shhhh..." it crooned. "Sleep."

The darkness turned to full velvet as she passed out.

FOUR

"You're a slave. Get that through your pretty little head. A slave. If I say you die for no other reason than my momentary amusement than you'll die. Your beauty, your skill, nothing of you belongs to you. I own you, Melina."

The voice was so sweet. Like the resonance of a loving mother. Warm, feminine, and refined. Soft hands rubbed her shoulders then twisted in her hair yanking her head back. She leaned over Melina and kissed her cheek. Her owner's light brown hair fell across her face the scent of sand and desert flowers. She put her lips next to Melina's ear.

"I've seen how he looks at you..." she whispered. "Stay away from my husband or I'll tie you down and peel your face straight off your skull, slowly."

Her mistress glided away. Melina held still in the submissive pose on the floor, watching her go, mordant loathing infecting her. Why did she hold still? Why didn't she kill her right then? She could... Why did she hold still?

Her mistress turned and looked back at her. She clapped her elegant hands once. Guards came in immediately.

"Take her to the arena."

Melina gasped and coughed. She rubbed her eyes as

her vision cleared. Sweat ran down her skin in thin, cold lines. She was in her room at her parent's house, kneeling on the floor as she had been in her dream. No. It wasn't a dream. She'd had dreams. Many dreams. This was something else. Shivers pricked her skin, fear bleeding into her stomach. No. It *was* a dream, she told herself firmly. Mel got off the floor, her knees aching, and climbed back into bed.

Restless, Sabra rolled over in the massive bed that had been hers since she became pack leader and snuggled against Shreve's side. He slept deeply. Jealous of how easy he slept she tried matching her breathing to his. As comforting as it was to be next to her life mate, she couldn't rest. The dawn was coming fast, too fast, and with it a day of responsibility. Her mind worried over her task of going to the Dryads and investigating the circumstances around Ansel's death.

But there was something else nagging her...Sophie. She said not to wait for her when she left with Tristan. Sabra didn't have a hard time acknowledging her oldest was a grown woman and in control of her own life...but still, something was off-kilter inside her with regards to her daughter. She always did what was asked of her without complaint, but Sabra saw the strain behind her smiles. She'd known since Sophie was a small child, that she was different. Knowing it didn't mean she really understood. She just wished Sophie would confide in her.

Sabra gave up on getting any more sleep. She pressed her lips to Shreve's shoulder for a moment before rolling out of bed. He roused and turned over, looking up at her as she began to dress.

"Caught some new information last night on the upstarts who think they are so sneaky," he said on a yawn.

"Are they planning on assassinating me?" she asked casually.

"Probably, but I don't know that yet," Shreve chuckled. "You don't seem too concerned, my love."

She shrugged and began to braid her long hair. "You watch my back. You always have, so I can get on with other things."

He stood and came over to her, kissing her forehead. "At least, I can still be useful to you after all these years."

"I love you." She leaned her head against his chest for a moment before smiling up at him. "You were *very* useful last night."

He smirked. "Yeah, yeah. You're always so easy on my ego...Seriously though, keep your eyes open. There is a threat and I don't have the names I need yet to act."

"I'll be careful. You've got the kids covered?"

He frowned then. "I've got Jorgie covered. The girls are a bit trickier at the moment."

She nodded and let go of him. "I'm not worried about Lacey. On the other hand, Sophie keeps me up at night...I've gotta run. See you at dinner."

She checked on Jorgie, sleeping in a lump in the very middle of Sophie's bed. Smiling unconsciously, she leaned over and kissed his sweet, warm cheek. He looked so much like his father. His hair was the same wavy black and he had the same hunter green eyes.

"Good morning," she said to the guards outside the double doors as she closed them behind her.

They both inclined their heads as she passed. She blinked and yawned, making sure she was fully awake before starting her descent down the long stone stairs to the heart of the mountain. When she reached the halfway point she wondered why they were still so stuck in the past. It took forever to go up and down these stairs. Tesla could make something for them to travel through easily and she had offered more than once, but the wolves voted to remain in the old ways. None of Regia's new technology was embraced in the Lair. The wolves and the dryads were the same in that regard. The dryads also had rejected any technology and lived in a *natural* way.

She was wishing for some of the missing convenience at the moment, not just for the stairs, but if she had one of those nifty watches, she could have already talked to Shi and Ler.

As she approached the ground level, Tristan was leaning casually against the wall, blocking her path.

"Where's Sophie?" she demanded.

He stood up straight and inclined his head to her.

"Where is she?" she asked again when he didn't answer.

"Forgive me. I'm just a little embarrassed to answer, ma'am...She's asleep in my bed at the moment. Our relationship became more... *serious* last night. I left her there to go get some food, so I could bring her breakfast in bed."

"Oh?"

He flashed her a charming smile and a light blush colored his cheeks. "I'm in love with her. I told her. She said it back." Emotion swelled in his blue eyes. "I asked her to be mine forever."

Taken aback, Sabra blinked at him a few times. "What did she say?"

His smile grew. "I'll let her tell you."

He turned on his heel and strode quickly away. She frowned at his retreating back trying to analyze how this news sat with her. After a moment she realized she really didn't know how she felt about it. Usually, her feelings were quick and solid, and she trusted them. She needed some alone time with Sophie, but that would have to wait until later.

The morning sunlight was warm on Sabra's shoulders as she walked through the wilds toward the boundary of the Wood. The stretch of forest in between the Lair and the dryad lands was beautiful, but you noticed the difference as soon as the boundary loomed ahead of you. All the trees in this part of the forest were silent, normal. But the trees of the dryads were much taller. Their branches reached further and higher. Their leaves teemed so full of life, the depth of their color almost brought an ache to the eyes. The pale sunlight, filtered through the leaves, transformed in color, bent and changed like prisms. But at night was the real splendor, when the moon caressed them, the veins of the leaves illuminated violet, teal, or indigo.

Her mind circled as she imagined what she'd been told that led to Ansel's death. Her heart ached for his mother but she had to put that emotion aside and keep her mind and eyes sharp for the truth. Her hand clenched and unclenched on the hilt of her sword as she walked.

"Excuse me?"

Sabra gasped and turned, not only surprised but shocked she'd not noticed the presence of another person. Her eyes darted about, seeing no one at first. He came around the side of a large trunk, crossed his arms, and leaned against it. She let go of her sword handle and eased her posture, the warrior in her recognizing the warrior in him. She didn't want to put him on edge needlessly. Stress layered under his black iridescent eyes. No matter what, the eyes always gave them away. Only dryads had eyes like that. Like staring into deep space, endless dark covered with opalescence.

"Hello," Sabra said easily, unable to resist smiling at such a handsome face.

"You're her right? The pack leader?"

"That's right. I'm Sabra. And you are?"

He hesitated for a moment and she wasn't sure he was going to answer.

"Eli."

She nodded. "I'm going to see Shi and Ler."

"Because of Ansel?"

She took a step forward. "What do you know about that?"

"I was there... It was an accident."

"Accident?"

"Yes."

She watched him close up the next moment. Indecision and a few other emotions flitted across his features and then settled into a mask of mistrust. He turned and began walking away. "Go talk to them. Perhaps we shall meet again. My condolences to Ansel's family."

Sabra stared after him and found herself smiling again unconsciously. He reminded her of a sword. The kind made from the best steel. There was something compelling about him. She wanted to hear his account of what happened to Ansel. Not that she'd believe him, but she wanted to hear it.

She turned and continued in, toward the Heart. She

was still quite a ways away and only realized then that she'd never seen a dryad that far out from the Heart before. Once she crossed the boundary, dryads began coming out from their trees as she passed. No one spoke to her. Some smiled thinly and nodded their heads, but most gazed at her with suspicion and unease. It was a marked difference from the last time she'd been there. The dryads were a tight-knit people. All of them must know why she was there.

She slowed her pace as the flames of the manifestation came into view. Goosebumps rose on her skin and she exhaled slowly. Coming close to the Heart always made her feel small. She'd only heard its voice once in her life, at Tesla and X's wedding, when it tied them together. The Heart had never spoken to her personally, not that she wanted it to. Sparks snapped around the top of the white flames as she came closer, indicating it was aware of her presence.

Ler stepped in front of her and took her hand in greeting. "I've been expecting you. I'm sorry I could not come to see you last night."

She smiled sadly as he directed her to sit on a fallen trunk, long petrified. Shi surfaced from a nearby tree and sat next to her, her hand on her pregnant belly.

"You are very...round."

Shi chuckled, her hand moving in circles on her stomach. "Very."

They all looked at one another for a moment. Sabra blew out a breath, not wanting to prolong this. "Three of the Lair's young men came home last night with a body. Ansel. His head was broken open. They said they were jumped by a gang of dryads obviously bent on killing all of them. They said they were lucky to escape. What do you have to say to this?"

"That it is *very* different than the account I received from our young men who were there," Ler said. "Four of ours, have been secretly meeting with four of yours to fight. They have on three other occasions aside from last night. The purpose was to test their skills. They all came of their own free will. The only rule agreed to was no weapons. Ansel fell onto some rocks, off balance during his fight with Lex."

"I see," Sabra said slowly. "Your nephew?"

"Yes," Shi answered.

"We don't want bad blood or discord between our peoples," Ler added.

"No. Nor I," Sabra said. "I...there were no bystanders, no disinterested witnesses?"

"None that I know of," Ler said.

"I will consult with Forest about this tonight at the party."

"The party to welcome Erin into their family?" Shi asked.

Sabra nodded.

"We were invited also, but of course we cannot go.

Too far away. Maddox will have to bring her here if we are to meet her anytime soon."

"I'll give him a nudge in your direction." Sabra sighed and stood. "I will issue strict orders to the pack to stay clear of your borders for the time being and to not act in vengeance of any kind. When we learn the truth...I hope all will be well as soon as possible."

Tristan ran, a cold sweat clinging to his back. Where was Sophie? He had to find her, and fast. Where did she go last night? He shouldn't have left her alone. His heart pounded hard against his ribs as he imagined her harming herself. She wouldn't...would she? He thought for sure she'd run home after he'd threatened her little brother, just to be close to him. Perhaps it was best she hadn't. Maybe she just needed some time to process everything he'd told her, settle with her fate. But still, where the hell was she? Fury scorched his throat. He'd teach her a lesson for making him worry, once he found her.

He stopped short and tried to clear his head. He couldn't be seen like this. Calm down, he ordered himself. Tristan focused on taking a few deep breaths and made his way to find Callen. He needed help. He needed more eyes.

Tristan banged on his door and waited. Callen answered, looking pissed and disheveled.

"It's too early," he snarled.

Tristan ignored his anger, pushed past him and

closed the door. "Is Lacey here?" he asked under his breath.

"No, I wish."

Tristan relaxed a fraction. "Good. Look, I need your help. Sophie didn't go home last night. I told her what was what and took what I wanted. I told her what would happen if she told anyone, but after I left her alone, she didn't go home... I just ran into Sabra. I told her Sophie spent the night with me. You have to help me find her. I need you to go out and scour the wilds."

Callen spit out a string of curses. "This is your screw up. Why should I—"

"Don't even start. I go down, and you're coming with me. All the way, bro. I'll burn you without a second hesitation."

Callen ran his hands through his hair and nodded. "Figures...fine."

Tristan waited by the door as Callen pulled on his boots and they headed out together.

FIVE

The tickle of tiny legs crawling up her arm woke Sophie. The gasp pulling into her lungs burned and felt dry. She sat up in the darkness, a sliver of light slashing across her chest. What happened to her? The pain in her wrist brought the memory of Tristan back, knotting her stomach with revulsion and rage. Pressing her legs together as hard as she could, Sophie refused to give in to the tears. The tears were there, running down her face, but she wouldn't give in to them. She refused to acknowledge them.

Shame coursed through her veins like thorns in her blood. She'd been raped. She hadn't been able to stop him. Her cheeks burned hot. Her mother would have killed him, her sister also. But not her. He'd gotten the better of her. She hunched over, holding her head in her hands as she remembered his threats. He'd trapped her. She rolled to the side and curled into a ball, holding her stomach. Was she pregnant? He'd trapped her within her own body.

But what came after? How did she get here? Her hands lifted to her throat. She'd created something. A monster. A nightmare with glowing eyes...No. It wasn't real. She'd dreamed it, or perhaps she'd been hallucinating. Nothing she'd ever painted had taken on a life of its own. None of her creations breathed or spoke. It hadn't been real.

Jorgie...She got to her feet, ignoring the pain radiating all through her body. She had to get home. She needed to hold her brother against her chest and know he was safe. She needed to wash Tristan off her body and focus on how to take him out and the faceless threat to her brother. She squinted at the sliver of light and followed it out of the cave.

The mouth birthed her out on a ledge. Eyes popping, she looked down. The water running from inside the cave slid past her foot and over the edge. How in the hell had she gotten up there? It wasn't that she was afraid of heights, she'd lived her whole life at the top of the mountain, but still, she was baffled. The perch she stood on jutted roughly ten feet from the mouth of the cave and then fell away into a cliff face. The Wood lay before her, the tops of the trees glimmering green in the morning sunlight.

She ventured to the edge and looked straight down. It wasn't that far up. Seventy-five feet perhaps. Had she scaled the cliff to the cave? Sophie looked at her knuckles. Her hand was still injured from the rape, but her other hand was clear. No nicks or scratches. She faced the mouth of the cave again. Off to the side, she saw where she'd come from. Rocks stuck out of the ground in an obliging natural ladder.

She wiped her hands on her jeans and took a deep breath before starting to climb. The top was only ten feet up and she pulled herself aloft and stood on flat ground. The Lair stood off to the East, only a mile or two away. The back of this smallish cliff sloped down toward the familiar forests in between werewolf and dryad territory. She'd seen this rock hill many times before, from a distance. She looked at the ground and saw her own tracks. Curious, she began to follow them, making mental notes of her surroundings as she went.

The cave had felt so empty, so hidden, and she wanted to come back. Perhaps she had finally found somewhere she could create her art and leave it. Her creations could stay there, in the dark, and she wouldn't have to re-absorb them.

Her mind set firmly on Jorgie, she pushed her body through the pain and ran back to the Lair. Only the early risers were up and moving around in the suburbs at the base of the mountain. She kept her head down and continued to run.

The entrance to the Lair was before her. She skidded to a halt. She must look appalling. She didn't want to draw attention, at least not yet. She hadn't thought how she was going to play this. She just had to get home. Get her arms around her brother and tell her parents what happened. Tristan would die and if there was a real threat to Jorgie, if her parents knew, he would be protected every second of every day.

Sophie faltered on the thought. Tristan had many friends. Everyone loved him and wanted his love. He had influence on lots of people...and he wasn't the person she thought he was. He was evil. She swallowed, fear coating her in bitter cold. What did she do? If she miss-stepped...her heart clenched as she imagined

Jorgie's eyes blank and lifeless. What did she do? She couldn't afford to make a mistake. Her brother's life was in her hands.

She continued forward slowly. The events of the night had changed her. Her physical awareness of who and what was around her reached a new level. She stopped, feeling Tristan behind her. She didn't fight or call out as he wrapped his arm tightly around her waist and pulled her off her course and behind a small house. She looked into his eyes, eyes she had once thought beautiful, and a part of her went dead inside.

"Where have you been?" he snarled under his breath. "Do you have any idea how I've worried?"

She didn't trust her tone of voice, or what she might say, so she just shook her head. He'd set her up perfectly. She couldn't strike at him. She couldn't scream.

The edge in his gaze eased. He looked her up and down and wrinkled his nose. "Poor baby. You look terrible. Come with me. I'll get you fixed up. Walk close behind me and with any luck, no one will notice you."

She couldn't see a way out of it, at least not yet. She exhaled making her heart hold steady. He gripped her just under the elbow and pulled her along behind him. She came without argument, sharpening her eyes to look for weakness. Honing her ears to hear clues as to who might be the shadow ready and waiting to hurt her brother.

She focused her eyes on the back of his head and nowhere else as he towed her down a dark stone corridor to his door. Not that they had been together very long, but she'd never been inside his home before. He'd not tried to invite her over even once. She hadn't given it any thought until that moment as she wondered why.

The living room was dark and small. He shut and locked the door behind them. She picked out the basic shapes of furniture as her eyes adjusted to the lack of light. He flicked on a lamp, washing the space in dingy lowlight. Sophie blinked and looked around. It wasn't the swish flat she assumed the Lair's heartthrob would inhabit. Everything was old, poor, and feminine as if the place belonged to an old woman.

Tristan faced her and rubbed his hands up and down on her shoulders. His smile was timid.

"I've kept everything the same. This was how it all looked before they died. You remember, don't you? You must remember." There was a plea in his tone.

She swallowed, racking her brain. She had no idea what he was talking about. A fire of hate burned in her heart. Facing him, breathing the same air, and not attacking...The wrongness turned her inside out. "I...I need to go home," she said quietly. "My family will start to worry about me. They'll come looking."

He shook his head. "I ran into your mother not long ago. I told her you were here, asleep."

"I need to go home," she repeated. "Please...You were right, okay. I will protect Jorgie. I won't tell anyone what you did to me."

He looked over her shoulder, his eyes sliding out of

focus. "Sometimes things have to be forced on us, for our own good, and we might not realize at first what an amazing gift it is. At first, we might fight, thinking it's nothing we want, nothing good for us. Like when parents make their kids eat healthy food. It all comes from love. Love so deep it would do anything." He blinked and looked into her eyes again. "You don't know how much I love you, or for how long, Sophie. I can see you don't believe me. You're trying to be strong, but you're looking for the way out."

Dread bit down in her stomach as she watched him, as she listened. He was so physically beautiful. But behind those ocean eyes thrived a monster. How had she never seen traces of this sickness in him or the danger? How had she ever been charmed by him?

"Oh, Sophie," he whispered, leaning in and kissing her gently on the forehead. "You're trembling. You're scared of me."

"Yes," she breathed.

"That will pass. Soon you'll understand…The bathroom is through there," he inclined his head toward a door on the other wall. "Go get cleaned up. You're a mess."

The door to the bathroom was thin and old. The lock feeble. But as soon as she closed it behind her, that door was her very best friend. The only barrier she was allowed between herself and her tormentor. There was no window in the small bathroom. No escape.

She checked the lock twice before turning on the tap and stripping out of her sweatshirt. The back of it was covered in mud from sleeping in a cave. She placed it on the counter and looked down at her jeans. A lump rose in her throat as she took them off. A patch of dried blood covered the crotch of her pants the size of a large rose. The evidence of what he'd done to her screamed from her clothes like a billboard. Even if she washed up, her clothes gave everything away. She'd have to wash her clothes and stay there until they were dry enough to wear.

Steam filled the tiny space as she turned on the shower. She wouldn't have even noticed the soap except it was her favorite. Her cold dread grew another layer of ice. He had her favorite soap in his shower. How did he know? And for how long? He'd said he'd loved her for a long time. Just how long was this *long time*?

The lock clicked and the hinges creaked as he opened the door. Sophie held perfectly still and watched his blurry silhouette through the translucent shower curtain. She had no weapon, nothing to defend herself with. What was he going to do? He moved around the small space for a moment but didn't approach the shower. She peeked around the edge of the curtain.

He smiled sweetly at her. "Just bringing you a clean towel."

He gathered up her soiled clothes and bunched them under his arm. "I think your clothes are ruined, sweetheart."

"Wait!" she called as he left the room.

He didn't come back. *Shit.* She'd go home in a towel

if she had to. Pride was disposable at the moment. She turned off the shower and started to dry off when like the soap she was taken aback. The towel was a pale violet and smelled of lavender, her favorite color, and scent. She wouldn't even take the time to try and convince herself it was a coincidence.

Wrapping the towel around herself, Sophie rested her head against the pitiful door for a moment and slowed her breathing. She was in a cage with a monster. Screaming and fighting would only get her hurt or killed, and Jorgie too. *Be still.* She told her spirit. *He can't touch you. You belong to yourself. He can't see your true face. Your body is nothing. He can't touch your soul. Be still. Watch and listen. Lie and smile. Escape will come in one form or another.*

"Tristan?" she opened the door and looked out.

"In the kitchen," he said loudly.

She ventured out and around the corner into the kitchen. He smiled and set a plate of toast in front of her. "I'm sure you're hungry."

Revulsion coated her stomach. She doubted she could eat anything and keep it down.

"No thank you. I just want my clothes back."

He frowned and pushed the plate toward her. "You need to think about the baby. You should eat."

"I don't feel well. I don't think I can," she said honestly. "Maybe later." Screaming erupted in her head. *There is no baby! Oh, gosh...please, no baby. Please. Please no.*

He shrugged and began to eat the toast himself.

"I'm getting cold, Tristan. Please let me have my clothes back."

He pointed with the remaining crust at a closed door on the other side of the living room. "*Everything* is in there. Go ahead."

The hair on the back of her neck stood up. The words were benign, but there was something about the way he said 'everything' that alarmed her. She turned slowly and walked to the door. As soon as she grasped the knob he was right behind her, his hands intimately on her waist.

"I'm nervous about you going in there. Look," he held his arm up close to her face. "I've got goosebumps…I just…remember what I said about not understanding things can be for our own good."

Her disquiet ratcheted up. She didn't want to go in there. "I remember."

"Go in."

Candlelight flickered in the corners of the bedroom. Sophie gasped and covered her mouth with her hand. Her clothes were laid out on the bed. Not the clothes she'd just taken off. Other clothes. Clothes she'd worn only two weeks ago. Black pants, her green top, her favorite fuzzy socks and her pink lace bra and panty set. But that wasn't even close to the worst or the half of it. The wall next to the bed was plastered with drawings. Drawings of her. Of them together. Doing things they had never done. A picnic on the beach. A candlelight dinner. A mating ceremony with her in a lavish dress.

And sex. Lots of drawings of them having sex. And one final drawing, unfinished compared to the rest, of her very pregnant.

The air was too thick for Sophie to breathe. Her pulse raced so fast it became a murmur. Her eyes darted off the wall to the foot of the bed where a life-sized carving of her stood. Transfixed, she moved forward and touched the smooth wooden cheek.

"Who made this?" she whispered.

"I did. Of course. Who else could capture you so accurately? You didn't know I sculpted did you?"

"No. I didn't know."

"I've made other carvings of you through the years, but this is the most recent. The others show you as you were, younger obviously. What do you think?"

Screaming filled her head again, louder, desperate, enraged, and terrified.

"You're very talented," she managed. It was the truth in any case. Sick, twisted, and talented.

He closed in behind her and wrapped his arms around her waist again, pressing his lips to the side of her neck.

"What do you think of my drawings?"

Against her will, she began to tremble. He tightened his hold on her.

"I…I…" she stammered. "It's just fantasy."

"No! I mean yes, but it could be real. We will be so happy, Sophie. So in love. No one could love you the way I do. No one would ever show you devotion like I do and will…Do you believe me?"

"Yes," she said without hesitation. She believed it with her whole heart. No one else would *love* her like *this*.

"Do you see? Don't fight it. Let me love you. And all this wonderful fantasy," he gestured to the drawings, "will become real...I will do anything, Sophie. *Anything* to make you love me."

She turned to face him. He wiped the tear from her cheek with the pad of his thumb.

"If you would do anything, why wouldn't you wait for me? Why did you rape me?"

His expression creased in pain. "I'm sorry. You're right. I should have waited, but I felt you slipping away, and I'd only just finally persuaded you to give us a chance. I couldn't let whatever mistakes I'd made in wooing you ruin our entire future." He placed his hand flat on her lower abdomen. "I felt something last night. Instinct and intuition. I had to seize the moment and I could tell you wouldn't make love to me, no matter what I said." A visible shiver rolled over him and excitement lit his eyes. "Our child was too important. If I didn't act, they wouldn't exist. I love our baby too much to not do what was necessary for them to live. Don't you see? I would have preferred our first time was different. Like this one," he pointed at one of the sex pictures. "That's how our first time was in my mind. It's a shame, but perhaps tonight we can make up for that. See how much pleasure I've given you? See your face? I know it will look just like that as you cry out my name."

"I see it, Tristan," she attempted to placate him. "It

looks wonderful. Thank you for the clean clothes. Can I go home after I get dressed?"

He frowned. "I want you to live here with me now. We're a family."

"Yes, but I have somewhere I have to be tonight. My parents and siblings and I were invited to my cousin's party to welcome his life mate into the family. We've accepted the invitation. I can't not go. It's important."

"Oh...yes. I forgot about that. I saw the invitation. Of course, you must go."

She caught herself before she demanded how he had seen the invitation Maddox sent directly to her parents, but then she reminded herself Tristan had her clothes and knew her favorite soap. His psychotic reach into her life was frighteningly deep.

"I'll let you get dressed." He backed out of the room and closed the door, leaving her adrift in the middle of his shrine to her.

She threw on her clothes as quickly as possible and felt a small relief just to be dressed. It was a thin barrier between her and this sickness. He was waiting for her just outside the door as she came out. The screaming filled her head again as he reached for her and pulled her to him.

Calm down! Shut up! She told herself forcefully. *Think. Don't react. Just think.*

Sophie exhaled and shut off her emotions. Her mind went hazy and she relaxed against him as though she wanted to be there. He noticed, pulling her tighter and kissing her neck.

"Come back here after the party tonight," he ordered.

"I will."

He looked her in the eyes. His gaze probed and dug deep. She kept her mind blank, her soul quiet.

"I always know where you are. I'll know when you return tonight. Don't make me come get you."

"I won't. I promise to come back."

"Good. Be prepared to spend the night when you come. You don't need to bring anything. I have enough of your clothes here to last a few days at least."

When she tried to look away, he caught her chin and brought her gaze back to his.

"I'm trying to adjust, Tristan. Honestly, I am." She thought about some of the things he'd said to her that morning. "We weren't a family yesterday, and now we are." She used his own psycho words about them being family. "Cut me some slack. I promised I'd come back, I think you know me well enough to know you can trust me to follow through on a promise."

His features turned contemplative, then he smiled. "True. Okay, you work on adjusting and I'll try to give you what you need to do that."

"Thank you…I'll see you later."

He let go and she headed to the door, slowing her steps so she didn't leave too fast. As soon as the door was shut behind her she almost let it all go. The screaming in her head had moved to her throat and was pushing to come out, but she couldn't let her guard down now. Who was watching her? She swallowed and made her way to the stairs that would lead her home. Keeping her head down, she spoke to no one as she went.

The guards stood at the entrance like always. Two hulking sentinels of men, heavily muscled and heavily armed. She didn't look at them. Obviously, they were useless. The guards worked in shifts. She didn't know how many there were. How many did Tristan control?

Sophie bolted the doors behind her even if they were useless as well. The locks had also betrayed her.

"Hello? Is anyone home?"

Silence answered. Her hands began to shake. The tremors jerked in her muscles, growing more violent by the second. The shaking moved up her arms and into her chest. She sank to the floor as the levy inside her broke, a tsunami of emotions overtaking her. Tears streamed from her eyes as if poured from a full pitcher. When her tear ducts dried out then her stomach pitched. Sophie ran to the bathroom and vomited until she was empty. Even then, her body heaved painfully over and over.

Physically wrung out, she finally stalked slowly up the stairs to her bedroom. Jorgie's stuffed bear was laying on her bed. She grasped it to her chest and curled into a ball, inhaling the sweet innocent smell of her brother.

Shame and rage mottled together as one word

solidified in her mind. Violated. That's what she was. Tristan had violated her in more than one way. He'd violated her body, yes, but he'd taken more than that. He'd stolen her peace, robbed her of happiness, raided her life plans, and hijacked her future.

Bitch, please. Get your sorry ass up. Where's your grit? Don't you have any? Whose daughter are you anyway? She thought about her parents. Two of the most respected and feared individuals in all Regia. And they hadn't been handed their fates. They bled for them.

A new strength sparked in her heart and she stood up, taking a deep breath. She was Shreve and Sabra's firstborn. Surely some of their strength was in her. But at the same time...

A feral glint lit deep in Sophie's brown eyes. A savage joy, bloodthirsty, and quantifiably crazy purred in her chest. She was their daughter and her father, so good and kind, wasn't always so. Tesla changed him when she saved his life before Sophie was even conceived. Her father was a clone of one of the most notorious monsters in all of Regia's history. Even though her father found his goodness and found his own path, before that his hands were guilty of innocent blood. Shreve was the very best father. Sophie had nothing but the utmost love and respect for her father. He'd always been honest with her about his dark past. She knew he was open about it to teach her things, moral lessons as she grew. It wasn't until that moment that she contemplated the identity of her father's original,

Copernicus. She wasn't proud. It wasn't something she could ever be proud of and if she was that pride would shock and appall her father if he learned of it. No, it wasn't pride but a desperate thirst. She needed to find a new measure of strength. If her father had been capable of all of his crimes, all the death, the evil, surely somewhere deep inside her lived the same propensity. She didn't want to conquer anyone or take power for herself at the cost of life. She just wanted to kill Tristan and destroy the threat to her little brother. If that meant she had to search in dark places and coax out inclinations and desires that should never be brought to light, so be it. She'd find her strength and tear it out of her depths with her own claws.

The familiar pull to create began building in her hands. She clenched them into fists. No. Not here, never again. She thought back to the cave. It was hers. However long it took to best Tristan, until she did and erased the threat to Jorgie, she wouldn't paint anywhere but there. Creating would sustain her when she felt weak or in danger of lashing out.

SIX

Midday sunlight glinted off the sweat on her skin and lit up the highlights of Erin's fiery hair as she jumped back from the sword slicing at her core. She ducked another strike and rolled, turning invisible. She pulled the glass spike from her bun, coming up behind Forest, grabbing her, and holding the spike to her throat. Forest laughed and sheathed her sword.

"Nice," Forest said appreciatively. "I think that's enough for today."

Erin became visible again and twisted her hair back up, stabbing the clear spike back through the top knot. "You were going easy on me, weren't you?"

"Yes. But you're just beginning. That said, I can tell you're practicing. You're a quick study. You know, if you were working for Fortress, I'd say you should be trained as an assassin. I see how you might be...your stealth and speed...You've been sparring with Maddox?"

"Sort of. I wouldn't call it sparring. He's instructing me. I feel a little self-conscious with him and kind of like his guinea pig since he's starting to train masters on the mountain part-time. Like he's learning how to be a teacher with me."

Forest dusted off her pants. "Him being at the mountain, working alongside his father, is making Syrus so happy. How is Maddox doing at work with you? With the adoptions? When I ask, all I get is a half grunt and *fine, mom*."

Erin giggled. "That's where *I* get to train *him*. At the Onyx castle, he's my guinea pig. He's doing fine. The kids realize he's the weakest link and derail him from his work often to play with them. He hasn't learned how to detach himself yet and tends to bring work home...he gets this far off look in his eyes sometimes and when I ask him about it, he's always agonizing over one kid or another and finding them the perfect adoptive parents."

Forest pushed her hair away from her face. "He's really making me proud."

"Me too."

The two women smiled warmly at one another.

"Is everything all set for the party tonight?" Forest asked.

"Yes. The army Maddox hired to get our place ready finished working their magic and took off this morning. Everything looks amazing. Can't wait for you to see it. And my dress...I'm still not quite used to the money I mated into. I can't deny I like the lack of stress around finances, though."

"Anything you need from me?"

Erin shook her head. "Just show up...Thanks for the combat training...Mom." Erin was trying to get used to calling Forest *mom*. She loved calling her that, but it didn't just naturally pour out of her mouth yet. She still had to think about it first.

"No problem, sweetie. I'm proud of how far you've come so fast."

Erin wiped the back of her hand across her forehead. "I'm working at it. I better get back home just to make sure everything really is going to be ready for tonight. I'm nervous. I've never hosted a party like this before and we've only just moved into the place. I'm worried there's not enough space to entertain properly."

Forest laughed lightly. "Relax. It's just family and friends, and your house is more than adequate in size. I've hosted larger numbers here, and this house is less than half the size of yours. Don't worry. Everything will be fine. Calm your nerves. Everyone just wants to meet you anyway, not judge your house."

Erin blew out a breath and nodded. "Okay. I'll try. Thanks. I'll see you later."

Forest kissed her cheek and turned to go into the house.

Erin walked through the gate and out from under the protective magic dome covering the property. She touched the brand new medallion on her wrist, opening a portal to her house and went through it. The end dumped her out in her garden. Her heart gave a little jolt, still in awe that this was her property, her garden, her house. The newly completed construction was a more traditional style than Tesla's house. The front porch wrapped around the front and sides and the windows on the second story were gabled. It was large, the space waiting and ready for the family she and Maddox would create. She wasn't ready for that yet. She wasn't even ready to think about thinking about it. But when the time came, they wouldn't have to move into a larger place to accommodate. They'd only moved in a week ago. It was still like a dream. Her connection to Maddox was new enough, she still marveled at that as well.

Her gaze moved over the lush landscape of her garden. The vast space was rimmed with a fifteen-foot-high rock wall to give them security but more importantly privacy. Their real security was invisible and covered their property in a magic dome. Round tables were placed here and there, ready for the party. Golden lanterns hung in the tree branches all over. White pebbles lined the bank of the thin bubbling stream that snaked through the garden. As soon as the sun set, the pebbles would glow faintly gold as well.

Her nerves rose up and bounced around inside her. She would meet the extended members of Maddox's family that night. This party was a big deal. It was to be like a reception since she and Maddox hadn't had a public marking ceremony. She touched the crescent lover's mark Maddox put on her neck and smiled to herself.

She was dirty from sparring with Forest. Best to get another type of dirty before she got clean.

I'm a very dirty girl. She messaged Maddox at work. *Going to shower. I don't think I can manage to scrub my back adequately on my own. Any suggestions, Player?*

He replied immediately. *I'm taking my lunch break now. Be there in two minutes.*

She giggled, taking her shirt off and leaving it on the ground. She walked to the house, stripping as she went, leaving her clothes strewn on the ground like a trail of breadcrumbs for him to follow. She left the front door open, hanging her bra on the doorknob before heading to the bathroom.

She set her watch on the counter and tapped it so sexy music began to play. She stepped into the oversized shower that was the size of a large bedroom and turned on the tap. 20 hidden showerheads jumped to life, perfectly spaced on the tiled ceiling, turning the room into an indoor rainstorm. The water shimmered and pelted her head and shoulders, instantly the perfect temperature. She closed her eyes and smiled when she heard him come in and close the door.

His heart spoke love to hers as he came up behind her, pressing his bare chest against her back. Maddox brushed his lips across her neck.

"Goddess," he breathed.

"What took you so long," she teased.

He ran his hand down her forearm and laced his fingers through hers. The gold medallion on his wrist next to the new one on hers was identical. Just one more symbol that linked them.

Melina gazed out of her living room window and

smiled. The view of downtown Paradigm was obscured by nearby buildings. It sucked as far as views were concerned, but it was hers, and that was what made it awesome. Her first apartment. A place that was hers and only hers. She couldn't afford a better view but that was just for now. She wasn't content. She would succeed in climbing the corporate ladder, and before too long, she'd be able to move to a flat off the main square where she could walk to all the hot and happening places. A flat with a balcony she decided as she stood there imagining it.

She turned away from the window and went back to unpacking. Her parents had wanted to help her a little too much and she'd only just booted them out, respectfully and with a kiss. She needed to put her things away on her own. They insisted she come back home on the weekend and she'd agreed.

She went to her new and stingy closet space, beginning to hang her clothes, thinking about what she might wear to the party that night. She didn't need to try to be sexy at Erin and M's party since it was just family and old friends mostly. She doubted there was anyone going that she didn't already know.

An all too familiar pang of jealousy hit her in the chest as she thought about Erin and Maddox. They were so happy. So in love. Not that it was a shock to her. All destined life mates were obsessed with each other like that. Especially in the first five years or so. She wasn't jealous of Erin having Maddox. She was very happy for them, but their joy made her lack of joy acidic when she was near them. She wanted a destined life mate. She wanted it more than she wanted anything else in her life.

It was why she held her heart away from every guy who buzzed around her. She enjoyed dating. She knew she was beautiful. Not that she was a vain bitch, or not too much of one anyway. But anyone she did consent to go out with more than once, she held at arm's length. She was a virgin and that was both chagrin and pride for her. It wasn't something she talked about. She knew all about sex and was certain she would both enjoy it and rock it when she did give it up. There were times and boyfriends that had tested her resolve on that, but she was saving herself for her mate.

Sophie?" Lacey half shouted behind her, fixing her hair for the party.

Sophie blinked and looked up at her sister's reflection in the vanity mirror. "What?"

Lacey laughed and rolled her eyes. "Where's your head? You're all spaced-out. I asked if you wanted me to braid this brown mop. *Twice*."

Sophie shook herself and then smiled. "Sorry. No thanks. I'm going to leave it down... That's how Tristan likes it." She added quietly.

Lacey sat down on the bench next to her. "Speaking of which, is he why you're all glazed? How are things with that stud? We haven't talked much lately."

Sophie smiled darkly. "Things are great. *Really* great.

I think we're taking a serious turn or will be soon."

Lacey raised her eyebrows and looked her sister over closer. "Look at you, skank. I've never seen that glint in your eyes. Is he really that good?"

"Wouldn't you like to know?"

She laughed. "I would, yes."

"Well, too bad. It's not your concern. You've got your own man to occupy you and your thoughts."

"Prude," she complained lightly standing up and went over to the closet.

Sophie left Lacey's room and went back to her own. Her parent's door was closed but she could hear their voices faintly and Jorgie was sitting on the floor in the living room, already in his dress clothes, playing with his blocks. He glanced at her. She smiled at him. He frowned back.

"What's the matter?" he asked.

"Nothing."

"Lying is wrong," his little voice scolded her. "You're not yourself. I can see it."

She stopped and sat on the floor next to him. A shaking began under her skin as she looked at his profile. She pushed it down hard. She couldn't be weak. Only behind a levy of strength could she make him safe again. She would make him safe, no matter what she had to go through.

"You're right. I'm sorry. Something is wrong, but I'll be okay. You can't tell anyone."

His deep green eyes searched her face. "I'll help you."

Her heart clenched but she schooled it, turning it back to stone. "Thank you. But I have to work through this on my own. It's important I do it alone."

"But I want to help."

She kissed the top of his head. "Okay, Jorgie. There's something really important you can do to help me."

"What?"

"Until I go back to being me, *really* me, as only you know me, until then, if I tell you to do something, even if it's weird, you have to do it as quickly as possible and without question. Even if you have to disobey mom or dad to do what I ask, you must. Okay?"

His eyes rounded and he nodded. "I swear."

She pulled him into a hug and kissed the top of his head again. "I love you the best," she whispered.

His little arms tightened around her neck. "I love you the best, too."

She stood and went to her room, looking over the contents of her closet. She decided on her brown cocktail dress and cat's eye jewelry. The shimmery chocolate fabric hugged her body and made her rich brown eyes pop. She always felt confident and sexy in this dress. It used to make her happy. Now she turned it into a weapon. Her arsenal against Tristan was sparse. She'd wield her appearance like a blade.

Her mind moved back to his shrine and something dark and poisonous began to slide in her bloodstream. She lifted her head higher and adjusted her dress so her cleavage showed fuller.

You're not ready for me, psycho. You don't see me coming.

"Mom, I'll be right back," she called to her parent's closed door after coming down from her room.

"Hurry up. It's almost time to go."

"I know. I'll be right back," she repeated.

Sophie left through the double doors and started down the stone stairs. Hyper aware of everything and everyone she passed, but she hid it, trying to appear oblivious. All of her senses sharpened and the poison in her veins warmed and ran thicker as she knocked on Tristan's door.

He looked shocked as he opened to her. His voice came out in an odd half word before his mouth just hung open as his eyes roamed over her. "Wow," he finally managed.

She smiled and moved closer, nuzzling the side of his neck. "I have to go," she whispered in his ear. "But I wanted to show you how I dressed for the party. Is there something you want me to change? My dress? My hair?"

He growled low in his throat, running his hands down her back, and gripping her ass tightly. "Change nothing. Have you started listening to me finally?"

"You said you like my hair down. I'll always keep it that way from now on."

He jerked her back and held both of her wrists roughly in his hands, his eyes flashing. "Are you messing with me?"

"No. I'm still adjusting, it's true. But you've been in my head all day since I left here this morning." It was a half-truth. He had been in her head. "I want to be happy. I think we can be."

He pulled her back against him and kissed her mouth. She pressed and kissed him back as if she was totally in love with him. As if she wanted him and needed him desperately. His eyes were opaque with lust when she broke away.

"I'll be back after the party," she promised quietly.

A hard edge frosted his blue eyes. "You better," he threatened. "If I have to come get you, you will be punished."

She looked down and eased her confident stance into a softer, submissive one. "I will be back. I promise. When we get back from the party, I'll spend an appropriate amount of time with my family, just a few minutes will be all that's needed. Then I'll come to you."

"Come back just as you are. Don't change your clothes first."

"Okay."

He growled low again. "You're torturing me in that dress. Hurry back so I can get you out of it."

She gave him a dark smile and backed away from him. He watched her go back up the stairs from his doorway. She hesitated for a second outside the double doors of her family home. *There's nothing wrong. I'm happy. I'm in love with my boyfriend. My smiles are real.*

She pushed through the doors. They were all standing in the middle of the room, her parents and siblings, waiting for her.

"Oh good, you're back in time," Sabra said. "The portal Tesla is sending will open any second. I was afraid you would miss it."

Sophie joined them, wrapping her arm around Lacey's waist. Shreve picked Jorgie up as a black gash tore the atmosphere next to them. They went through all together, the rushing pull of the portal moving them swiftly through the dark before depositing them on the ground in a lushly landscaped garden party.

"Wow," Lacey said looking at the house and garden, then at her sister. "Say what you want about Maddox, but he's got style. This place is gorgeous."

"Agreed," Sophie nodded emphatically.

Sabra and Shreve instantly moved into the small crowd. Jorgie ran to the stream and jumped it in one leap. Lacey headed toward the inviting front porch where Maddox stood, introducing the stunning redhead on his arm to everyone who approached. Sophie gazed at her cousin and his new life mate before taking in the party as a whole. This type of event was so much better than her sister's engagement party. At least outside she could breathe and the sounds dissipated instead of bounced. The beauty of the garden was soothing. She would have liked to spend time there alone. Just her, the trees and flowers, and the sweet bubbling sound of the stream.

Her heart trembled as she thought about Tristan and how she would have to go to him soon. Too soon. Here she was surrounded by all the people who cared for her the most and she couldn't ask for help.   She hung back close to the massive rock wall surrounding the property and took a few deep breaths, looking for Rahaxeris. In this group, she would be most comfortable hanging around him. Not that she was *uncomfortable* around her extended family, but all of them would force her to chit-chat. Rahaxeris would allow her to be silent next to him without plaguing her with mundane questions she didn't want to answer.

She spotted him a little ways away, detached from the crowd. His straight golden hair brushed over the shoulders of the black robe he wore. He was old, she didn't know how old exactly, but his sharp features and red eyes had lost none of their edge. He was her grandfather in an unnatural, clinical sort of way. He was a full-blood elf, her aunt Forest's father. But he had contributed his DNA to the creature Sophie's father had been cloned from. So, to her and her siblings, he was grandfather. He was loving to his family, but he terrified everyone else. Talented, skilled in torture and magic, he was probably the most powerful person in Regia, second only to Tesla.

Grabbing a drink off a tray offered by a server as she

passed, Sophie made a beeline for him.

"Sophie," he said quietly, giving her a small smile.

"Grandfather." She took a bigger gulp of her drink than she intended. She immediately felt steadier, just being next to him.

They looked on the nearby huddles of chatting people together in silence. A terrible pressure began building in her throat. She wanted to tell him everything. He was the only one she could trust. He would know what to do. She edged closer to his side.

"Grandfather..." she said again, her voice low.

He gave her his full attention. He blinked once and narrowed his red eyes at her. His nostrils flared slightly, and he wrapped his long sharp fingers around her wrist, pressing down on her pulse. The next second he took the drink out of her hand.

"You shouldn't drink in your condition."

Her breath arrested in her lungs. "What?" she rasped.

"You're pregnant, Sophie."

His hand moved up her arm and supported her as everything began to spin. She tried to focus her gaze on him.

"I won't tell anyone," he reassured her.

"Thank you."

"Come see me tomorrow in Kyhael...Let me help you. There's a deep fear in your eyes. You hide it well, but I know you, sweetheart. Let me help you."

She took a few deep breaths. She couldn't afford to fall apart. Heart racing, she glanced fearfully back at the people closest to them. She couldn't do this.

"Open a portal for me please, grandfather. I need to be alone for a while."

"Where do you want to go? Home?"

Something was building in her. The pressure to create pressed painfully under the skin. She thought of the cave.

"Not home. Send me to the wilds near the Lair."

He jerked his head to the side and walked toward a large tree next to the rock wall. She followed, glancing to see if anyone was paying attention. No one was looking their way. He walked behind the tree and struck the air.

"I'll tell your parents you got sick suddenly, and I sent you home."

"Thank you."

She walked into the waiting portal. The rushing blackness took her away. Sophie half stumbled as the portal closed behind her. She exhaled in the darkness of the forest, allowing herself to just breathe for a moment. Then came the panic. She took off her pumps and threw them before falling on her hands and knees.

"No!" her scream echoed through the trees. *"No! No! No!"*

Every swear word she knew rushed up her lungs and poured from her mouth. A tangle of words, every syllable saturated with hot blood from her raw heart.

She sank back and sat on the ground, wrapping her arms around her knees. Her vision tunneled but she didn't cry. Instead, the moist membrane on her eyes dried out and desolation held solid inside her pupils.

Life was growing inside her. She didn't want it. Not ever. She pressed her hands to her stomach, not gently. Not a tentative caress. Not the first spark of awe. No wave of warmth and softness at the knowledge she was going to be a mother came to her. Instead, she felt disgust. It wasn't a child, it was a parasite. A virus using her as a host: Tristan's infection.

All the passion of her panic slid away like an ebbing tide leaving a flat despondency behind. Her plans to out psycho Tristan crumbled into tiny fragments. She closed her eyes and exhaled slowly. Sophie hadn't yet really considered what pregnancy would mean in this trap he created. It was a perfect maneuver on his part, she conceded. Holding the fear of harm to Jorgie wasn't enough for him. A baby on top of that gave him not just the upper hand but an entirely new set of cards, and he held them all.

What was left to her? What choices? Did she have any?

Hazed with despair, her mind slowed. She didn't know how to fight now. Sophie got to her feet suddenly desperate to get to the cave. She had art. Tristan had taken everything else from her, but he couldn't take that. He couldn't take something he didn't know existed.

She had always hidden her strange ability out of

fear. Now she would hide it for another reason: Identity. Even if no one else in the world ever saw what she made, it came out of her and her alone. Over this last vestige of herself, she would hold absolute ownership.

She looked around, searching for the right direction to the cave and began walking, not troubling to find her shoes first. The ground under her feet didn't bother her in the slightest. The pressure to create began to build again. This was her window. It might be the last time she was alone for a long while. This would be the only honesty to her life now. She wouldn't hold it back. Once she reached the cave, she would purge it all without restraint. No holds. No boundaries.

All of her senses heightened as she walked. Whatever she was about to do, whatever she created in this short breath of time, she would treasure every moment. Every detail she would commit to memory. An hour only, two at most and then it would be over.

She found the way. As soon as she knew she was going the right direction, Sophie began to run. The velvet darkness of the cave welcomed her in and she felt as if she had left Regia altogether and entered a safe haven, a world all her own. It was a very small space in terms of square footage, but that didn't matter. Art wasn't bound by measurement of inches or feet. Even the tiniest work of art could be a universe, a single brushstroke could make a road into the deepest emotion.

The art pushed in her veins and throbbed in her

fingertips. She put one hand on her stomach again and a wave of violence rose in her arm. She reached out and grabbed the dark colors off the stone wall of the cave. A mix of black, gray, and brown clung to her palms. She spread images on the air, the dark angry hues of her spirit swirled into the color she pulled from the stone.

The first images were ugly, of course, they were. She drew herself out without restraint. The hideous things she created were beautiful in their purity. For a while, all that came out of her was filthy. The lines twisted and cringing in pain. She purged her heart and did not reabsorb any of it, grateful she was able to force those feelings out and even more grateful she didn't have to take them back. She breathed easier. The tension in her shoulders evaporated. She didn't have to apologize for what she felt, not in this place. And she didn't have to carry this weight anymore. Oh, she knew more stress would come, new hate, and new lies. But she could bring them here, tear them out, and leave them.

Sophie closed her eyes and listened to her heartbeat. All the rage was gone and now came the sorrow. The tears were warm under her eyelids. As the saline slid down her cheeks, she touched it with her fingers, pulling the essence of her tears. She added no other color this time. She painted the image of a baby with the transparent pigment of her tears. The lines of the child were rounded and simplistic. She took her time, adding lines to the image very, very slowly. She painted close to her face, her emotions now were foreign to her. What she felt was confusing and complex: an amalgamation of many all merged into one.

The life inside her wasn't her enemy. A ragged resignation breathed through her. She wouldn't blame the child, but she didn't think she could ever love them. Tristan had created a prison for her, and this baby was the bars and locks. How could she ever love her cage?

Sophie finished the painting of the baby by encasing it in a transparent womb, and then she turned away. Her mind reached a flow state now that she had emptied herself of everything she didn't want to carry inside. She began to experience the truth of herself, as if she was a well overfull. But now that she had drained, she could see the bottom and there was something there. Strange lights, new colors, shades, and hues, deep and honest and pure.

Eyes closed, she held her hands straight out, open, fingers splayed. There would be no forethought this time. She would just open the current. Only when she was finished would she look at it.

It moved up through her body from her heart rushing to her hands. Heat smeared across her palms and fingertips. The urge to look was strong, but she resisted the temptation. Her mind moved over words she felt identified her.

I am Sophie. Half-wolf. Half-shifter. I am young. I am strong. I am caged. Daughter, sister... Mother? I am lost... I am an artist. No. I am art. I am Sophie and I belong to no one and nothing except the art within me. I hide in the dark. I will always hide in the dark.

She thought about Tristan. *I am a sacrifice.*

Her hands moved over the feeling until she was completely spent. Sophie slowly opened her eyes and gazed at what she made. Her mouth parting in a small shock that quickly turned into a smile of pleasure, relieved that what she had created with her eyes closed was indeed something beautiful.

It was black, the edges undefined, and smudgy. It wasn't a bird and it wasn't a butterfly but something similar to both. Verdant green lines illuminated inside the wings like the veins of a leaf on a tree. It just hung suspended in the air for a moment, then it moved. Sophie gasped and stepped back. The wings beat slow and fluid. The smeared black background appeared detached from the green skeletal structure as if it couldn't keep up with the movement. Like watercolor, the shadowed background drifted free-form while the outline above was defined and sharp.

She followed it as it moved around the cave. It didn't really fly, more like floated, its movements akin to the languid grace of a jellyfish in the water. What had she painted? What did it represent? Hope? No that wasn't quite right. Longing. That was it. A longing for freedom mixed with uncertainty... a horizon wide open.

Her time was running out, and she had to go back to the beast that caged her, but she had never felt more centered. Sophie turned in a slow circle, regarding every work of art she created that night. This was her own little, secret world.

None of the art moved except the winged creature.

It drifted lazily up to the ceiling and clung to the stone, seeming to slide into it.

"Stay here," she whispered, feeling slightly foolish talking to the art.

Before she left, her eyes fell and held onto the painting of the baby. She exhaled and forced her emotions to remain in a neutral place. She didn't want to give in to the hatred she felt for the child. It's a boy, she thought and then shook herself. She had to go. It was time to play the part again. It was time to hide her heart, to detach her soul from the window of her eyes. It was time to not just tell lies but become them.

"I'll come back."

She left. The silent trees of the wilds in between the Wood and the Lair caressed her with shadows as she walked toward home. The whole area felt empty. She saw no sign of life or heard any movement. Her mind turned to Tristan and how she would handle herself throughout the night while she was stuck with him. Should she tell him about the baby? Would he be able to sense it as her grandfather had? Sophie decided to hold on to the information and keep it to herself for the time being. She didn't fear his response, it was what he wanted after all, but perhaps in some way she couldn't yet see, the pregnancy might become some sort of leverage she could use against him.

Sophie touched her stomach again and pondered the amount of time it would take before the baby would be due. Her fingers drummed on her abdomen mimicking a pulse. The child was a clock. As soon as she thought it, she latched onto that notion. It wasn't a cage, it was nothing but a clock. A reminder of the deadline she was approaching. She must find the means to free herself and secure Jorgie's safety before the child was born.

Bracken crunching under footfalls caught her attention, but she was too wrung out to be startled or care if there was danger headed toward her. Her gaze shifted through the shadows. There was something. The way it moved broke through her apathy. She blinked, but it seemed she couldn't truly see what stalked closer. It wasn't a shadow and yet that was all she could compare it to. Whatever strange flesh it was built of the moonlight didn't grasp or touch it in any way. The dark thing held still one moment then shifted to the side or forward too quickly. Its movements jerky one second, beautifully liquid the next. Her mind tripped as it approached. It can't be, she thought. She'd only dreamed creating that thing.

The silhouette's glowing green eyes fixed on hers and it smiled. It was like looking in a distorted mirror. It was her true face, but it was vulgar, twisted, and filthy. The illumination of its eyes glinted a proud insanity.

"Mother," it whispered in an exact copy of Sophie's voice.

"I am not."

It tilted its head. "Denial is a thin coating. You won't keep it long."

"This isn't possible. I'm dreaming again. Hallucinating. You're not real."

The long twisted ribbons of the thing's hair swayed as if blown by a strong breeze, but there was no breeze. Her form hazed, and she turned in a circle, laughing like a maniac. Then she moved so fast Sophie jumped to the side as she came up behind her, placing her midnight hands on Sophie's shoulders. Alarmed, she pulled away and faced it again. Its touch had felt like warm water.

"Do you love me, mother?"

Sophie ignored the question, her mind still bogged in rejection that this could possibly be real. "What are you?"

"I'm yours. I'm you."

"You're not me."

"You created me in a moment of rage and despair. I am pure. I am undivided. I know what I feel and what I want and there is nothing else. I *am* feeling."

"I must reabsorb you."

It darted out of her reach and laughed again. "The time may come for that, but this is not it. I would kill you or at the very least, the child inside you."

"How could you know that?" Sophie argued. "How could you possibly know anything if all you are is an emotion?"

The shadow shrugged. "I am pure. I was too strong to remain inside you. I had to break out. I did, too, if you don't remember. I tore you open the moment I was born. You want to swallow me back up? There's not enough room for the both of us in there. Or should I say the three of us? I wouldn't want to kill my sibling. I'm anxious to meet them."

At a total loss, Sophie just shook her head. "No," she hissed.

"Yes, mommy. Oh yes. Just think what might be inside you. Perhaps they will be *just like me*."

Sophie tried again to reach out and grasp the thing, but it was too fast. It slid through the shadows of the trees and away. In a second, she couldn't see it anymore. She held still, watched, and listened. Nothing. The forest was quiet all around her again.

SEVEN

After the sunset, all the dryads gathered together close to the Heart, as they did every night. There wasn't anything special about tonight, it wasn't a solstice or festival. It was just the usual socializing, future planning, and gossip swapping social hour it always was. The loudest and most animated of the group stuck close together next to the flames of the manifestation. Eli hung back, not interested in engaging tonight. He wasn't angry per se, but since Ler ordered him to get rid of Tristan's axe, he felt submerged in a harshness that was beyond mere annoyance.

He wanted to move, to act, but he had no direction. He needed to fight, but, at the moment, he was a warrior without a war. Apprehension hardened inside his mind and he couldn't shake it loose. He wasn't the only one. Whispers of what had happened that night with the wolves had reached every dryad. They all knew, and stress created a backdrop inside all of them. Eli could see it in their eyes and hear it in their voices even if they were talking about other things. The worry seemed to weigh heavier on those who were new parents.

His attention settled on those who rocked infants in their arms or tried to corral toddlers. All the new parents were their own clique. They all exuded an air of pride and spoke to one another as if they shared important secrets that those who were not parents yet could not understand. This didn't annoy him. He didn't care. Nothing inside him seemed anxious at all for fatherhood, despite the constant cultural pressure to procreate. He liked kids, just other people's kids. When he thought about the little ones, all he felt was an obligation to protect them.

In the group of new parents, his eyes settled on Shi. Her hand rested on top of her pregnant belly, unconsciously moving in slow circles. She was the closest thing he had to a mother. Because of that, his protective nature was unwavering when it came to her. Part of him wanted to go and sit beside her, just to absorb some of her warmth, but he couldn't be greedy. Shi was adopted mother to them all, but she also had two of her own children and another on the way. After 10,000 years of being caught in a tragic love affair, Shi and Ler finally had a family of their own.

He saw his friends and considered joining them but before he moved forward, Ara caught his gaze. She looked at him from the side of her eye and he got the feeling she had been looking at him for a long time. He looked away but, after a moment, he looked back. She was still looking at him and her eyes burned with intention. He sighed and turned away. Her attention scraped at his already raw mood. Guess Lex was right, she was interested in him. It made him feel angry and guilty even though he hadn't done anything wrong. And he wouldn't do anything wrong either. Ara was with

Rom and Rom was his friend. He wouldn't touch her.

His teeth ground together as he imagined being with her. His mind thrust the fantasy on him against his will. Her eyes had let him know she wanted it from him. He shook his head and banished the errant images from his brain. He wouldn't do that. He wouldn't do that to his friend. And he wouldn't use her even though he could. She wasn't what he wanted. He didn't know exactly what he wanted but he knew it wasn't her. He hoped her infatuation would fade quickly, and she would be loyal to Rom.

Eli decided he'd rather be by himself and began heading away from the Heart. He walked at a leisurely pace through the shadows, avoiding eye contact with those he passed.

"Hey, Eli! Wait." Lex called coming up behind him.

He looked over his shoulder and slowed.

"Where are you going? It's early."

"Just not in the mood tonight. I'd rather be by myself," Eli said.

They walked companionably together in silence toward the outskirts of the Wood. When the noise of the crowd was far behind them, Lex grabbed Eli's arm and gave him a serious look.

"You didn't get rid of that axe did you?" Lex kept his voice low.

"What do you care? Did Ler ask you to interrogate

me about it?"

Lex gave him a dirty look. "How long have we been friends? When have I ever..."

"I'm sorry. That was shitty of me. I'm just on edge... Yeah, I still have it."

"Good," Lex exhaled. "That's good. I can't understand his reaction to it. Keep it hidden."

"I will. Did you hear any of what Sabra said?" Eli asked.

"Not really. I caught snatches of their conversation, eavesdropping you know. All I heard was she said she would look into it. I didn't get anything else, sorry."

Still desiring to be alone, Eli gave a fake yawn. "I'm just gonna call it a night, man. You should go back to the Heart. Go run your game on the females and see if you can get lucky."

Lex chuckled and shook his head. "I'm right on top of that. But why do I get the idea you're trying to get rid of me?"

Eli stopped next to his tree and leaned against the trunk casually. "I'm just not feeling that well."

Lex looked up at Eli's branches, his eyebrows pulling down in a look of concern. "Dude, are you ill? Your tree doesn't look healthy. You don't have much color."

"Yeah, I've noticed. I think it might be taking that axe to the arm. I mean, the Heart healed me, I feel mostly fine, just not totally myself yet. Don't worry."

Lex continued to scowl up at his branches for a moment, then he shrugged. He nodded to Eli, turned, and began walking back toward the Heart. "See you tomorrow."

Eli watched Lex walk away. He waited until the shadows swallowed him up before sliding into the trunk. Guilt assailed him and he berated himself for being a disloyal friend and a liar. This wasn't his tree at all despite that everyone he knew believed it was. No one knew where his tree was, the location was his most guarded secret. So many times, countless times over the years he came so close to telling someone the truth, particularly Lex. But the words never came out. His instinct was resolute on this point but consciously he didn't know why. Why couldn't his friends know the location of his tree? He knew where all of theirs were.

Eli sighed and tried to let go of the guilty weight in his stomach. He moved the guilt aside to make way for anxiety. Lex thought his tree looked unhealthy, Eli would have to do something about that in case someone else noticed as well. He was usually more diligent. He couldn't afford to neglect his maintenance of this tree, otherwise, it would become obvious it wasn't truly him in a very short time.

Nestled deep inside the rings, splinters, and sap, Eli exhaled, pushing a measure of his life-force into the silent and stationary heart of this tree. Vibrant green light spread through the wood, reaching up through the canopy, pushing into the veins of the leaves and also down through the trunk's girth, pooling in the roots.

He lost consciousness for a moment, physically taxed from giving so much of himself. After a few minutes, he woke feeling groggy. Eli reached into the hollowed out crevice he'd cut long ago and touched Tristan's axe. As soon as his fingers made contact with the weapon, ice entered his heart and the death memories of his father threatened to take him over. He forced himself to continue touching the axe even though he was afraid of it. His fingers moved down the length of the handle and lightly over the blade. His own fear was offensive to him. He wouldn't allow himself to indulge in this kind of weakness. All dryads feared axes. He would no longer count himself among them.

A scorching fury ignited in his brain. He wouldn't just master his fear. Conquering it wasn't enough. His whole life, over and over, he'd been forced to witness his father's execution. The beat of the axes, keeping perfect time as they cut down his father, was always with him. The gory music of death was wrapped deep inside his identity. He gripped the axe handle tightly with both hands. Right then and there Eli resolved that his fear was dead. Even though he still felt it, he would not acknowledge its existence, not ever again. And more than that, he would master this weapon and turn it against his enemies. A dark smile spread his lips. The dryad who fought and killed with an axe. A morbid pleasure spread through his chest, and he chuckled lightly to himself. He would offend everyone he knew.

Eli held still and waited for the night to mature before he dared to venture out and go to his real tree. He needed to wait for the rest of his kind to fall asleep, on the off chance someone came looking for him. He dozed on and off, lulled by the vibrations of his people, humming deep in the ground. The hum grew fainter and fainter as the congregation began to disperse, climb into their trees, and fall asleep.

He roused fully when the hum died down to only a few dryads. He climbed out of the trunk and stretched. His gaze drifted up to the canopy. Infusing the tree with his life-force worked. The leaves were vibrant again and in the darkness, mimicking the glow of a true dryad's tree. He was about to take the axe out of its hiding place when he felt someone approaching.

"Eli," she whispered.

He ground his teeth together and swore internally before turning to face her.

"What are you doing here, Ara?" he asked shortly, even though he already knew why she was there.

She came close, serious energy radiating from her. "I think you know."

He shook his head. "Rom is my friend."

She crowded him, heatwaves dancing on the surface of her skin. His body responded regardless of his determination to leave her the hell alone. Her midnight eyes sparkled with desire and knowledge. She smiled darkly at him. "I know how to keep a secret. Don't pretend you don't want me. The attraction between us is too strong to deny."

Bullshit, he thought. If she wasn't acting like this, talking like this, he never would have thought about being with her. And now she had just put him in the worst possible position. Damned if he did, damned if he didn't. He tried to think through it. There was no way to come out of this unscathed. How did he prevent as much damage as possible? He swallowed hard and braced his hands on her shoulders.

"You're beautiful and sexy, Ara. You know that. And I would enjoy you...if you were mine. But you're not. I won't have pleasure at the cost of pain to someone else. I just can't."

She pulled out of his grasp and wrapped her arms around his neck, pressing against him and kissed his mouth. His brain clouded and he clasped her to him, kissing her back roughly. *Damn her... No. No way was this happening.*

He braced his hands on her shoulders again and pushed her back. She gazed at him with taunting heat in her eyes.

"I'm so hot for you, Eli. You're what I really need. Rom isn't half the man you are. I knew kissing you would be like that. Don't bother lying. You're burning up for me, too."

"I'm sorry. This isn't going to happen. I never did anything to lead you on, or at least not intentionally."

She put both her hands flat on his chest and ran her fingers down his torso. He grabbed her by the wrists and forced her hands back, anger now pulsing through him.

"Didn't you hear me?" he demanded. "Rom is my friend. Don't you care how much this would hurt him?"

She licked her lips. "I only care about you. I care about our future together."

She was really pissing him off now. "Future? You're

way off. There's no future for you and me."

A frown pulled in her brow and she narrowed her eyes. "What are you saying?"

"I'm saying no. No to anything and everything that could transpire between us."

"Why? If you're so worried about your honor, I'll dump Rom tomorrow. I'll end it. Okay?" she smiled warmly and moved toward him again.

"I. Don't. Want. You." his voice was hard. "Is that clear? I'm not interested. I have never been."

Color rushed into her cheeks and she put her hands over her mouth. Ara shook her head and tears slicked her eyes. He cursed her in his mind. He didn't like having to be so harsh, but it seemed she wasn't going to give up otherwise. The moment dragged out, tense and awkward. She swallowed and straightened her shoulders, her expression shifting into a derisive sneer. The next second she lunged at him, a cry of fury in her throat.

He blocked her attempt to strike him and shoved her backward. She stumbled but she didn't fall. Breathing hard she took a step back, a nasty smile on her lips.

"Think you're too good for me? Is that it? You should have thanked your good luck when I came here. Everyone wants me. You have no idea what you're passing on...You'll be sorry for this. Reject *me*? I'll make you pay...so much, Eli."

"I see what I'm passing on. No dignity, no loyalty, and no class. *You* should count yourself lucky someone like Rom wants you at all. This was your mistake, don't make it worse."

She continued to back up. "Like I said, you'll pay. Just wait and see."

He sighed as she turned and ran back toward the Heart. He hoped humiliation would get the better of her through the night and she wouldn't do anything stupid in the morning. If she kept silent, so would he. If she didn't and she lied about what happened, he wouldn't turn a deaf ear. He'd defend himself and his honor if she forced him to.

Eli gazed into the shadows after her, the weight of what this could mean for him in the morning falling on his shoulders. He exhaled and grimaced. Hell hath no fury... he waited a few minutes, just holding still and listening, making sure she was really and truly gone. The moon moved overhead as time passed. The entire forest gave a deep sigh as all went sleepy and quiet.

He took Tristan's axe from its hiding place and headed out of the Wood, toward his real tree. Eli needed to reconnect the two halves of himself. Keeping his tree's location secret meant he didn't get to be whole as much as the rest of the dryads, and the amount of time he spent torn in half probably wasn't advisable. The longer he went without reconnecting, the more agitated and strung out he became.

Passed the boundary of the fringe of the Wood, nestled in a clutch of towering, ancient, silent trees, the other half of Eli lived. His heart beat steady and he breathed easier as he drew close to his base. The glow in the veins of his leaves was faint, but it was still visible. His height also gave his tree away as dryad. He set the axe down on the ground over his roots, before sliding into the trunk. He exhaled and closed his eyes as his two halves realigned. Regrettably, maintenance was required to disguise him and he would have to see to that now.

He inhaled, pulling energy and life out of the wood and into his heart. It was a reverse action of what he had to do on the other tree, his fake base. Centered and resigned he slid back out of his trunk looking up at his branches with a critical eye. If any of the other dryads knew what he was about to do, and that he did it regularly, they'd consider him completely and possibly dangerously insane. Perhaps he was. He didn't like to think about it too deeply. Grimacing, he began to climb his trunk. *Just get it over with quickly.*

Eli ran his hands over a few of his branches, testing their strength, and assessing vibrancy. Biting down on his bottom lip he grabbed a thick limb with both hands and snapped it off. The cry of pain pushed hard in his throat and sweat instantly covered his skin. Damage or injury to the tree caused simultaneous physical pain in his corporal body. He dropped the limb to the ground, panting. He gave himself only a moment to school his breathing before breaking another branch. And then another and another. He slumped after six, weakened and nauseated. *Come on. You can't stop yet. Four more.*

It wasn't just the physical pain, this type of self-mutilation broke his heart. Every branch he broke was akin to cutting off his own fingers. They were a part of him. Living pieces of himself that he decided to kill. The discarded branches lay in a pile at his roots when he finally finished breaking himself, for the time being at least. The illusion was satisfactory. His tree wouldn't draw the eye now.

Exhausted, Eli lay back, his branches supporting him comfortably. Why was secrecy so important? Why was he so aloof from the rest of his kind? Every time he pondered these questions, answers were insubstantial. He couldn't answer why all that came to him were flashes of his father's execution and sometimes a woman. He never saw her face. She was always sitting, looking down at her hands. He looked over her shoulder at her palms. Her skin looked like carved wood. Words were on her hands. He tried to read them, but, as soon as his eyes focused, the words faded like sand washed by waves, replaced by lines of new words. His heart warmed every time he saw her in his mind. Sometimes he felt certain she must be his mother.

Eli's heart pulsed heavy with grief for the parents he could never know. He blinked his eyes, his vision returning to the here and now. Or so he thought. Frowning and sitting upright, he rubbed his eyes and blinked a few times. What was that?

The small creature drifted on the air toward him. He'd never seen anything like it. Wings like a black fluid haze with glowing green veins or perhaps the glowing part was a skeleton. He blinked again and reached out with one finger as it came close. It didn't flee from his hand. His fingertip touched the edge of its wing. His lips parted and he held still, amazed. Touching the thing felt like sticking his finger in warm oil. It was a pleasant, comforting temperature.

Slowly he twisted his wrist, so his palm was flat under it. The thing alighted on his hand. It beat its wings laboriously a few times then the bottom of it liquefied and ran under his skin. Startled, he tried to bat it away with his other hand, but it was too late. The entire creature had absorbed into his palm. He held his hand up close to his face and made a small cry of alarm in his throat. It moved again. Its smudgy wings beating slowly through his hand. It slid up to his forearm. He grabbed the crook of his arm trying to keep it from moving further. It stopped where his hand blocked, pulled up through his skin and out, drifting back into the air.

Amazed, delighted, and a little apprehensive, Eli laughed aloud. "What are you?"

It flew close to his face. He blew on it gently. It beat its wings a little faster and circled around his head. He held his hand out for it again, not wanting it to leave. It came back to his palm, alighted and slid under his skin. Perhaps he should have been afraid, but his initial anxiety vanished. It moved up his arm again and this time he didn't try to block it. The warmth of it eased his physical pain as it smeared over his shoulder and across his chest.

Eli pulled his shirt over his head and watched the bird thing move over him. It looked like an odd tattoo. It slowed its exploration of his chest and seemed to settle on the top of his shoulder, its darkness spread along his collarbone and a little up the side of his neck. He exhaled and closed his eyes enjoying the fluid, comforting sensation it created. What the devil was it? Whatever it was, he wanted to keep it, and he wanted to keep it a secret as well.

After a few minutes, he noticed it had a pulse, or something similar. A constant, sleepy throb ran deep in the veins and out through the wings like the ebb and flow of waves. Eli smiled, bemused. It was like having a new pet.

He jumped down, picked up the axe, and climbed back up into his canopy. He leaned back again turning the weapon over and over in his hands. The feel of the wood handle was uncomfortable to him. He didn't like the sensation as if it was made of a bone of a dead friend. The wood didn't come from a dryad, but still, it was distasteful. *Get over it.*

He continued to mess with it long into the night, the texture of it, the weight, and how it moved. He would practice with it until he could wield it admirably. Eli shifted it from hand to hand, not sure which side he preferred, and it didn't matter. He was ambidextrous. He needed another axe of equal size. He'd fight with two. One in each hand. The only problem was where was he going to get another axe?

As he pondered the problem, the bird thing began pulling on his arm. He looked down at it. One wing lifted off his skin while the other stayed rooted underneath. The free wing pulled and beat. He frowned and touched it lightly, trying to help it free itself or settle back on him again. It resisted both actions and began to pull harder on his arm.

"What?"

The thing surprised him with a show of force he wouldn't have thought possible for the insubstantial wisp. It tugged vociferously on him and refused to let go.

Eli smiled. "Alright, alright. You want to show me something or lead me somewhere. I get it."

He jumped down from his branches, landing lithely on his feet. He contemplated leaving the axe by his trunk and then decided he needed to start getting used to having it with him. He needed a belt equipped with the right sized loops for this axe and the other one he would acquire. For the time being, he rested the axe on his shoulder and followed the direction his new pet was pulling him.

Eli snickered to himself as he walked, amused at this odd turn of events. It led him toward the rock face with the thin waterfall. He stopped and looked up where the trickle of water slid off the edge from the cave mouth behind it. The bird thing yanked hard upward toward the cave.

"Seriously? You want me to go up there?"

It yanked hard again.

"Fine, but this better be worth my while."

He had to set the axe down then before grasping the rock with both hands, instantly finding purchase and hefting himself upward. It wasn't really that high up, seventy feet give or take. The steep rock face gave a decent amount of natural handholds and in a minute, he mounted the shelf where the cave opened and the stream slid past his feet.

Eli looked out over the tops of the trees and spotted his own canopy. He was used to seeing this place from the vantage point of his highest branches. He always liked this little cliff in his view of the world but he hadn't come here since he was a boy. Why had his pet wanted him to come here? It continued to pull on him. He followed its direction into the cave opening.

At first, he saw nothing out of the ordinary, nothing than what he expected to see. But then he walked around the snaking corner and stopped dead, his mouth falling open and his breathing arrested in his chest. The first second was shock, the next was awe.

Eli's eyes were wide, his gaze absorbing the uniquely beautiful images greedily. Oh, yes. A deep sense of rightness breathed into him as he walked around the art hanging on the air. It spoke to his soul. Who could make such things? He desperately needed to know, because whoever it was, he understood them. Something deep inside him, a place he didn't even know existed until that moment, woke up and recognized this, acknowledged it.

Slightly winded, he sat down against the wall. Time lost its relevance. His eyes slowly and intently probed every tiny detail of the images. It wasn't the beauty that struck him or the skill. These designs and pictures were not brushed with paint but with pain. Each drifting and suspended dance of light and color was a raw, honest, brutal display of emotion. He understood why the creator of such things hid them. Part of him felt despicable for lingering like this. It was so intimate. So real. As if he looked directly into the artist's soul.

He gazed back down at the bird thing, now resting peacefully on his forearm, and was assailed with questions. More than how was why? Why had it come to him?

He had to meet the artist. He was utterly compelled and at the same time afraid he would be disappointed. His mind had built this person up so high already as if they were some divine, otherworldly dream. *She*, he thought. Surely the artist was a woman.

Eli leaned his head back and exhaled. He tried to imagine her. What race would she be? How old was she? He knew he was tired. He felt it. He should go back to his tree and sleep, but he couldn't leave. His heart wouldn't let him. Not yet. He envisioned a woman, little more than a shadow there in front of him, her arms open, beckoning him to come close and hold her. And damn he wanted to. He scowled and shook his head. What the hell was wrong with him?

Rahaxeris sat down and picked up his book, opening it to where he'd left off earlier in the day. He'd enjoyed the family gathering and getting to meet Erin. She was easy to like, and he looked forward to getting to know her better. Having Maddox settled was a great relief. He was worried about Sophie but he knew she would come to him in the morning.

His mind began to slide over the words on the pages, slipping away from the here and now.

Something moved in his peripheral vision. Startled, for the mere fact that he *was* startled by something, and that it was able to creep up on him. He turned his head very slowly and looked at what was looking at him. He set his book down just as slowly and stood up.

The female figure looked like a flat cutout, a silhouette. She was all darkness, like the heart of a shadow, only her eyes glowed a strange green light. She breathed, causing her defined edges to blur. He'd never seen an entity quite like her, that fact alone was chilling. Then she smiled.

"Hello, grandfather."

His cold blood ran a bit colder. It spoke with Sophie's voice.

"What are you?" he asked calmly.

"Feeling. I am only feeling."

"Where did you come from?"

"Sophie. Obviously."

"Sophie made you?" he pressed.

The thing laughed and spun in a circle like a little girl.

"I climbed out of her. She tried to take me back, but I wouldn't let her. I haven't fulfilled my purpose yet."

He tried to decide how he could capture this thing so he could study it. "What is your purpose?" he moved closer.

"Killing," it hissed. Then it laughed again.

"Killing whom?"

It closed its eyes, the expression on its shadowed face going euphoric. "The baby's father."

EIGHT

Sophie sat on Tristan's bed, gazing at the life-size carving of herself. She was numb, thankfully. Candlelight flickered over the erotic drawings on the wall, seeming to give them life. Did they freak her out and disgust her? Sure, but she had to look deeper than that. She had to understand him. Movement rustled outside the bedroom door. Was he coming in now?

As soon as she'd arrived at his apartment, he'd ushered her into the bedroom without explanation and locked the door. Why had he done that? She had to pay attention to everything he did. Her eyes probed deep into the details of the shrine. This space was the truth of him. The sickness inside him spilled out and saturated the walls and floor. She remembered how he'd said he was nervous to show her this room. Sophie believed he was completely honest at that moment.

She lay back on the bed and looked intently at the wall of pictures. She narrowed her eyes at the bottom corner of the one closest to her head. He'd dated it. Her gaze jumped from picture to picture. He'd dated them all. She rose up onto her knees getting closer to the pictures. The door opened behind her.

"What are you doing?" Tristan demanded.

"Learning," she answered mildly.

"Learning what?"

"How you love me. Your desires for us." She turned to face him and lay back down.

His hard expression eased slightly. "Learned anything so far?"

"Maybe...I'm humbled by you, Tristan. The amount of what you feel for me...well, it's more than I ever thought anyone would or could feel for me. I'm sorry I didn't understand sooner." Her words were so over the top, but she had a feeling his desire for her love was so sick, he would accept this. He would like it.

His demeanor relaxed and he closed the door, leaning casually against it and looking her over slowly. "How was your cousin's party?"

"As expected. Idle chit-chat, food and drink and introducing everyone to his new life mate."

"What did you think of her?"

Sophie shrugged, keeping it in her mind that this was normal. She wanted to be here. No, it was more than that. This was her home and her man. Just be easy. Let it come naturally. You're not afraid of him. "She's very beautiful. Maddox is a lucky man. I didn't really get a chance to talk to her much. It was the kind of affair where everyone wanted her attention."

He sighed and crossed his arms. "It annoys me that I couldn't have been there with you. I should be with you from now on at any family gathering."

"Of course."

His gaze warmed, but that only lasted a second. Everything about him hardened abruptly and he pointed at her bare feet. "I told you to come back here exactly as you had been. You didn't listen! Where are your shoes?"

"They were hurting my feet. I left them back at home." Her mind raced for a second. He was too deep in her business and he cared about and noticed things no one else would. "I gave them to my sister. They fit her better. I'm sorry. I honestly didn't realize it would bother you. I should have known better."

Some of the hardness left his eyes but his mouth still held a tight line. "I forgive you. But you still have to be punished so you remember not to do it again."

She swallowed. "Punished how?"

He looked around the room quickly, frowning. "Nothing too serious. Ah, here."

He grabbed a picture frame off the bookshelf, opened the back, took out the picture and set it down before dropping the glass on the floor. Tristan stepped over the broken glass, grasped both of her hands and pulled her to her feet. He kissed her mouth softly and smiled.

"Stand on the glass."

Her nostrils flared as she pushed her reaction down deep and ignored it. She looked down and nodded her head once. The first second wasn't bad, only a few small cuts into her feet, then he pushed down on her shoulders. She swallowed her cry of pain and remained silent as blood pooled on the floor under her.

"You won't forget your shoes again, will you sweetheart?"

"No," she whispered. "I promise."

He faced her, pressing a kiss to her forehead. "Good girl."

Tristan leaned down, picked her up and carried her back to the bed. He knelt by her feet and began to gently pick the glass out of the cuts. She closed her eyes and focused on breathing. She'd make him eat glass before she was finished with him. He left the room and came back a moment later with bandages. Once her feet were wrapped up, he climbed on the bed next to her.

Great. Here we go. She thought bitterly as he moved on top of her and kissed her neck. She kept her eyes pinched shut and let everything inside her drift. Until she defeated him, sex was something she would have to endure with him. She knew and resigned herself to the reality. But in her mind, it wouldn't be him. She could imagine she was with someone else, *anyone* else.

He reached under her and pulled the zipper of her dress down.

"Sophie," his voice commanded her to open her eyes.

She met his gaze.

"I love you. Don't be scared. This won't be like the

first time. I'll be gentle."

She reached up and touched his cheek. "Thank you."

He moved slowly. She wished he'd just hurry up and get it over with but he seemed hell-bent on drawing it out and playing the patient and skilled lover. She would have to find another measure of strength she hadn't yet considered. If she had a hope of deceiving him, she would have to engage in bed. Passive, with her eyes shut, wasn't going to work. *Damnit*. But this time, no, not this time. He had to prove he would be gentle like he said he would. She could be reserved and nervous this time. She could close her eyes. She had a good enough reason. He had to prove himself and his prowess.

"I'm nervous..." her voice was quiet and shaky.

His touch slowed, the pressure of his hands more comforting than a caress. "I'll be gentle. I promise."

A piece of her broke loose when he entered her, a fragment detached and dissolved like mist in a breeze. *I am a sacrifice*. Her mind moved to the dark entity she encountered in the forest. It was what she wanted to be. Free, honest, feral. Sophie took comfort that it was her creation. Some part of her roamed the world and did as it pleased. *I want to be her*. While his body was joined with hers, every internal scream of rage and denial in her head she ignored. *My body is nothing. The real me, my true face, my soul, my art, he can never touch*. The screaming quieted as though muffled. *My body is nothing*, she thought again and again. Nothing about sex was what she'd imagined it would be like. She'd certainly never had any aberrant fantasies of being forced. This wasn't what physical love should be. This wasn't what she longed for. There was something else. She clung to a new type of fantasy now, gaining a stronger opinion on what kind of partner she wanted. Her mind drifted on the wish she had a destined life mate and the shred of comfort that Tristan was not him.

She exhaled in relief when he finished and moved off her. Making her stand on broken glass beforehand aside, he *had* been gentle. He ran his fingers lightly over her skin, a frown on his face.

"I'm sorry. I don't know your tastes yet. I'll learn how to please you."

She offered him a weak smile. "I know you will. It wasn't you. I was just too tense, I think."

"Will you be open with me? Will you tell me what you like and don't like in bed?"

"I don't know any of that yet. I've never been with anyone but you."

"Oh." Instead of this news giving him pleasure, his face fell. "If our first time had been different I would have realized that. I was preoccupied."

"Sure. Rape has many elements," her tone was acidic but she was too raw to care if he hurt her again. It felt good to say it.

To her amazement, he laughed. "That's true." After a moment, he stopped laughing and looked at her seriously. "I don't want to rape you again. So don't force me."

"Me force you to force me?"

He chuckled. "That's funny." His mood shifted quickly and he was serious again. "I've been with other women, lots of them, but it was never like this. And it was never *here*, in this room. No one has come into this space except you. My heart is yours. It has been since we were children...you remember when we met, don't you?"

A cold warning spiked in her blood. Her life might hinge on the next thing she said. His eyes filled with desperation. Slow. See what you're really dealing with. Behind the beautiful blue of his irises swirled the sickness and the heartache. She couldn't discount his pain. His insanity didn't invalidate or cancel his emotions. His love for her was real. Sick but real.

The moment dragged out as she strained her memory. Slowly she reached up and framed his face with her hands.

"I can't remember how old we were, or the season. Remind me of the details."

"I was seven. My parents had just died. Your mother came to me. She was trying to comfort me and make sure I would be taken care of. She was doing her duty to a displaced child within her pack."

Her mind jolted.

"Yes. I remember. My mom brought you to our home for the afternoon...you were so sad. I wanted to cheer you up. We played a few games on the floor."

He leaned over and kissed her deeply, his tears fell on her face. "Yes," his whisper was full of relief. "I knew you remembered. I just knew it. I fell in love with you that day. I determined, no matter what happened, one day you would be mine, and we would live together at the top of the mountain. Do you remember what you said to me?"

"No."

His smile was warm and full. "You said I could be anything I wanted if I set my mind to it. You said I could have anything if I fought for it with all my heart."

She returned his smile. "Those were the things my parents always told me. It was all I had to offer you...but I believed that. Then and now, Tristan."

He laced his fingers through hers. "You see, you were right. I have fought for you with my whole heart and now I have you. And I have set my mind to something else that I don't have yet, but I'm close, Sophie. So close. You're lucky your parents said such things to you, believed in you. Mine never did. No one believed in me until you."

"I'm sorry your parents weren't supportive. Still, I'm sure you must miss them."

He turned his face to the side, his cheek tightening. "I showed them...I think maybe I miss them sometimes, but they are always with me."

Her blood chilled at his demeanor and tone. What did he mean, he showed them?

Loud knocking sounded on the front door. He slid out of bed and threw his clothes on at top speed. He gave her a severe look. "Stay here. Keep quiet."

Tristan left the room, shut the door, and she heard

the lock slide home. She got up, wrapping the blanket around her and limped on her injured feet to the door. She pressed her ear against the wood.

"When do we go?" a low male voice asked.

"Tonight," Tristan answered.

"How will we pick those we kill?" another male voice asked, something about this voice was familiar to her, but she couldn't tell who it was.

"Just follow my lead," Tristan said. "It might take us a few times to be able to find a good target at the right place and time. We have to strike just right the first time if we want to have a single hope of starting a war."

"A *small* war," one of the others scoffed.

"We've been over this," Tristan snapped. "Do you want to rise to power or not?"

"I want revenge. You're the one after power."

"And I will have it, too, so do what I say, and you'll benefit. Sabra's time to lead this pack is almost over," Tristan declared fervently. "Are you with me or not?"

The other two voiced their commitment. She continued to try and listen but then they all left. The front door opened and slammed shut. She held her breath. No noise or movement sounded past the door. Sophie gripped the doorknob and jostled it. The lock held firm, keeping her caged in the bedroom. They were plotting murder and to overthrow her mother. Growling, Sophie slammed her shoulder into the door. It held as strong as a brick wall.

Tristan stopped walking and closed his eyes, turning his face to the night sky. The moonlight kissed his face and sank through his skin, flowing into his blood, singing in his bones. Pride surged into his brain and glinted in his eyes. Werewolves were superior to every other Regian race. None of them understood this. None of the other races knew the ecstasy of this intimacy with the moon. They were the chosen. His lip curled into a sneer as he thought of the dryads. They were so arrogant. They claimed to be the children of the Heart. What good was that? The wolves were the children of the moon. He'd take the moon over the Heart any day of the week.

His pulse beat steady as he methodically removed his clothes. Callen and Satran behind him followed his lead and began to strip as well. Tristan shifted first. His body stretched upward until he was almost twice his normal height. His arms elongated, claws pushed out of his fingers, and his physical strength surged. He looked back at the others as they finished shifting into beast form. Not man and not wolf but the deadly monster in between.

They moved forward silently into the forest toward the Wood. The time was perfect. In the dead middle of the night, the dryads would be asleep inside their trunks. Tristan was looking for a dryad still up and preferably all alone to kill.

NINE

Nel woke slowly, unsure what had roused her. Was Sam up again? Groggy and annoyed, she yawned and stepped out of her trunk. She looked up at the moon and scowled. She couldn't have slept any longer than a measly hour. Just enough to make her feel even more tired than before she'd fallen asleep. Her ears pricked for Sam's cries. Her daughter wasn't awake as far as she could tell, so why was she?

Nel rubbed her eyes, about to climb back in her trunk. A long, twisted shadow rushed over the ground freezing her heart, lungs, and her whole body in place. The beast's low growls sank terror down her spine. What did she do? Did she run, to draw the beast away from her daughter's tree? Did she call out to her mate, Dez? Or would that only get him killed, too?

Her eyes locked on the steam coming from the beast's snout, rising rhythmically from the shadow ten feet in front of her. It was right next to Sam's sapling of a tree. *Please don't wake up, baby. Please.* She begged her daughter in her mind. *Mommy loves you. Don't wake up. Live, sweetheart. Live to the fullest. Mommy loves you so much.*

Nel's muscles tightened as she decided to run, to save her child's life, by giving her own. The monster in the shadow bared its teeth at her, the moonlight glinting off the long white fangs, dripping with gold dryad blood. She gasped, her eyes darting to Dez's tree. All the color of his leaves were gone, his corporal body torn open next to his trunk.

She sobbed once, covering her mouth with her hands. She had to save her daughter.

Nel turned and ran but she only made it two strides as another beast jumped out of the shadows and grabbed her. Towering over her, it sank its three-inch talons into her shoulders and lifted her off her feet. It turned her around in its arms so she faced back toward the other beast. It slunk from the shadow toward her, a bloodthirsty madness in its eyes.

Her breathing came in and out in short jerks, but she remained quiet. She would not scream or cry out. She would not wake her daughter. But her efforts didn't matter.

"Mommy?" Sam's sweet, sleepy voice sounded in her ears as the three-year-old climbed out of her small tree.

"Run, Sam! Run and hide!"

The monster in front of Nel surged forward and clamped its teeth on her throat while the one holding her from behind stabbed into her stomach with its claws and tore her torso open. The world turned sideways. Snouts and teeth filled her body, gnawing, ripping, drinking. Flat on her back on the ground, her vision darkened. The last thing Nel saw was a third beast rising up behind her baby, scooping her fragile little body up in its arms. *Make it quick*, the last vestige of her conscious pleaded to the monsters. *Don't make my baby suffer. Please...please make it quick.*

Her heart gave out and she died, drowning in heartbreak.

Tristan lifted up the little girl and held her carefully in his beast hands. She gazed up at him with wide eyes, but she didn't cry out. He put his snout close to the messy curls on her head and inhaled. He turned as Satran and Callen finished with her mother and began walking away. She didn't need to see that. He continued to stare down at the young thing, captivated. Why didn't she scream? Why did she just look at him like that?

His heart warmed. He loved her. The feel of her body structure in his hands, the smell of her, her round soft cheeks. She blinked slowly up at him, mesmerized or just in shock. Dryads really are beautiful, he thought, falling into her black, opalescent eyes.

Tristan didn't get far before his companions rushed up on his heel.

"We need to hurry," Callen's words slurred through his grisly chops. "What are you doing?"

"Let's go! Just kill her," Satran added.

"Shut up. Look at her. She's perfect. I'm going to keep her."

"She won't survive," Satran argued. "She'll reach the

end of her tether any moment."

"Shhhh...I know. And we will see what happens when she does."

They continued forward through the darkness toward the Lair. Regret and love filled Tristan. She was a prize and she was his. He would keep her. Whatever was left of her when he'd taken her too far...whatever was left, he would keep.

He felt it. The moment the pull to her tree began to tug her back. Still, she didn't cry out but her little body tensed, and she gasped. She jolted and splayed her soft hands flat on his chest as if she could push him back the other direction. He never stopped, but he did slow his pace, to have every second remaining with her. To experience fully the moment she died.

Pain rushed like a current into her eyes and opaque tears slid down her cheeks. A strangled cry did break free of her then.

"Shhh..." Tristan stroked the back of her head with his elongated claws. "I love you."

She broke. All three of them heard it. Her bones snapped under her skin all the way through her. The sound filled him up and chills of pleasure covered him. Her breaking bones sounded like the snapping of dry twigs and she hung limp in his hands. All the color drained from her. She looked like a lifeless doll now a pale greyish brown. She turned monochrome. Her hair, skin, and eyes all turned the same color and the vibrant scent of life hissed out from her pores like steam leaving behind the sweet dull smell of petrified wood.

Tristan cradled her closer to his chest and shivered again. *Oh, my sweet thing. I love you so much. We shall never be parted. I will keep you with me, always.*

Sophie woke in the dark, faint rustling noises behind her. She rolled over and rubbed her eyes.

"Tristan?"

"I didn't mean to wake you. Go back to sleep."

His back was to her, kneeling on the floor in front of an open chest. His hands moved inside it and then he pulled them back and shut the lid. He turned and looked at her. Oddity came from him like a strange smell. He was excited, but it was childlike. She was immediately on edge at the glint in his eyes and a chill swept over her. What had he done?

He came to her and gently smoothed the hair off her forehead. "Go back to sleep, my princess. Everything is all right. I promise. Don't be scared. Things will start to happen soon. Very soon. But if you stay beside me, nothing bad will befall you. You must always stay beside me, Sophie."

"Yes," she breathed. "I trust you to take care of me."

He leaned over and kissed her temple. "Good girl."

She turned back to the wall as he lay down beside her and wrapped his arms around her. His hands held tightly as though he thought she might try to run away any moment. She closed her eyes trying to think of something peaceful. Some small shred of comfort but nothing came. His hands on her, so possessive and loving, felt like he'd dipped them in acid. Had he just killed someone? Were the hands he caressed her with guilty of taking innocent life? If so, was tonight even the first time, or had there been others? Many others even? She wouldn't let Jorgie be one of them.

He was pressed against her. She was caged in his arms...if only that was all. He was inside her in the life he planted there. So where was she? She closed her eyes, feeling her heart pound. Her mind raced through the darkness, over the ground, through trees, and over rocks to her cave. That's where she existed.

Sophie woke early in the morning, relieved the night was finally over. Everything felt so much bigger at night. The day would clear her head, wipe away her fears, and she could think. She had to get away from him for a while. Surely he wouldn't try to keep her locked up here? He would be smarter than that. Her family would come looking for her.

Sophie stretched as she got up out of bed. Her body felt weird, not bad but strange. Whether it was the pregnancy or just being sexually active or both, she felt a subtle change. The room was dark, the only light coming from under the door. She collected herself and worked to convince her brain of the lie that everything was fine, that she was happy. She moved to the door and tried the knob. It was unlocked.

She cracked the door and listened. Tristan was in the kitchen. The light sliced through the darkened room and she hesitated only a moment. Her eyes fell on the trunk that he'd been putting something in in the middle of the night. Did she have enough time to open it and look? She held her breath, listening closer to his movements across the apartment.

Heart in her throat, Sophie turned and crouched in front of the chest. She lifted the latch and opened the lid barely an inch. An odd smell came from inside. Not a bad smell, it was something natural but unfamiliar to her. She knew it was something she had never smelled before.

"Sophie?"

She bit down on her lips as she closed the lid as quietly as she could and re-clasped the latch. She was determined she would find out what was in there. Soon. She stood up and met him at the door with a warm embrace and a kiss on the cheek.

"Good morning," she said sleepily.

"You're up early. You could go back to sleep for a while if you wanted."

"No thank you. I'm quite awake and I'm hungry."

He smiled. "Come have breakfast with me then."

She sat demurely at the table across from him while they ate to the very basic and bland breakfast he'd made for them. It was the second time he had made and offered her food. She wondered if the time was coming when he might become more misogynistic and demand that she make all of his meals. She schooled herself to be ready for it if and when the time came and to easily accept it without argument.

A long, low rumble vibrated through the stone of the floor and walls.

"Was that thunder?" She asked.

"I think so... There it is again. Do you hear?"

They sat there quietly for a few moments just listening to the storm begin outside. Tristan stared off into space, his face contemplative. Disquiet slithered at her stomach at his expression. She didn't trust anything he thought about that hard to be anything good.

"There are some important things I need to see to today. I'm sorry, sweetheart. I have to go... Actually, now that I think of it this is a good thing. You should go home and do whatever it is you normally would do today. Let your family see how happy you are. Tell them about us, so they won't be shocked when we announce our intention to mate."

Sophie licked her lips and swallowed. "Okay. Do you want me to come back tonight?"

"Of course I want that, but I'm not sure how the day will go. So... Come back here around eight and see if I'm home. If I'm not, just go back to your folks."

"I'll do just as you ask, Tristan."

He got up and came over to her, leaning down and

kissing the top of her head as if she was a child. "Good girl. I'll miss you so much today."

She tilted her head back giving him an unmistakable look. He leaned down and kissed her lips. She kissed him back passionately. He broke away from her and went to the bedroom. After a few moments, she followed and stood in the doorway, watching as he finished getting dressed. He looked at her, his expression shifting over a number of emotions quickly. Then his eyes turned cold and stern.

"Hurry up and get dressed. I have to leave and I'm not going to leave you here alone."

"I'm sorry I didn't realize. Where are my clothes?" She asked.

He pointed at the dresser against the wall. "Your clothes are in the bottom two drawers."

She opened the drawer and quickly grabbed a pair of her jeans and a shirt. She got dressed at top speed so as not to anger him. He opened the closet door and pulled out a pair of her shoes that he'd obviously stolen from her room who knows when and handed them to her. She slid them on and left the room, waiting for him by the front door. He rushed by her obviously lost in thought and flustered. She followed him out and waited patiently behind him as he locked the door. He turned and caught her chin in his hand.

"Remember my instructions, Sophie."

She nodded and looked down submissively. "Yes, sir."

"I love you."

"I love you, too." The words slid easily out of her mouth now. They were nothing. Words with no meaning as if she spoke in a language she did not understand. The words didn't matter.

He turned away from her and headed quickly down the stairs toward the ground level. Sophie stood still next to the locked front door and just waited, listening to his retreating footfalls as they echoed off the stone, growing fainter and fainter until she could no longer hear them. She leaned back against the wall and exhaled. She was free, for a few hours at least, she was free. She didn't dare hope that she would actually get the night away from him as well even though he had said it was a possibility.

She thought about going home. She wanted to more than she dared admit to herself. But it was midmorning. No one would be there. Her parents would be busy already in their respective duties, Lacey was probably with Callen or her girlfriends helping her with mating ceremony details, and Jorgie would be at school. She decided she would go down to ground level and see if she could catch the gossip. She wanted to go see her grandfather, check that, she had to go see him because if she didn't he would probably come find her now that he knew she was in some sort of trouble. She couldn't let that happen. And as much as she wanted to confide in him and seek his help, the prospect was terrifying as well.

Rahaxeris didn't have the same type of sensibilities as most people. His moral ambiguity was what she needed more than anything right now. If she asked him to keep silent, even when no one else would have given the same information, she could trust him to do as she asked. Should she just go there now? Get it over with?

Her heart felt heavy and exhausted as it pumped. She would do all that was required of her no matter how unpleasant, no matter how ugly, but right now, at this very moment, she had a rare window to do as she liked. Her spirit was already deep in the cave where her art lived. For just a little while, even if she didn't create anything, she would stand in the dark and just breathe.

Sophie walked casually down through the heart of the Lair, keeping her pace easy, while she kept a sharp eye, looking for Tristan so he didn't catch her. The few people she passed nodded or greeted her quietly, but thankfully none of them tried to really engage her in conversation. She moved faster as soon as she was outside of the mountain, keeping to the alleys and side paths through the suburbs until she hit the wilds. Then she began to run.

The storm overhead blanketed the sky in a dingy charcoal gray. Thunder growled intermittently and lightning struck in the distance, but no rain fell. The darkness of the morning coupled with the shadows of the forest almost made Sophie believe it was actually nighttime. Her footsteps were confident, her direction sure. She knew exactly where she was going and how to get there as quickly as possible. It didn't take long.

TEN

Eli… Wake up, Eli. The Heart whispered. It's beautiful, guttural voice breathed deep through the ground around his roots.

He woke suddenly. Had he imagined the Heart's voice? Or had the deity actually spoken to him?

Are you fully awake now, Eli? The Heart's voice whispered again.

"I am," he answered respectfully. The next second he inhaled quickly as he felt it. The pain of grief that could only come from death, traveled through the ground and constricted around his roots. "What has happened? The weight of tragedy fills me."

Yes. Murder was committed last night. Three dryad lives were lost, no, they were taken, violently taken without provocation. You need to join your people. Come close to me. Draw near the manifestation and show solidarity.

"Yes, of course. I will go now… I… I don't know what to say to you. I am amazed and humbled that you would decide to speak to me so openly."

I will be speaking to you again very soon. We have much to discuss, and I am anxious for it, but right now you must do as I have told you and join the people. Do not press me to speak. I will speak when the time is right. The Heart said.

"Thank you. I will obey."

Eli climbed out of his trunk and stretched. He blinked a few times and looked up at the sky. Thunder rolled through the clouds over his head. A strong gust of wind blasted him from the side, making his branches sway and a few of his leaves detach and fly. He had to do what the Heart told him. He had to join everyone but he certainly didn't want to. Three dryads had been murdered during the night. He'd rather stay right where he was and not know who. At the moment, all he felt was sorrow but once he knew the identity of the victims, the sorrow would vanish behind a curtain of rage.

Lightning struck, catching his eye, and thunder rolled again. The second the lightning was gone, something else caught his gaze and held it. Up on the cliff, in front of the cave where the art lived, a woman stood. Was she the artist? He couldn't see much to her, just her shape, and the wind blowing her hair. She was standing dangerously close to the edge. Panic flooded him. Was she going to jump?

The birdlike thing on his shoulder gave a little jolt. That was all the encouragement he needed. Eli ran toward the cliff face but as he reached the bottom he quickly decided the best thing to do would be to move off to the side and not come up right in front of her so as not to scare her. He would come up from the side and approach her quietly in a gentle, non-threatening way. He jumped and grabbed at the rocks hefting himself aloft. Adrenaline coursing through him, he scaled the cliff face very quickly.

He pulled himself over the top of the hill and stood up. Gritting his teeth and trying to be quiet, he moved closer to her and looked down over the edge to where she stood on the rock shelf 10 feet beneath him. Carefully he climbed down and stood a few feet behind her. She stood rigidly and hadn't moved at all. She gave no sign that she knew he was there. Thunder rolled again, exploding overhead light cannon fire. She must be the artist. He couldn't let her die. She was too special.

"Don't jump," he said gently.

She didn't turn or make any sign that he'd startled her. Instead, she shook her head and made a little sound like a huff of exasperation.

"Can I be of service to you?" He asked.

She shook her head again but still said nothing. He frowned, taking stock of her then. Desolation seemed to cling to her skin. Dark emotions swirled in the air around her. He couldn't tell if he should tackle her to the ground or if she was fine, and he should just walk away and leave her alone. He was leaning more toward tackling just in case she was about to jump.

"So you're here to play the hero?" she asked snidely.

"That's me. I can't help myself. So are you going to step away from the edge and cut me a break here?" He kept his tone light.

"No. I don't think so... I used to think only the weak committed suicide. I've never been that girl. I don't think I am that girl now, but I do wonder... If I did just remove myself would that solve things?" Her voice was so flat. It put him on edge more than crying or screaming would have. He needed to distract her even if he had to be ridiculous and say things he would never have to a stranger.

"I doubt that would solve anything. You have a really fine ass, I'm sure you have a boyfriend that would miss it."

"I'm sure he would...More than a natural amount... But he's psychotic, so there's no knowing."

"Is that why you're up here? A boyfriend? Whoever he is and whatever he's done he's not worth this. You'll move on and find someone who really appreciates you. Or you'll find your destined life mate."

She shook her head again. He wished she'd step back. He wished she turned around so he could see her face. He didn't know what to say, he'd never tried to talk someone out of committing suicide.

"I think you want to live," he said decisively.

"Go away... Or don't, I don't care. I don't care about anything." Her voice took on a dreamy resonance as if she wasn't quite coherent. "I hate crowds."

Eli frowned, unsure if he'd heard her correctly. "You hate crowds?"

"I hate crowds," she said again. "They make me hurt. Too much noise, too many smells, the air gets heavy. Everyone looks at me with expectation. They expect things that would be easy for someone else, but for me, they feel so hard. And if I did the things they wanted... I would hate my life. I'm so weak. It's pathetic how weak I am."

The words poured from her uninhibited and raw.

"I like how honest you are," he admitted. "It's a little strange, but I like it."

"It doesn't matter what I say to you, whoever you are."

"That's true. So, why don't you tell me more?"

"I don't like sex. I mean, I've only had it twice and the first time was rape so, yeah, that definitely didn't live up to my expectations. And the second time was… just something to endure. I feel like there's something else that should be there. Well, I don't love him, so there's that. I could never love him."

"So leave him," he said easily.

She laughed but the sound was bitter. "Gee, thanks! Why didn't I think of that? I can't. I'm trapped."

"How?"

"I just am."

"Okay. What else?" he urged. "Tell me something you'd never admit to anyone."

"I'm jealous of my sister. She's gorgeous and the badass I wish I could be. And she's found love. All our people are proud of her. They wish she was princess-wolf and not me. I wish she was, too."

"That doesn't sound too scandalous. Seems normal enough. Surely you can do better than that. When will you get an opportunity like this again? Spilling your guts to a complete stranger?"

"You want something juicier? I've got something for you...I want to tap into the dark insanity of my heritage. I want to become a killer. I want to disembowel my enemy with my bare hands and leave his body out in the public square where everyone can see what I'm capable of...then they'd all leave me the hell alone. How's that?"

"Hmm...not bad." He waited for her to say something else but she was quiet for a while.

Her shoulders slumped again. "I'm scared my brother will die and it will be my fault. If I just remove myself from the equation now, he'll be safe."

Eli acknowledged to himself that he was interested and wanted to ask her more about her troubles but she still hadn't moved away from the edge and her desolation seemed to be heavier than before. She still might jump. And just as he thought it, she leaned over, looking straight down.

"I think there's a difference between jumping and falling, don't you? I think there is. It's the last choice. I wonder what it says about me. Fall or jump..."

Eli took a step toward her and then another. "You know," he said casually. "You're forgetting the third option." He took another step toward her.

"What's that?"

"Being pushed."

He rushed forward grabbing the back of the waistline of her pants firmly in one hand and shoving her with the other. She lurched forward, her feet slipping over the edge, just as he jerked her backward. She gasped and spun around striking at him. He clasped her tightly to his chest and smiled smugly at her.

"See? I knew you wanted to… live…" His voice died away and all the blood drained from his face.

She blinked a few times, staring openly into his eyes. All the air was sucked out of his lungs and he couldn't inhale. All he could do was hold on. Every inch of his body that touched hers rushed, a sensation under the skin that surged. This sensation was hungry and desperate and senseless. He'd never felt anything like this and he knew only that this force inside him wanted one thing… And that was her.

She was gorgeous, her beauty was wild like the storm overhead. He tried to swallow but he felt choked. He tried to blink but his eyes refused to close for even one second. There was no ground under his feet only a down rush. She said nothing, she just stared. Her expression mirrored how he felt. His pulse slammed too hard and too fast and he tightened his grip on her. Shivers ran over his back, up his neck, and down his arms to his hands.

Eli had never felt desperation before, but now it filled every inch of him. How could he feel greed like this? He would never have thought it possible to experience such a forceful, drastic change in one moment. To see something that touches so deep. Something that reaches straight into you and pierces straight through. He knew her. He'd stood in the middle of the manifestations of her soul. *I've got to have this. I have to have her, no matter what it costs me.*

She didn't try to get away. She just held still in his arms and stared into his eyes. Thunder cracked again and jolted him to reality. What the hell was wrong with him?

"You're the artist." He said quietly, finally finding his voice.

She blinked twice, her eyes losing the soft dreamy edges that had just been there, and roughly pushed against him. He let go.

"How do you know about that?" She demanded.

"I've seen it. I've been in the cave… And there's this…" He turned his head to the side and pulled his loose collar open so she could see the bird thing on his skin.

Her eyes rounded in disbelief and she took a step back from him shaking her head. "Impossible," she breathed. Then her cheeks flushed and her eyes burned. "Thief! How dare you take my art? Give it back! It's mine!"

"Whoa! Calm down! I didn't take it. It came to me. I wouldn't have the faintest idea how to *take it* anyway. I don't understand how it slides under my skin the way it does."

Frowning, she came closer, her eyes narrowed on his

neck. She reached out and touched the bird thing where it rested over his collarbone. A warm electric spark flared under his ribs at her touch.

"What's your name?" she asked.

"Eli. And yours?"

"Sophie."

He swallowed hard again as she retracted her hand from him.

"I think you're incredible." He confessed. "The things you create…"

Her expression crumpled like she might begin crying. Pain hooked into his chest and desperation rushed on him again.

She wrung her hands. "I…This is terrible. I never wanted to show anyone. I purged my soul in that cave, and you've seen it. I confessed things to you just now that I wouldn't dare ever tell anyone…You're a complete stranger and yet…the fact that you've seen my art…you know the reality of me more intimately than anyone."

"I won't take that lightly, Sophie. Or treat it with carelessness. I swear. I'm sorry for…violating your sanctuary. It was unintentional."

She pointed at his neck. "It came to you how?"

"I was just resting in my branches, looking up at the sky, and it floated down and alighted on my hand. Then it melted into me. It moves through me. And it pulls on me. It has a will of its own. Sometimes it leaves me and flies away…I…I've grown attached to it. You don't mind, do you? I mean, I want to keep it, but I also don't know how to remove it, if it being with me offends you."

"I can't explain how serious this is. Do you have any idea what that is under your skin? Do you have the slightest understanding what I felt when I made it?"

He had felt it but he hadn't put words to it until that moment. He didn't want to answer wrong. Eli closed his eyes and put his hand over the bird thing, really focusing on what it was. "It's longing."

He opened his eyes and looked at her apprehensively. She gaped at him like he'd just doused her with cold water. Her breathing came in and out in quick little shudders.

"Yes," she whispered. "You do understand…I don't know how." She shook her head. "…you keep it. I'm not offended. Frightened, but not offended."

"Frightened of what?"

"I'm sorry. This is all wrong. I just wanted to come here and create for a little while, since I had a window. I wasn't really going to jump. I don't think I was. I'm sorry for the trouble I caused you. Thank you for stepping in. I'm beyond embarrassed. Is there some way I can repay you?"

He scowled, somewhat insulted she would suggest he would want any repayment. But then…he smiled at her.

"Will you promise to always tell me the truth? No matter how much you might want to hide it?"

She shrugged. "Sure. What the hell. I promise. I doubt I'll ever see you again anyway."

His voice lowered, his gaze heating. "You doubt it, huh?"

Her eyes narrowed. "Charm? Save it. So, you're enamored with my art? Fine, but keep it in a normal sphere, please. I've got enough to deal with right now without adding another stalker up my ass."

He blew out a breath and chuckled. "Wow. Why do you think you're weak exactly? And just how many stalkers do you have?"

She just shook her head again and looked away. "I feel the time slipping past me. I have obligations to meet. Not yet. Just a little while still."

She couldn't leave yet. He couldn't let her get away so quickly. Not since he'd found her. He gestured to the mouth of the cave. "This is where you are just you, right? No matter what's happening out there?"

"Yes."

He took a step closer to her. "Let me be a part of that."

She frowned. "Why would you want to be?"

His gaze reached out and grabbed hers with an enticing force. The air between them trembled, expanding and contracting. The edges of something invisible grabbing and tugging at the skin. Pulsing heat urging them to move closer. Daring them to deny its tempting gravity.

"It's not a matter of wanting, it's beyond that... I see it in your eyes. I feel it in this space between us."

"This is impossible," she argued feebly.

"You're right."

"There can't be *anything* between us."

"Of course there can't," he agreed.

"So what are you saying?"

"Let me be here with you. Tell me the truth, as you promised and let me watch you create."

A frown creased her brow. "Do you have any idea what you're asking me for? I can't give anything else. My art is the last shred of me that is mine alone. I need to keep it that way."

"I don't want to take anything away from you." He looked down for a moment then his gaze darted to the mouth of the cave and then to the ledge she'd just been precariously standing on. "Things are bad for you. You wouldn't have been up here threatening to jump if they weren't. Look, I'm a fairly simple guy... a warrior. I feel an inherent need to protect those near me...When you're here in your cave, I'll protect you."

"That's thoughtful, but—"

"It's not. My desire to give something back to you is purely selfish. I feel compelled. Like I *need* to give to you."

"If you want to give me something, then give me back my solitude."

He closed his eyes and sighed. "Alright. It hurts to do as you ask, but I will. If that's what you really want."

"It is." She lifted her chin defiantly.

"Okay." He turned and walked away, grasping the first stone he needed to pull himself up. He made it halfway to the top, over the cave.

"Wait!" she cried.

ELEVEN

What was she doing? Sophie watched him begin to climb the natural ladder, her heart burning bright. He was so...so much. He made her skin tingle and buzz and her pulse race. She'd never felt such strong and instant attraction to anyone. And he was an effing dryad! Her life was already a tangle of explosive fuses. He would be the fire that ruined everything. He would burn her down. So why did she call him back after she'd effectively asked him to leave?

Because she damn well wanted to. Rage flared through her veins. He wanted to be a part of the tiny corner of the world that was hers? This gorgeous man wanted to be near her? He wanted the truth? Fine. She'd speak it, to him, and to herself.

"Wait!"

He jumped down easily and faced her, smiling. Her heart gave a little start. He was so hot. He had one dimple in his cheek and a cleft in his chin. His dirty blond hair hung past his shoulders and his eyes...goodness. The midnight sky of his eyes offered her the open horizon she longed for and washed her in dark heat. And he was strong and solid. When he pulled her back from the edge and held her against him, she felt it. He did have the seasoned body of a warrior. He could hurt her if he wanted.

He was a stranger.

He was a risk.

She didn't care. She didn't just throw caution to the wind, she smashed it at her feet with a vengeance.

"Alright. You can watch."

She didn't know what she was doing with him exactly but she knew it was reckless... Reckless felt good.

She turned on her heel and strode into the cave. He walked close behind her. She didn't look back at him and he made no noise, but she felt him like the heat of a fire on her back. Was she dreaming? It felt like it. Every element of this present moment was bizarre.

Her art floated, suspended in the mineral air, illuminated and pulsing. She walked into the midst of it all and let it surround her. She glanced nervously at Eli. He moved to the side, leaning against the wall. She closed her eyes. What did she feel? What did she want to let loose?

She curled her hands into fists, the pressure filling them up. *Don't think. Don't restrain it. Just let it happen. Don't be ashamed.* Was it possible he could really understand the subtle nuances in her art? He'd known the bird thing was longing. Perhaps he only knew that because he could feel the emotion of it since it was inside him in a way. What about the rest? Could he really see?

She pinned him with a sharp look. He raised his eyebrows questioningly. "What?"

She walked to the back of the cave next to the dark opening she hadn't dared venture into yet and pointed at one of her paintings. The edges of the abstract form jutted sharply. She thought it looked angry but she wasn't feeling anger when she made it.

"What is this?" she asked him.

He came closer and looked at it. "Shock as innocence was lost."

"What...I mean...how..." she stammered.

He smiled. She recovered.

"What about this one?" she pointed at another one with deep teal lines that looked like the surface of the water.

"Fear your lies will unravel."

Sophie swallowed hard, her breathing hitched. "Okay, what about that one?" she pointed at the painting of the baby.

He gazed at it thoughtfully. "There is a lot connected to this one."

She crossed her arms feeling a small spark of smugness. "Stumped?"

"No...but there is no easy answer as if I could answer one hundred different times and each answer would be right... It is the unknown. A direction you are bound on, but the path is in the darkness. You cannot see the way.

Have I passed your test yet?"

Shivers lifted on her skin and she nodded. He went back to where he'd been and leaned back against the wall. She moved to the center and her hands relaxed open, she lifted them. Emotion swelled and surged out. It was a mess. A disjointed tangle of confusion. The lines of muddied color and light painted her own eyes, filled with fear and sorrow and despair. At first, they were brown as they were in real life. Then she glanced at him. Her lips parted. The force of his gaze pushed slowly into hers quickening her pulse, disorienting her thoughts. He shouldn't be here like this. It felt illicit. As if he was a voyeur. The thought was arousing.

She pressed her lips tightly together and flicked her fingers over her painting. *I don't care what happens now. He'll see this. I don't care what's next. Let him see.* A new layer of green brushed over the brown as she poured the nameless feeling she'd had deep inside when he held her beside the ledge. Her gaze cut to him and she watched him look into what she'd just added. No shock came into his eyes or features. He stared at her new painting for a moment then he looked straight into her eyes.

"That's a dangerous invitation...I want to kiss you. Right now."

She smirked. "You're oddly direct."

"If I was walking along and fell into a pit, it would be stupid of me to act as though I hadn't. Don't you think?"

"I suppose it would."

He pointed at the image of her eyes. "You create such a thing with wild abandon and you accuse *me* of being direct?"

"Why do you want to kiss me?"

His eyes were black naturally, but at that moment, the color tunneled even darker. Black burned blacker. "You know why…" His voice was as dark as his gaze. "Attempt to deny it. Either that or say it."

She trembled, feeling as though she were falling. "Oh, gosh," her whisper shuddered. "I don't know what's happening to me. I'm *going* to say it."

He crossed his arms over his chest and waited, completely unembarrassed.

"You want me…You connect with my art. You see what I'm feeling when the meanings are hidden. I excite you. It doesn't matter that we just met. You think I'm beautiful. It doesn't matter this is impossible. Language is unnecessary. Words…cannot mask."

He stopped leaning and stood upright. "I'm convinced I'm dreaming, Sophie." He took a step toward her. She took one toward him as well, so they were only a foot apart. "You said you were raped. Because of that, I'm not going to reach out and take what I want, even though I could. Even though you've invited me in with your demeanor and dared me with your painting. I'm going to ask and honor your answer. May I kiss you?"

Permission. Did she dare give it? She had already, but if she never said it…Her gaze roamed over him and settled on his neck where she could see the tip of the smudgy wing of her longing. Then she looked at his pulse thumping in the vein under his ear. It was steady while hers was erratic. She looked at his lips, unconsciously licking her own. Trial... Venture... Risk... Taste.

Shivers rose on her skin and she swallowed. "Yes."

He didn't hesitate and he didn't rush. It was a simple action. Just his mouth against hers. Nothing more than a pleasant pressure. Nothing more at least for the first second. Blood and hunger flooded into her lips as he overtook all of her senses. He smelled like the forest after the rain and he tasted of life. Thriving, reaching, verdant life. Perhaps she was naïve, but not for one second did he seem to be *trying*. He wasn't trying to show, or impress her with his prowess. He wasn't trying to heat her up so he could move to the next level as quickly as possible. There wasn't any trying. He kissed her without any ego.

As if she had stumbled across a hidden treasure, amazed, tempted, and greedy she had to have more of this unknown taste. Like a child, coaxed into trying a new flavor, and at the first touch of it to the tongue realize in a rush, it's their favorite and always will be. That was Eli's kiss. His mouth, the shape, the taste. She could gorge on this until she broke apart. Every other kiss she'd experienced had been poison and this was pure water.

His hands held her as he possessed her slowly. It wasn't like being with Tristan. It wasn't like any other time she'd been in a man's arms. Against him, surrounded by him, she relaxed as she never had. Safe. Small, utterly feminine, and protected. That's what she felt. His strength was hers now. He'd lend it to her.

Thunder cracked outside. Reality jolted her with freezing cold and she pulled away from him, horrified. Too late.

"This is impossible. This can't happen for so many reasons. We can't—"

He captured her mouth again fast and hard. Then he broke away chuckling. "Do you feel better now that you stated the obvious and also irrelevant? Are you sorry? Cause I'm not. I'm not sorry at all."

"No," she whispered, shaking her head. "I'm not sorry, and yet I've never felt more regret."

She tilted her chin up, her lips begging his. He kissed her again and she wound her arms around the back of his neck. *Yes.* She thought desperately. *This. So much this.*

"I have to go, while I have the will to make myself. I have to see my grandfather, then I have to see the rest of my family, and none of them can know what I'm hiding."

"What are you hiding, Sophie?"

She groaned, pulled away, and walked to the mouth of the cave, staring out. He stood beside her.

"I don't know you. You know too much about me, but it's all in the abstract. I have to go."

"I'll promise you the same as you have promised me. I will tell you the truth. You can ask me anything and I'll answer."

Her lips quirked up. "Is that so? Did you mean what you said about my ass?"

He circled her, slowing down behind her as he went, taking his time gazing at her body. A seductive devil was in his smile. "Absolutely."

She giggled. The lightness of the sound and feeling shocked her. How long had it been since she'd laughed?

"When will I see you again?" he asked.

Words were pushing in her throat. Haughty statements that they wouldn't see each other again and other things of that nature, but she couldn't bring herself to say them. They would see each other again. She didn't know when or how but trying to deny it was pointless. She turned her body so she faced him fully.

"I know I'll think about you until we meet again. But in my mind, I've put you here, in my cave. You exist only among my images, as if you are one, too. I'm probably more than half crazy, Eli. The lies I live..." she shook herself. "It doesn't matter. Nothing matters in this place. If you and I are ever in this place again together, it cannot matter. Can you accept that?"

"I accept nothing," his voice was rough. "I'm not supposed to be here. I care about loyalty, perhaps above everything, and yet I commit betrayals, some subtle, some opaque, some I have no gage to their severity. Touching you will no doubt be added to the strikes against me." He reached forward and took her hand, bringing it to his lips. For a moment he stared at the top of her hand, rubbing his thumb over and over the place he'd just kissed. "This feels something like fear. It's not..."

He dropped her hand and walked away abruptly. She stood still and watched him leave the cave. Objection shouted all over her skin as he left. The absence of him made her feel as though something had just been ripped from her.

Eli pulled himself up with the rocks that jutted out of the ground. He stood on the top of the small mountain and looked out over the Wood. He just stood there for a few moments under the angry clouds, excitement and elation running all through him. Sophie. Unusual, talented, vulnerable, beautiful, seductive, forbidden... These were the words he ascribed to her. He felt a rush as if his veins were filled with a tingly breeze. He felt high. The sensations inside him were totally foreign. He'd never felt such things before. He would not have thought it possible. The ecstasy of what he felt was short-lived as he abruptly remembered where he was supposed to be and why.

Guilt slammed into his chest like a physical blow. He had no right to feel what he felt. He had no right to spend time with Sophie. How could he desire her? How could he be so despicable? Was this how Ler felt when he first laid eyes on Shi? He'd never felt any pity for Ler. At least not until now.

Urgent to join his people, Eli began running. The physical exertion did nothing to shake his guilt. He hadn't done anything wrong. He hadn't put himself in her path for any reason other than to save her life. And he had... Or maybe he had. She might not have jumped. But still, he'd only reacted, his protective nature taking over and he had rushed to help. What happened after wasn't his fault. And it wasn't hers either.

So what did that mean? It meant he should never see her again. He knew that was the answer as soon as it came to him. The answer was hateful to him. The answer was pain and he felt nothing but wrath toward it. He ran faster, harder, burning through his emotions. What was he thinking? What was wrong with him? So what if he found her enticing? So what if he tasted bliss on her lips? So what if she was the most special creature he'd ever encountered?

She said if they were ever together again it couldn't matter. That was the only way, he acknowledged. It could only be a game between them and that was all. His traitorous mouth smiled without his consent. He'd play. He'd play as long as she played. And it would never be anything except a game. Never. He swore it to himself.

He slowed his pace as he entered the boundary of the Wood. He felt it in his feet, the anguish in the ground, the grief that wrapped around every root in the soil. His lungs constricted as he prepared himself to learn the reason, to learn the identity of those who had been lost. It was easy to find his way to the place everyone gathered. There was so much weeping, it overtook his hearing, the sound sliding down into his heart where it planted a bitter seed.

Nel and Dez were laid out on the ground beside one another in between their trees. Whenever a dryad died it felt like a double death because there was always two bodies, the corporeal form, and the tree. All the color was gone from Nel and Dez. All their leaves had fallen to the ground in the bark had turned a gray. Their corporeal bodies, savagely torn up, likewise had lost any variance of color and were now petrified like statues.

Across the crowd, Eli caught Lex's eye and jerked his head in a *come here* motion. Lex came over to him and the two of them moved off from the congregation to speak privately.

"Where have you been?" Lex kept his voice down.

Eli ignored his question. "What happened?"

"Wolves, at least two, in beast form. No one heard or saw anything but they left tracks."

"What about the little girl?"

Lex grimaced. "She's dead too, but nobody has found her body yet... I think they took her out of the Wood."

Objection and outrage flared in his brain but he pushed it to the back, cold reason taking over.

"Why would they do this? Why would they kill the child?" Lex asked helplessly, his voice breaking.

Eli closed his eyes and tried to think. "Revenge... I think it was Tristan, Callen, and Satran. I think they did this to get revenge for Ansel."

"But that was an accident!"

"You think those bastards care?"

Lex grabbed his arm. "Do you think this is all? Do you think they're satisfied? Or do you think there will be more?"

"I can't even begin to try and comprehend the thoughts and motivations of individuals that could kill like this. People they had no grudge against. People who had done nothing and could do nothing to them. I can't imagine the inner workings of someone who could kill a little girl like that... Tristan likes to provoke and he's good at it. You know that as well as I. If he was behind this, he's trying to instigate something."

"Well he's gonna get what he asked for," Lex snarled. "No one is going to let go of this. Whoever is behind this... if they wanted to start a fight, they just succeeded."

Weighed down with grief and outrage in equal measures, Ler climbed into his trunk where Shi waited for him. She collapsed into his arms and cried quietly. He stroked her hair and rubbed her back.

"Guard duty has already been assigned for tonight," he told her.

She sniffled. "What are we to do, Ler?"

"We have to do whatever is necessary to protect ourselves. And yet saying words like that, whatever is necessary, sends a chill through me. I've stood on this line before, where circumstance or enemies have pushed you into a place you don't want to be in. I'm so afraid of making a mistake, Shi. I'm not the King, but you and I are the oldest, and they all look to us as if we are their parents. But the first generation is grown now..." He closed his eyes and rested his cheek against the top of her head. "They are young adults, but they are adults."

"Yes," she breathed. "I feel their unrest. A thirst for revenge has been whetted among them. It's right for the young men to feel the need to fight and protect. You can't do it all on your own, Ler. And it would be wrong of you to try. Our warriors are strong and skilled. And though it scares me... Terrifies me to say this, you must let them claim their lives as their own. For they will anyway, but everything will be better if they don't look to you as holding them back. You must guide them and work with them."

He pulled her closer, the baby in her tummy kicking hard enough he could feel it, too. This baby would be their third child. And he hoped that there would be even more in the future. He thought about Sam, she had been the same age as their son, Haz. They had often played together. And now she was dead, her life ended just as it barely began. His need to protect, his need to kill anyone who threatened his children was just as strong as it was throughout the community in all the young men.

Ler feared he wasn't up to the task to keep his head cool. His love for Shi had already been the catalyst for a genocide once. He *could not* make a mistake.

Twelve

Rahaxeris watched the silhouette of Sophie move about. She sank into the stone walls and slid across them like a real shadow. He didn't know if he could cage her, and if he could, he wasn't sure that he should. He wanted to keep her there at least until Sophie showed up so she could explain what the devil this thing actually was. He didn't trust the entity's explanation of anything. She was like a smudge of criminal insanity. He kind of liked that about her, but still...

"So... You said your purpose was to kill the father of Sophie's baby?" He asked casually, trying to engage it in conversation.

She slid out of the wall, darted in an unnatural fashion toward him, and then draped herself in a lounging position across the table in front of him.

"Did I say that?" She giggled.

"Yes, you did. And it caught my attention. Why should you want to kill him? Who is he?"

"Sophie made me. At the moment I was born, what she wanted most was his blood..." She closed her glowing green eyes and rolled down the table like a child rolling down a hill. She giggled again and sat up. "There's not much to me. I'm not a real person. I'm not really alive. And when I fulfill my purpose I think I shall cease to be. So," she paused, her tongue darting out of her mouth. The action seemed to distract her. She stuck her tongue out and licked each of her fingers in turn. Then she looked back at him again and smiled. "So, maybe I shall take my time. I could cause some trouble here and there before I kill him. Havoc... I could create some. The idea excites me. Perhaps I should go and get started now."

Rahaxeris really didn't want this thing to leave now that it confessed it was bent on raising hell. "Sophie said she would come to see me. I expect her soon. You should stay and wait for her with me."

"Oh I don't know," it said loftily. "I don't have anything to say to her. I don't think she'd be very happy to see me again. She's trying to avoid reality."

The silhouette slithered through the middle of the table and skipped down the hall. He got up and followed it, irritation and a light panic filling him as it went into his personal chambers.

"Excuse me." He said angrily as she slid straight into the wall where he kept his most personal memories.

After a second she came back out her creepy eyes glinting with a knowing taunt. "That's quite a juicy story buried in those walls. Are you proud of that history, or ashamed?"

He scowled at her. "Neither," he said thinly.

She laughed, spun in a pirouette, and then darted at him again, her midnight face mere inches from his.

"I see you," she whispered. "You don't want anyone to know how much love you truly feel, do you?"

"Of course I don't. There's no point..."

"Why are you so alone? You're still attractive, darkly alluring. Why do you keep yourself closed off to the possibility?"

He pondered the answer to her question for a moment and then decided to answer honestly. "I would never dishonor the love I had for Liasia. Yes, she is dead. I could find someone else and it would not hurt her in any way, neither would it bother my daughter... My solitary life is a monument to Liasia. If I was to open myself up to love again, slowly, over time the monument would start to show wear. It would begin to erode. If I take the eyes of my heart from it for even one moment, it will change. I would consider that sacrilege. My life has been coated with blood and regret. But not her... Not one moment I spent loving her do I regret. So I shall remain as I am. My memories, that you so blatantly accessed a moment ago, they sustain me. They always will."

Rahaxeris could hardly believe he had just confessed such things but as he had spoken, the thing in front of him had held still and listened attentively or appeared to at least.

"Lovely. Emotion is all I am comprised of. I understand your words."

"Will you stay here for a little while, please?" He asked. "Just wait until Sophie comes."

It licked its lips again and rolled its head in a circle three times. "Hmm... No. But I might come back sometime."

He focused his power and put his hands on her

insubstantial form, grasping her by the forearms. It was like trying to hold oil, but he did hold her. She screamed, bent at the waist in an unnatural contortion, and sank her teeth into the top of his hand. Despite the odd slicing pain, he didn't let go.

"It doesn't matter how powerful you are," she screeched. "You will not hold me against my will!"

"I guess we'll see about that. I'm holding you now."

She laughed an evil, maniacal sound. "No, you're not."

She fell through his hands as if she had suddenly become sand, pooling on the floor at his feet. He reached down to try and pick her up again but she absorbed through the floor as if the stone was soil. Scowling at the place where she had just been, he sighed and went back to the main room, considering if he should send for Tesla about this. She would know what to do. He sat and contemplated, deciding he would wait until he talked to Sophie first.

Sophie herself showed up a few minutes later, out of breath from running. He opened his arms to her and she fell into them immediately. She held solid for a moment only, then he felt her crumble and she began to sob against his chest. He ran his sharp hands down the back of her hair over and over. He waited silently for her to cry herself out, bemused. Sophie had always been his easiest grandchild. She never got into any trouble and compared to the others she was as normal as anyone he could describe that word to... At least until now. She wasn't normal at all, not by any stretch of the imagination. He just hoped that she wasn't in the same league as Tesla where it came to unique freakiness. For her sake.

"I'm sorry," she rasped quietly. "I didn't mean to break down on you like that."

He shook his head. "It doesn't matter." He let go of her and looked into her face. "Tell me your trouble, and I'll see if I can help."

She swallowed and her bottom lip trembled. Fear tunneled deep in her eyes. "You can't tell anyone else."

He hesitated for a moment, unsure. "Alright. Whatever you're going through, I'll keep your confidence so long as you allow me to help you, if I can. Those are my terms."

"Okay," she exhaled.

She walked a few steps away from him and began pacing back and forth. She opened her mouth a number of times, closing it sharply over and over, shaking her head and wringing her hands.

"Sweetheart, pick something to tell me... Tell me about the baby, or tell me about the creative ability you've been hiding."

All the flushed color from her cheeks drained away and she gaped at him for a moment. Then she squared her shoulders, her lips thinning in a determined line. "How do you know about my art?"

"Oh, I'm well acquainted with a silhouette that bears a striking resemblance to you, especially your voice, in all of its strange and insane glory. She just left. Not before she startled me and raided through my personal memories that I store in the walls."

Sophie put her hands on her head and groaned. "I've never made anything like her before. Nothing that large. Nothing that talks and moves about on its own the way she does. Usually what I make a small, just images or designs that float in the air. I get overwhelmed, everything bottles inside me, and it has to come out somehow. But up until a few days ago, whenever I had the compulsion to create anything, I have always reabsorbed it for fear of discovery."

She gazed at him apprehensively but he didn't say anything. She swallowed hard and continued.

"I don't know what to do about the shadowy version of me that is running loose. I tried to reabsorb her but she got away. She said I couldn't reabsorb her. She said she'd kill me, or the baby, if I tried. I think she might be dangerous, but I don't know for sure."

"She said her purpose is to kill your baby's father," Rahaxeris said warningly.

Sophie blinked at him a few times, then to his astonishment, she began laughing. She laughed so hard she clutched at her side and tears of mirth began running down her cheeks. He frowned at her.

"Sophie?"

"I'm sorry," she snickered. "I wish she would hurry up and get it over with."

"Explain," he demanded.

All laughter faded from her and she began pacing

again. Sophie put both of her hands on her abdomen. "Tristan is a psychopath. He sensed my fertility, and because he's obsessed with me and has been for years, he raped me so he could knock me up. He's trapped me, most effectively, grandfather. He's really charismatic. He has lots of friends and influence in the Lair. I'm scared of what he can do. Not for myself. This isn't about me. He threatened Jorgie." Her voice broke and she gasped and put her hand over her mouth. "He said if I told anyone what he did to me, or if anything bad happened to him, that bad things would happen to Jorgie. He said he has someone who already watches Jorgie and will step in and hurt him if I don't fall in line..."

"You are not thinking clearly, Sophie."

She held her hand up to silence him. "I've been playing him. Tristan is starting to trust me. He thinks I love him. I've been making him believe it. I'm not just being idle. I'm not just lying down and let this happen to me. But at the moment I don't know what else to do. For the time being, abhorrent as it is, I have to sacrifice myself to this beast, to keep my baby brother safe. All I need to know is who this person is. This pervert who is waiting in the wings. Once I know their identity, or identities there might be more than one... This is one bride who will be dressed in blood."

"I don't understand why you haven't told your parents about this. Why didn't you go to them for help? It makes no sense that you wouldn't trust them to do everything possible to protect Jorgie and you. You're their children. Your parents are two of the strongest and most deadly individuals in all of Regia."

Her expression crumpled and she rubbed her temples. "Of course I wanted to go to my parents! Of course, that was my first thought... It's just... I'm not exaggerating when I called Tristan a psychopath. His bedroom is a shrine to me. One he has built meticulously over many years. He has a life-size carving of me that stands at the end of the bed. But it's not just that kind of stuff, he's taken my clothes out of my room, somehow, even though I've never invited him in. Either he was able to get past the guards when no one was home, the guards are in his pocket, or it was someone else. You see? I don't feel I can trust his threats to be idle." Her eyes pinned him and beseeched him to understand. "Until I can learn who does his bidding in the background, so I can take them out, I can't risk taking any action beyond what I already have."

He pursed his lips and nodded gravely looking down at the floor. "Yes," he said slowly. "I'm afraid perhaps you are correct. You have done right so far, as hard as that is, I cannot even imagine what you are suffering right now, Sophie... I'm very proud of you, sweetheart. Very proud. Did he only threatened Jorgie?"

"No. He threatened my whole family, but he knows me so well since he's been stalking me for years, he knew Jorgie would be the greatest leverage."

"Yes," he said again. "You're right to move slowly, to gain his trust."

"What can you do to help me? Can you offer me

anything at all, grandfather?"

"I shall think on it. I promise I shall not stop thinking about it until all of you are safe and you are free from the clutches of this monster. At this moment, the only thing I have thought of is to have Tesla make you and Jorgie portals. The kind she has made for Maddox and Erin. The ones that are embedded in their wrists. Then no matter what was happening, you could escape. Jorgie could open portals and get free if someone was after him or hurting him."

Sophie's eyes lit with hope but it only lasted a second and she shook her head. "I fear his eyes... I've seen Maddox's portal. Tristan would notice. He notices every detail where it comes to me in particular. I wouldn't be able to hide anything on my body from him, nor would I be able to conceal something else, like jewelry with the same kind of power. Like aunt Forest's portal ring."

He closed his eyes and slowed his breathing, trying to detach his emotions around this situation. Under his cold surgical exterior, he felt the rage and the bloodthirst any other man in this circumstance would feel. "Does Tristan know about the baby yet?"

"No, not yet. I wasn't yet sure if I should tell him, or if I should wait, and perhaps use the news to get me out of a bad situation with him if one arose. I just wasn't sure. He wants the baby so I don't fear his reaction to knowing that there is one."

Rahaxeris' heart softened as he gazed at his beautiful, sweet granddaughter. "How do you feel about the baby?"

"Too many things. It will be a while still before the evidence of their existence is obvious to the rest of the world, and it will be a while still before I feel the effects of pregnancy." Her voice was as hollow as her eyes.

"I could remove it from you… Since Tristan doesn't know."

Sophie went very still and held his gaze unflinchingly for an unnaturally long moment. Her hands moved to her stomach, seemingly without her knowledge. Many questions and emotions swirled in her eyes. Finally, she shook her head slowly. "No…" Her hands clenched into fists, gripping handfuls of her shirt over her lower abdomen. "They are not the one that is guilty in any of this. I will not strike an innocent."

The next moment she rushed toward him, tears streaming from her eyes. He gathered her softly against him and offered her whatever comfort he could while she sobbed.

"From the first moment I knew the child existed, I hated them. But that was unjust… And now I feel guilty for feeling that. It doesn't matter that I didn't choose them. I'm their mother. I already feel the natural instinct to protect, and it's so damn strong, grandfather… There's more… I didn't realize it until just now when you offered to kill them… There's love. I love my baby."

"I'm sorry, Sophie. I did not mean to injure you when I offered that."

She sniffed and pulled away from him wiping the

tears from her cheeks. "I know. I should go now. Tristan is busy today, doing terrible things I'm sure, but I have the day free... Perhaps the night as well I'm not sure."

"I promise to work on your problem with my whole heart and mind." He gave her a reassuring smile and caught her chin in his sharp hand. "You will be safe again, soon. I swear it. We'll figure it out. Don't panic if you see me at the Lair in the next few days. Just act naturally, and trust me. I'd burn the world down to protect Jorgie, too, and you... Go enjoy your freedom, short as it may be."

A strange expression crossed her face like she was caught between embarrassment and excitement all of a sudden.

"What?" He asked raising one eyebrow.

She blushed. "Oh, it's nothing, just an idle curiosity... Umm... About Dryads."

"What about them?"

"Um, when they are in their corporeal form, are they *exactly* the same as everyone else, you know, *anatomically*?"

"Yes..." He said slowly. "Why?"

Her cheeks flushed a deeper shade and she shrugged unconvincingly. "Like I said, just curious."

She hugged him tightly around the waist again briefly before letting go and heading out the door. He stared and narrowed his eyes at the place she had just been. What was that? She'd gotten all goofy there at the end. He dismissed it as none of his business and headed to the library, his mind already frantically searching for a solution for her. He pulled books down off shelves, stacking them on the table, as his mind moved over some of his old skills. Skills he had not used since his days as the high priest of the *Rune-dy*.

There were a number of things he could do to protect Jorgie. He just needed to find the right one for this situation. His grandson was young, too young really to have any kind of judgment Rahaxeris could count on. Whatever he decided to do, that action or magic must work no matter where or what Jorgie was doing. Inspiration struck and he went back to the shelf plucking his cookbook down from the top.

Rahaxeris would have enjoyed the novelty of his work over the next hour, given that he had not done anything of this nature in over 100 years. Yes, he would have enjoyed it, if it weren't for the reason why he needed to. Jordan was his youngest grandchild. The thought of anyone threatening him ignited a fire in Rahaxeris' heart. But it wasn't any fire. This bloodthirsty flame of vengeance was cold, calculating, and expertly cruel.

He smiled to himself as he poured the sweet red liquid into a circular mold. He leaned over and blew on it, whispering an incantation into the candy as it hardened. As soon as it was cool, he popped it out of the mold and wrapped it in a square of shiny gold paper. He slid the candy into his pocket and looked at the time. If he was correct in his assumption, Jorgie should be getting home from school right about now. Rahaxeris hit the air with the flat of his hand, opening a portal straight into his grandson's bedroom and went through it.

The bedroom was empty, but he could hear the boy talking to his older sister, Lacey, in the living room beyond. He waited patiently behind the door. After a few minutes, Jorgie burst into the room, throwing his jacket and backpack at his bed as if they were repulsive to him. Rahaxeris smiled to himself and very slowly and silently pushed the door shut. He held his finger up to his lips as Jorgie turned and saw him. His grandson's eyes widened in surprise, but then the boy smiled. Rahaxeris crooked his finger at the boy. He came close and hugged his grandfather around the waist quickly. Rahaxeris leaned down so he was face to face with him and pulled out the piece of candy.

"I brought you something special... Something very important," he whispered." This is magic. You need to eat it."

Jorgie eyed the candy suspiciously for a second. "Will it hurt?"

"No, not at all. But it might tickle. You're not ticklish are you?"

Jorgie nodded. "Sometimes I am. What kind of magic is it?"

"Protective. Like I said, it's very important. You need to eat it now."

His big green eyes grew a little wider. "This is a secret, isn't it grandfather?"

"It is, clever boy. I know I can trust you not to tell. You have to do this for Sophie."

Jorgie took the candy. "Sophie's in trouble. You know about it, don't you? That's why I have to eat this?"

Rahaxeris smiled warmly at the boy and ruffled his hair. "That's exactly it."

Jorgie nodded and put the candy in his mouth. He moved it back and forth between his cheeks and then swallowed. The barrier of protection that slid over his skin was invisible, but Rahaxeris could see it clearly. Jorgie shivered and snickered trying to hold in a giggle as the spell tickled him for a second.

"You're a good boy. I love you."

He reached up with his little arms and hugged Rahaxeris around the neck quickly and then let go. Rahaxeris straightened up, winked at the boy, opened a new portal, and left.

The protection of the magic wasn't absolute, but it was damn good. The barrier over his skin would deflect any blade. He could still be bound by rope or chains, however, and if someone truly wanted to hurt him and was determined, means could be found. But if it came to that, this would buy time, thwart and confuse the perpetrator.

Thirteen

On the surface was grief, heavy and suffocating like a humid summer day. All the dryads felt it, breathed it in without being able to stop, even though they choked on it. Eli had never experienced anything like it in his whole life. Not even his death memories came close. Those were dreams, dismissed after waking, like fantasies that didn't belong in the here and now. There was too much going on inside him and he couldn't stand to be around anyone else, now that he had done his duty.

Many of the other warriors seemed to look to Eli for instruction. He'd never intentionally sought leadership. It just sort of happened organically. The warrior's meeting that morning had seemed endless to him. After hours of arguing and planning and more arguing, the only conclusion that was agreed to was that the warriors would take turns standing guard all around the boundary of the Wood during the night.

The fact that this was all, irritated Eli, but he didn't know what else they could do at the moment. The entire Wood had been searched, every inch. So, they all knew it was true, Sam's body had been taken. The passion of the outrage filled them all collectively. Eli was by no means immune to it, he felt it acutely, but it seemed to him that he was the only one that understood their limitations were so great compared to the wolves. Passion could only take you so far. If there was anyone else who seemed to understand that the way he did, or probably more than he did was Ler.

Extracting himself from everyone else, Eli climbed into his faux trunk and exhaled in the silence. It was then his mind turned to Sophie. He ran his tongue along the inside of his mouth and over his teeth. His lips tingled, the flesh remembering the feel of her lips, the taste of her tongue. His mouth grew hot and he swallowed. He looked at her inside his mind, he smelled her, and he touched her. For a little while, he was lost inside a fantasy where there were no thoughts, no reasons, no barriers, and no guilt. But it didn't last. He curled his hands into tight fists. Why did he feel like this? How could he possibly feel desire for a she-wolf? And the timing couldn't be worse, damnably so.

He thought back to everything they had said to one another and marveled at the urgency of it all. He'd only just met her, and yet it felt as if she stood on the edge of a blade. As if there was no time to test, to try, and to flirt. Under the surface, he felt as if he had to grab her now because now would be all there was. Why did it feel like that?

Eli cursed himself. It was impossible. He couldn't spend time with her, especially now. If tension escalated with the wolves and actual fighting broke out, any time he spent with her would be traitorous to his own people. The same would be true for her. There was no reason to risk it... Absolutely no reason at all. And yet, as he thought it, some deep place in him flared and argued there was every reason even if he couldn't name them.

Guilt sank heavy into his skull like iron drifting to the ocean floor as he thought about Sam, Dez, and Nel. He owed them vengeance. He owed their memory the force of every blow he could land.

Eli...

He jolted as the Heart's voice came into his mind.

I told you we would speak. Are you ready?

"Yes. I am listening."

I am grieved, and I am angered beyond what I have felt in a very long time. Since the resurrection of your race, I have waited. You are special to me, but I hoped I could wait longer, perhaps the next generation or the one after.

"I don't understand," Eli admitted.

I know where your tree is. I'm the one who put it there. You have always wondered why you felt the need to hide. I put that desire in you. You must be prepared for a life removed. The memories you have of the woman, with the words on her hands... I'm sure you have guessed that she was your mother.

"Yes, that was my guess."

The vision you have of her, of her reading. That was her job... Her birthright actually. She was the historian, granted access to all the ancient knowledge of the dryads. She alone could read the archives. The words existed inside her. Along every ring of her trunk words were carved, the knowledge tattooed into her veins. I have kept this hidden from you, but I can no longer for it is your birthright as well. I had hoped it would be unnecessary for you to access this knowledge, but it is necessary, and you have proven worthy.

Eli swallowed hard. "Are you sure of that? I doubt that I am worthy to carry any such honor."

I know you. And no, you are not perfect. But, as I said, this is your birthright .and I shall not keep it from you any longer. You do not have to give anything up to accept it. You do not have to stop being a warrior. Being the historian comes with responsibility, it's true. But the knowledge you will have access to will only grant you power beyond what you ever imagined possible for yourself.

"Where is the history? How can I read it?"

It is already inside you, etched along your rings. It was always there but I kept you from being able to see it. You can read it when you are inside your real tree. Or you can read it on your hands, wherever you are, as your mother used to.

His guilt suddenly felt heavier than ever. "Are you really sure about me? My heart is divided. I desire to be loyal but... I don't want to betray you even unwittingly. I'm not worthy to be the historian...And what if I never have children? Who will be the Historian after me?"

I appreciate your candor but I would ask you not to argue with me, or question my judgment. If you remain childless, I shall pass the history to another I deem worthy. You are the historian, Eli.

"Forgive me."

He waited for a few moments but the Heart was silent. So, he guessed that was it. Anxious and curious, Eli climbed out of his mock tree, looked around surreptitiously to make sure no one was close by, and then headed off toward his real tree. He became excited and began jogging. What did this mean? What kinds of knowledge did he now possess that no one else did?

The answer to that question came to him before he reached his tree. Eli skidded to a halt, his vision darkening. He felt compressed. Words filled him up and ran through his veins. He fell to his hands and knees unable to breathe. His pulse pounded in his ears. He could hear nothing else, and the rhythm slowed. Then it stopped. His heart held still when it was supposed to pump. Just one second, one beat that was lost, then his heart restarted.

He rolled onto his back and clutched at his head as centuries of history and knowledge poured through his brain. It felt as though his blood was filled with thorns. Had the Heart lied? Was it going to kill him?

His whole body jolted once, a spasm jerking every

muscle. Then it was all gone. The pain, the discomfort, the inability to breathe, all of it faded away and he could breathe again. Eli stared up at the sky where the traces of the tail end of the storm still lingered. He got to his feet, slowly feeling the movement of his body, testing it.

He pulled his shirt off and searched his skin for the bird thing, worried that something happened to it or it had somehow left him. He exhaled in relief as it moved slowly over his solar plexus. He put his shirt back on and finished walking all the way to his tree. Climbing inside, the words filled his vision. He didn't have to read it, to know it. The knowledge was there, deep in his consciousness like his death memories.

It was like answers to things you had learned as a child. Things you thought you had forgotten, things you didn't think about. And yet, if asked about it, the memory would be jolted and you would know again. That's what the history was like for Eli. He was amazed, overwhelmed, and somewhat fearful of what this would mean for him.

He climbed back out of his trunk and raised his hands up. Just as he had seen in his death memory of his mother, words covered his palms as though they had been carved. But they were by no means stationary. The words moved, replaced with new ones as soon as he finished reading what was already there. He found accessing the information through words written was more comfortable, but not necessary. Any questions he had, all he had to do was think them, and the answers would rise up through him and he would know the answer instantly.

The entire afternoon slid past Eli like mere seconds as he sat with his back against his trunk, his hands resting open in his lap, like an endless open book. Why was there so much they didn't know? Did his mother know all of this as well? Did she have everything? And if so, did she hide it from the others? Or did the Heart coach her on what could be common knowledge among the dryads and what was a need to know basis?

His eyes slid over the words and suddenly the whole world seemed to just stop. What? That can't be true. He narrowed his eyes at the words, reading them over meticulously and then again. He rubbed his eyes and read them again. *Aloud,* the history urged him. *You must read the words aloud.*

"Fehrum agat naihl."

As soon as the words hit the air Eli felt the shift inside his body. He got to his feet, a new measure of strength surging through him. All he had to do was think of what he wanted to manifest on his skin and it appeared. Carved wooden armor immediately covered his chest. He touched it tentatively with his fingertips, afraid he was somehow hallucinating. He imagined different pieces of armor, likewise, they surfaced on his skin as he thought them. Curved spikes twisted the tops of the vambraces covering his forearms. He held his hands up, his fingers outstretched and watched as his fingernails lengthened, sharpened, stretching out and pointing like claws made of wood. Green tipped the very ends of his talons in what he recognized as natural, plant-based neurotoxin.

The moment he decided to return to normal, he did. His claws shrank back and his armor reabsorbed into his skin. What had he just become? Not that he was complaining. With these new advantages, it seemed likely he could hold his own against a wolf in beast form. He scanned the generational memories to see if there was more power he could access. There was...

"Crux pherraum." Excited, Eli spoke the strange words aloud. At first, nothing happened. What had he just said? What did it mean? The answer came from deep inside him. *Weapons*. His pulse instantly sped up. Holy shit! Could he manifest weapons at will the way he could armor?

He held his hands out and closed his eyes. It was as easy as imagining it. In his mind's eye, he envisioned a staff. The next moment he felt its weight in his palms. He opened his eyes and looked down at it clasped in his hands. Eli laughed aloud. This was incredible! He twirled the staff a few times before allowing it to reabsorb into him.

At first, it made sense to him that all he could create would be made of wood, but he was wrong or at least in a way. Just for the heck of it, he closed his eyes and imagined an axe. Again, the weight of it fell into his palms. Astonished, he lifted the blade up toward his face and ran his finger down the smooth side. It wasn't metal. It was stone. Gray petrified wood, perfectly smooth and polished, the edge as sharp as steel.

Gripping it in one hand he manifested a second in his other hand. Smiling to himself he centered his balance and made a basic front strike with one axe and then the other. The weapons vanished when he desired. He didn't need Tristan's axe now. He would still keep it for a while, just in case it was needed as proof sometime. But he didn't need or want to fight with it again.

Where had those words come from? What language was it? He closed his eyes as the answer thrust to the forefront of his mind. Darksong, the ancient tree. The words were Dradhi, the language of the first, the original dryad. An image of it appeared in his head. Where the manifestation now burned, there used to just be Darksong. The Heart of Regia was there as it always had been, under the ground, but its lifeforce pulsed into Darksong alone, instead of burning. The flames came after...after what? He asked himself, the answer going opaque, hesitant to expose the truth. He pushed on it, demanding.

Fragments flashed. The history had been scrubbed.

Eli's lips parted, his vision darkening again. Snatches of knowledge moved through his consciousness in short bursts. A quarrel, a dispute, rage, and heartbreak. Why?

Darksong was grounded. He didn't walk outside of his tree. But the wood spoke. The bark twisted with mouths, not one but many. His bark was blackened as the Heart burned him, taking away the beauty of his foliage, twisting his branches into sharp, contorted angles. What was his crime? At first, there was no answer.

What was his crime? Eli asked again. Nothing. Then he saw her. A woman of unknown origin. Knowledge of her race was completely stricken from the history. The answer would not show itself to Eli no matter how hard he pushed. What was it? What was her part? Why did the Heart take offense and punish Darksong? Was it forbidden love, as Shi and Ler had been?

No... That wasn't it. He didn't know what it was and the answer would not reveal itself but it wasn't love.

Who was she? She moved with unnatural grace but not slowly. She was thin, her arms and legs were over long so she looked stretched. Her hair fell down her back all the way down past her knees, the color of moonlight. Her skin was deep blue and shimmered with stars, constellations, and galaxies. The stars on her skin moved even when she was stationary. Then she turned and he saw her face. Except she had no face only night sky where her eyes nose and mouth should have been.

Eli shivered and recoiled mentally as though she truly did face him in real life and real time. It didn't matter that she had no eyes, she looked right into him. And it didn't matter that she had no mouth, for she smiled at him hungrily.

He struggled to force the reluctant knowledge. Who was she? Tell me.

A quiet laugh echoed through the history *inside* him. The resonance of her laugh chilled and taunted him simultaneously. The image of her flickered and vanished leaving behind her name... Destiny.

Sophie shifted into a wolf and ran home from Kyhael. It was a long way and took her quite a while to get home. When she finally arrived back at the Lair, the evening was just beginning its dance of color. Telling her grandfather what was happening to her was a great relief, just to say the words aloud. Even if he could do nothing, just knowing he was trying gave her strength to carry on. Her mind began to spin on the possibilities of the evening and the night.

She would do as Tristan told her to, she would go to her family. She would be a part of them. If only for an hour or two she would slide into the weaving of the ties of blood that she belonged to. The lies would come as easy as breathing and she wouldn't worry about them. The words didn't matter. The only thing that mattered, the only thing she would allow to matter tonight was just existing side-by-side with those she loved the most and those who loved her. She wouldn't struggle against lying to them, it was necessary. She wouldn't feel anger or guilt about the deception.

Sophie carried a spark of hope. Somehow, someway, she would get loose from Tristan, and soon. Then she could tell the truth and the lies would be forgiven and forgotten.

The guards she no longer trusted, standing outside her family home open the doors for her. Her heart expanded as the familiarity hit her senses, the voices, the smells, and the textures of home. All of it was real and pure, a stark antithesis of Tristan's shrine. Everyone turned and looked at her as she came in.

"There you are," her mother said.

Jorgie jumped up from the couch and ran to her, wrapping his arms around her waist.

"Um... Tristan's busy. So I thought I'd come home for dinner."

Her father gave her an intense questioning look. "You say that like you don't live here anymore. Are you moving in with him?"

"I am," she answered casually.

Shreve scowled and looked away from her, his cheek pulled tight as if he was fighting to contain what he wanted to say.

Yes, daddy. You're right. I'm making the wrong choice. You want to tell me so. You want to demand I listen to reason. But you won't say anything, will you? No. You won't because I'm all grown up. My mistakes are my own. I know what you want to say and probably so much more. And you're completely right, daddy. I love you so much. You're the best father ever. I promise you'll understand by and by.

She said all this to him in her heart, wishing she could say it aloud right then.

Shreve stood up, walked across the living room to his and Sabra's bedroom and closed the door behind him. Her heart sank. She knew he wouldn't yell or make demands on her, and he wasn't being passive aggressive by leaving the room. She had a sense he was more hurt than angry. Hurt that she could make such a large decision without even asking him his opinion or how he felt about it, whether she listened or not. At least that was her assumption on how he must be feeling.

She sat down on the couch next to her mom. A frown creased Sabra's forehead as she read some letter or petition from the people, occasionally scrawling notes in between the lines. Lacey glanced at her for a moment, a small smirk on her lips, before looking back down at the notebook in her lap where she two made notes and sketched designs of things for her upcoming mating ceremony. Jorgie plunked down on the floor cross-legged, concentrating on a puzzle scattered in front of him.

A small shred of relaxation breathed into her lungs. For a few moments, she would pretend that there was nothing wrong at all. She had been pretending *that*. She was pretending it, but at that moment, she would fool herself. Sophie would lie and believe her own lie.

After a few moments of comfortable peaceful silence, Jorgie began to whine it must be about dinner time. As soon as he said it, her stomach growled in agreement. Her mom put her papers away and walked to the front double doors. She stuck her head out and gave orders to the guards to bring dinner for the family. Sophie heard them mutter their compliance and begin to shuffle way.

Sabra made to close the doors but before she could latch them, a boot blocked them. Sophie caught herself before she gasped as Tristan's voice filled the room. He laughed jovially as her mom stepped back from the doors and let him in.

"Didn't mean to startle you," he chuckled. "I was just hoping to find Sophie." His gaze caught hers.

She slid seamlessly back into the necessary

deception and smiled warmly at him. His eyes held no mistrust, only a deep well of love. Obvious, obsessed, twisted love. She got up and rushed into his arms as though she'd missed him desperately.

"Would you like to join us for dinner, Tristan?" Her mom asked.

"That would be lovely. Thank you… Actually, I was really hoping for an invitation. I was prepared to fish for it if I had to." He smiled, turning the charm on hard. Everything about him oozed charm. He would've been an expert salesman. He knew just how to regulate his voice, tease with his beautiful blue eyes, and put people totally at ease with his demeanor.

Sophie cursed herself for not seeing through him before… Before it was too late… Before he'd ruined her whole life.

"Don't be silly," Sabra said. "Of course you're welcome." She looked over her shoulder at Lacey. "Is Callen joining us for dinner as well?"

"No. Not tonight. He's busy doing something or other."

Tristan held her *close* to his side. She nestled next to him and rested her head on his shoulder. He turned his face into her hair and inhaled. His grip on her tightened. She fought not to wince and looked at him questioningly.

"Sweetie," he said softly. "I need to talk to you. In private. It's important."

"Okay. Let's go to my room."

He kept his arm possessively around her as they crossed the living room. From the side of her eye, she saw Jorgie watching them. His eyes narrowed. She could see him working it out. She shook her head, just a tiny, almost imperceptible movement. He blinked and looked back down at his puzzle. Darn kid was too smart.

Sophie didn't bother turning on the light in her room as they entered it. She really had no idea exactly what it was he wanted and she fought down her trepidation. Before he could say or do anything she turned, wrapping her arms around his waist, pressing intimately against him, and nuzzled his neck.

"I missed you so much today," she whispered before catching his earlobe between her lips.

He responded to her physically. Clasping her to him and kissing her hard. Mentally she sighed in relief that he wasn't angry, or if he was she had distracted him. For a few minutes they made out in the dark then he pulled back from her, lifting her wrist up to his face, and inhaling at her pulse.

"What?" She asked.

He let go of her wrist, pressing his index finger on

top of the pulse in her neck. She held still, totally passive. He moved behind her and pressed both of his hands to her lower abdomen. She knew what he was doing and a string of bad words uncoiled in her mind like a ball of yarn. The animal side of them was already making it evident. He let out a deep sigh, the sound satisfied and content.

"You're pregnant, sweetheart. Why didn't you tell me? Had you not yet realized?"

"Oh! No, I didn't realize. Are you sure?"

He chuckled quietly. "I'm sure. It's probably not obvious to anyone else yet. But of course, I've been looking for the signs. Being this close to you, I can smell it. Pregnancy hormones are radiating off your skin. Just barely, but still undeniable... Oh, Sophie, I'm so happy. No, that's not right. It's so much more than *happiness* I feel."

She smiled, fake happy tears building along her bottom eyelids. "I'm so excited."

"Shall we go tell your family?"

"Oh, no. Not yet, please. My parents are very traditional. They won't like it coming before a mating ceremony."

He nodded and gave her a soft, understanding smile. "Okay. The news will keep, but not long. You know everyone will know it very soon. Your hormones will continue to build until any wolf who passes you will know, even before you begin to show."

"Of course you're right, Tristan. We'll tell them, just please not tonight."

He leaned down and kissed her again slow and soft. She closed her eyes and thought about Eli. It wasn't Tristan. It wasn't his mouth. She imagined she kissed Eli. She despised the here and now. Her mind drifted through the forest to her cave, where her dryad waited among her art. Her heart latched onto him, even though she didn't know him at all. He was her defiance. She got lost in her memory of kissing Eli.

Tristan pulled back and gazed at her somewhat stunned. "Wow, Sophie. You've never kissed me like that before...I believe you truly must be happy."

She fought not to grimace. This was gross and dirty. She would never let her imagination run away with her like that again. She wouldn't kiss Tristan the way she'd kiss Eli. The two were divided. She would keep them that way.

"Dinner," Sabra called from downstairs.

He took her by the hand and led her as though she couldn't find the way in her family home on her own. They sat down at the long table side by side along with her family. Her dad sat across from her. She kept her eyes averted, but she could feel his gaze on her often. She couldn't betray her lies for even one second. Steeling herself, she lifted her head and acted *natural*ly. I'm in love. They need to see how much. They need to see it's real. They don't know he's a monster. No objections will be raised so long as they believe I'm in love.

Small talk punctuated dinner. Tristan conversed easily. Slick as ever. She focused on teasing Lacey about her mating ceremony prep. She was pulling it off. The stern gaze from her father eased or moved to the background, but he continued to look as though he was unhappy with Tristan's presence. He would probably act like that no matter who was sitting beside her. She was his little girl, grown or not. He'd been like that with Callen at first too, she reminded herself.

Tristan got to his feet, lifting his wine glass. "I have an announcement."

Her stomach dropped. He reached for her hand. She smiled and gave it.

"I thought it best for this to be here. Just family first..." he paused, seemingly for dramatic effect. "I'm in love with Sophie. I've asked her to mate with me and she's accepted."

"Oh, sweetheart!" her mom said getting to her feet and coming over to her clasping her in a tight hug.

I'm happy. I'm in love. This is what I want. I want nothing more.

"I'm so excited, mom! You have to help me plan our ceremony."

"Of course! Hey, you and your sister can plan together."

Lacey came over to her then and hugged her as well. "You said things were getting serious between you two. I guess you meant it. Where's your cuff?"

"Oh, um...I don't have—"

"Right here," Tristan said, pulling a carved wooden bracelet from his pocket and slipping it over her wrist.

Lacey looked down at it closely and nodded approvingly. "Nice choice, Tristan."

He didn't seem to hear her. He stared intently at Sophie, waiting for her reaction. She ran her fingers gently over the carvings. "Beautiful. I love it...I love you." She sounded so sincere, she almost fooled herself.

The cuff was very light, but it felt so heavy to her. Now, everyone would see they were engaged. Her eyes darted to Jorgie. Her resolve shored up. Her little brother didn't look at her. He kept his eyes on his plate and ate his dessert.

Tristan shook Shreve's hand, giving him the typical

assurances he would always love and cherish Sophie. Her dad didn't say much.

"Well, I'm sorry to have to go now, but I've got some stuff to handle this evening," Tristan said to everyone. "Thank you all so much for such a warm welcome into your family."

He towed her behind him through the double doors and down the stairs a ways before pulling her into a dark corner. He kissed her fiercely for a few minutes.

"That was amazing, Sophie. Better than I had imagined it. And most things hardly ever are better than I imagine...I've got to go. I have a ton of shit to deal with still, and I'll be gone all night. I'm sure of that now." He kissed her again. "I'll miss you tonight."

"When will I see you again?"

"I assume I'll be home tomorrow morning. Come for breakfast."

"Okay." She answered easily. "I will."

He let go of her and continued on down the stairs. Alone, she swallowed hard. Her hands began to shake. *No. Not yet. Not here. You can't lose it here. Hold on.*

She had free time. All night. She didn't intend to waste it sleeping. The evening was ending, darkness on the horizon flowing up, pushing the serpentine strokes of the jeweled sunset colors away. She wouldn't be that. She wouldn't be the sunset that was shoved aside by the night. Her hands pressed into her abdomen and she felt her pulse through her palms. She was going to be a mother. Somehow, even if she was stuck with Tristan, somehow she would maintain her identity and not just buried in a dark cave. Her child would know who she was even if she had to hide it from everyone else. Her child would know her. And what was she? She thought of Eli... She was defiant.

Sophie eased back the pressure building in her hands. She would let everything out but not yet. Tristan had crashed into the peace of her family and broken its shape with his announcement. Broken or not, she needed to go back there, at least for a little while.

The guards opened the double doors for her as she came back. Her family was still seated at the table, talking about her. They all looked over at her as she came in and quieted. She didn't return to the table but flopped onto the couch in the living room. She smiled over at all of them.

"Yeah, I know you were just talking about me. It's okay. I didn't really prepare you for that. I know it was a bit of a shock. And yes we are moving quickly, but when you're sure, you're sure. And I've never been more sure about anything as I am about me and Tristan."

Her father nodded at her resignedly and poured more wine into his glass. He stayed at the table while the rest of the family came back into the living room, surrounding her in a natural way, each of them going back to what they had been doing before dinner. Lacey made notes, Sabra went back to her official reading, and Jorgie continued with his puzzle.

The whole family stayed like that for a half an hour without anyone moving or speaking to one another. They had accepted her engagement. All of a sudden, it felt harder than it had before and her cheeks flushed with the pressure of tears. She got up quickly and went her room before anyone noticed. She buried her face in her pillow and just focused on breathing.

"Sophie?" Jorgie whispered, having snuck into her darkened room beside her. He leaned down putting his little face *next* to her ear. "Don't worry. Everything will be okay." His voice was so quiet she had to strain to hear the words. "Grandfather put protection on me."

She rolled onto her side and pulled him down next to her. "What do you mean?" She whispered.

"He said I had to do it for you. To help you. He put magic over me. I'm protected. So you don't have to worry about me."

"You didn't tell anyone else did you?"

"No. It's a secret."

She snuggled him close and kissed the top of his

head. "I'm so glad you're protected, but that doesn't solve everything. You still have to do what I tell you to, okay? If I tell you to do something, even if it's the weirdest thing you've ever heard, you have to do it immediately. Okay? You promised me that remember?"

"I remember. I promise. I just want you back. I want Sophie. The real Sophie."

"I want her back, too."

The next two hours were like a haze as if she was drugged. She came out of her room and interacted with her family some more, but she was an empty shell. Her mind and heart were deep inside her cave, and all she was doing was waiting for them to go to sleep.

Sophie lay in bed, in her pajamas, listening. Her ears reached out for the silence and embraced it tightly. She got up and stood in front of her closet for a few minutes debating what she should wear. Why was she doing this? She was going to create because she had to. She hoped she would see Eli because she wanted to. But whether or not she saw him depended on if he came to her. How would that work? Would he just know? Would the art that lived on his skin let him know she was there? Waiting for him?

She shook herself. She was crazy. Why would a hot guy like him want to spend time with her anyway? She was pregnant. What they had shared that morning was just a bizarre, random moment of insanity that should not be repeated. None of her internal recriminations stopped her for even one second.

Sophie took off the cuff Tristan had put on her wrist and set it on top of her dresser. She reached into her closet and pulled out a black slip of a dress. Since she was going to indulge this insanity, she felt like dressing for it. The silky fabric slid over her skin, the hem falling to her ankles. She remained barefoot and covered her shoulders with a full-length hooded cloak. Finally, she pulled from her shifter blood and changed her face till she couldn't recognize it.

Shrouded in black, she moved through the house and swiftly through the double doors. She moved quickly away from the guards, not acknowledging them in any way. The stone stairs were cool and smooth under her feet. The sensation reminded her of how Tristan had made her stand on broken glass. Her feet were completely healed but she hoped he would never injure the bottoms of her feet again. It could make it hard or impossible to run away if she needed to. She met no one on her way down and as she reached ground level and headed out into the night, again she did not address the guards or show them her face.

Callen opened the door when Tristan knocked and stepped aside to let him in. As soon as he shut the door, Tristan grabbed him by the arm.

"How many?" he demanded in a whisper.

"All of them. Twelve in total, including you and me."

Tristan exhaled and let go of Callen. "Good. You've told them everything?"

"Of course. They bought it immediately. Satran is in there right now, keeping them fired up. All of them are with you. Or so they've said."

"Excellent. We only need their loyalty for tonight anyway. I'm not sure how many of them will survive."

"I thought that was already decided."

Tristan chuckled quietly. "I've decided the outcome I want for tonight but I hardly expect everything to go according to plan."

"How did it go upstairs?"

Tristan smiled broadly. "Perfect, actually better than perfect. Sophie is completely mine and now her family knows it. She's pregnant and cuffed."

"I guess we have effectively infiltrated the first family, eh? I've got Lacey. You've got Sophie... I still don't see how it's fair. How do I know you are going to honor your word to me?"

Rage flared a warning in Tristan's eyes. "Knock it off. This was never a competition who could grab the daughter with the most power and you know it. Sophie is mine! She always has been. That's the difference between you and me, Callen. You don't love Lacey you only love power. I'm not judging you for that. I want the power as well, I admit it. Even if Sophie wasn't Princess-wolf I would do all I could to secure her to me. I have always loved her. It's just my good luck she just so happens to be the firstborn of Sabra and Shreve, but it truly is just coincidence. Or perhaps it's fate. Either way, I will be pack leader and you shall be my second in command." Tristan tilted his head to the side and crossed his arms over his chest. "You've said you were fine with that. Have you changed your mind?"

"No. I stand by what I said."

"Good, because we've got a big night ahead of us. Last night was just the beginning. The dryad's hearts will be broken. They will be enraged and afraid... We've shown them we have no code, no boundaries. Tonight we'll seal the deal. We'll kill as many dryads as possible, stage a scenario that never happened, and create a political shit storm for Sabra. This is only the beginning of her downfall."

Callen nodded appreciatively. "I'm ready, and so are all the poor, expendable bastards waiting in the next room."

FOURTEEN

The day slipped past Eli like the flow of water. He shifted between reading and training. Already a formidable fighter, new heights of skill slid seamlessly into him from the history. Knowledge, instinct, speed, and execution all matured to a level he never dreamed possible for himself. An axe in each hand, he fought invisible adversaries for hours. His favorite part of these new abilities was his precision. Every movement, every block and strike an impressive display of accuracy.

He blinked and looked up. It was dark. Night had fallen around him without his notice. He began striding toward the Heart. He wasn't supposed to be on guard, but he wanted to check those who were had what they needed and were positioned at the proper places to ensure the most protection during the night to the dryads who slept. He would give them the words. It would only take a few moments. All they would have to do was say the words aloud and each of them would transform the way he had. One phrase spoken and they would gain the ability to manifest armor, grow claws of deadly poison, and whatever other types of weaponry they could conceive of at will.

He saw Lex as he jogged toward the boundary of the Wood.

"Hey, where have you been all afternoon? I haven't

seen you since this morning."

"I can't even... It's a really long story. I can hardly believe it myself." Eli said.

Lex quirked an eyebrow up at him. "You look all keyed up. Did you finally decide women are worth your time? Who is she?"

"What? No, it's not that. Look." He held his hands out so Lex could see the words.

Lex frowned as he gazed down. "What did you do to yourself?"

"That's just it! I didn't do it. The Heart did this to me. It's because of my mother. She was the historian when she was alive. Now so am I. I'm the historian! This is my birthright. Eons of dryad history lives inside me now. I have access to the archives. To generational memories... It's absolutely insane what I've learned today. I'll tell you all about it but before it gets any later I have to give you the power."

"Power? What power?"

"This..." Eli closed his eyes and envisioned armor covering his body. He felt it solidify over his skin and opened his eyes in time to see Lex step back, his mouth hanging open. "Hold on! Don't lose it yet! There's more." Eli closed his eyes again and thought of his new axe.

Lex's mouth continued to hang open and his face became rather pale. "You... You can give me that power?"

"Yes. All you have to do is repeat after me. *Fehrum agat naihl.*"

Without hesitation, Lex repeated the words. Eli watched with a satisfied smirk on his face as Lex jolted once and then shivered.

"Close your eyes and just imagine the armor you want and it will appear on your body," Eli instructed.

He did, carved wooden armor manifesting on Lex. He opened his eyes and touched the breastplate. For a moment he just ran his fingers over it, tentatively, as if it might vanish. Then he looked up, his eyes bugging and whooped loudly.

"This is unbelievable!"

"I know! But that's only half of it. Now for the weapons. Say, *Crux pherraum.*"

Lex repeated the words, another shiver instantly going over him.

"It's as easy as the armor. Just imagine what you want and it will appear in your hands."

He closed his eyes and a sword manifested in his hands. Lex ran his fingertips along the side of the sword. "Holy crap! It's wood. Petrified. It's freakin sharp, too! This is going to tip the scales. Those wolves are not going to be ready for this."

"Definitely. I'm going to go around to everyone on guard and give them the words."

"So that came from our history? What language is it?" Lex asked.

"It's our original language, Dradhi. Long story, I'll tell you about it tomorrow. Now I need to..." Eli's voice trailed off. The bird thing on his chest was moving. It throbbed next to his heart in tandem with his own pulse. It felt as if it wrapped its wings around his heart, the sensation at first warm and comforting, then it constricted tightly. He choked on his breath, then it released him, unfolding and moving up to his shoulder where it tugged at him. Sophie...

"Eli? What's the matter with you?"

He shook himself and looked back at Lex. "I... I have to go. Can you go around and give these words to the others on guard? Please? I have something..."

Lex scowled at him quizzically. "I guess. What's gotten into you? Why are you so desperate to get away?"

Eli ignored his questions. "*Fehrum agat naihl.* Got it? Repeat it."

Lex repeated it a few times. "Okay, I got it. What's the other one?"

"*Crux pherraum.*"

Lex repeated this one a few times as well.

"Share it with everyone on guard tonight. Do it quickly. Do it now." Eli said.

Lex crossed his arms, about to demand an explanation from his friend, but before he could, Eli turned on his heel and sprinted away into the darkness.

The ground under her bare feet felt startlingly good, even when it hurt, even when it was sharp. Sophie gazed up at the moon as she walked inside the shadows. Every element of her awareness stretched up higher, farther, and also deeper. *I'm alive. The night is mine. I will consume it.*

Her eyes sharpened the closer she drew to her cave. She was looking for *her*. The dark, feral thing she'd created. Where was she? Did she still exist? Was she capable of killing Tristan, as she had told her grandfather was her purpose?

Sophie was relieved she had decided to tell her grandfather the truth, he'd come through for her. She didn't know when she would get the chance to ask him what he had done to protect Jorgie. She couldn't trust that problem no longer existed. At least not yet. But still, she was comforted that there was at least some safeguard over her little brother.

She inhaled deeply as she entered the cave. Time had not held steady for her that day. It jerked her around, agonizingly slow, endless, pointed and dizzyingly fast at other times. Had it truly only been this morning that she was right where she was now, kissing a stranger?

She walked around the small space lightly touching the images hanging in the air. She contemplated each one in turn. She faced the image of the baby, going perfectly still. Her spirit stormed behind the surface of her cool exterior. Tristan was a monster. Something of him, fragments, mixed with her, created something new, *someone* new. Should she fear them? Should she fear her own child? Would they take after their father?

There were no answers.

Sophie turned away from the baby painting. All thoughts must be shut off. Her problems did not belong here. Her lies could not be permitted in this space. Would Eli come back? She wanted him to. It would be better if he didn't... It didn't matter if he came or not she told herself. She came here to paint.

Sophie lifted her hands, her emotions rising up through her. *Bleed... Bleed out.* Muddy colors pushed out of her fingertips as she gave herself permission. The lines of the design twisted around and around each other like an intricate knot, the strands tangling and tying to one another. The image detached from her fingers and hovered in the air in front of her face. She didn't like it. Of every image she had ever made this one was the first to lie. She wasn't being honest with herself. She didn't come here to paint.

Sophie reached up, about to grab the image to reabsorb it but then she stopped herself, retracting her hand. No. If Eli came she wanted him to see it. She wanted to know if he would understand the way he had before.

The light that came from her art snagged on the crevices and edges of the cave's walls. She unfastened her cloak and hung it on the wall where the rock jutted out. The cool, moist air felt good against her bare arms. Even if Eli didn't show, she wasn't alone. Sophie placed her hands on her stomach.

I'm sorry little one. I'm not good, not like I should be. I promise I'll try. I don't know how to be yours. But I'll try to learn. I won't ever hurt you. And I'll stand in between you and your father. Even if he breaks me. I'll be the wall, and I won't let him through. You're not his. You're mine.

She closed her eyes and leaned her head back. She thought about her life before Tristan. She couldn't say that she had been happy, or at least not completely. Family love, occasional family drama, school, friends, personal interests, siblings, etc... Sophie always assumed her life was basic. Not so very different from anyone else's. What she wouldn't give to have it back now.

Her life had become a strange dream. Random moments of *oddity*, some of them saturated with beauty and desire. The rest of it was nightmarish, forcing her mind, spirit, and body to detach from one another and live separate. As it was in nightmares, she was trying to run but she was paralyzed. If only something could jolt her awake.

Her breath caught in her lungs she heard someone approaching. Shivers rushed to her skin, a flush of warmth followed. Had he come back? Eli...

Sophie turned away from the mouth of the cave so her back was to him as he came in. She closed her eyes and listened. His gait had been fast and urgent when she first heard him approach, but as he entered the cave, he moved slowly toward her. She waited for him to speak. Anything, a greeting, a question. He didn't say anything. He came up right behind her, not touching, but he was so close she felt the heat from his body and his breath on her shoulder as he exhaled.

She turned her head and looked at him from the side of her eye. He was gazing at the image she had just created, the lie, a small frown on his face. There were no preliminaries between them. Nothing ordinary. She turned her body toward him and lifted her chin defiantly.

"You don't approve." It wasn't a question.

He looked away from the image then, moving his gaze to her. "It's not my place to approve or disapprove. You're the artist...I can't say I particularly like it."

"I don't like it either. I thought about destroying it, but then I was curious what your reaction would be... If you came back. You did. Why?"

"You called me."

"Hmm... Why did you answer?"

He smiled, the dimple in his cheek coming out to play. He took a step back, his gaze heating as his eyes roamed over her. "Why did you wear that dress?"

"I wore it for you." Sophie could hardly believe she had just said that so matter of fact. "Do you like it?"

"Yes… Very much. Probably too much." His voice was as matter-of-fact as hers. "I don't know if I'm reading you correctly. Are you offering yourself to me?"

Sophie began shaking and her eyes widened. Was she? "I… I don't know what I'm doing, except being defiant."

His expression turned contemplative and he was quiet for a while. "You're as much of a thief as I am. I think we both understand this is stolen. This time, the kiss this morning, my thoughts, all of it is stolen, which is why feel so desperate for you. Like a treasure, glinting in front of a pirate, taunting him to seize it because this is his only chance. That's how I feel about you, Sophie. This is a game like you said this morning. It can't matter when we're together. You set the rules, I'll play."

She didn't answer. Her eyes began to burn with tears, and her chin trembled. She had said that, and she had come here dressed to entice him, so why did it hurt when he said it as simply as she had? Everything in his expression softened then, his eyes filling with warmth and understanding.

"I can't say I really like the way that sounds either," he replied to her unspoken response. "I will openly admit that I have never seen a woman as beautiful as you. You spark desire in me and I want to have everything that has transpired in my fantasies of you today. But that's not all. You fascinate me. I want to know everything about you." He looked down at the floor and sighed. "If you offered me something fast and easy with no strings and no heart, would I go for it? I'm not proud to admit I would, but I wouldn't be happy about it... Because... I think you're too special to be used like that."

His words were like the rain, soothing her suffering. "I want to talk to you."

"I want to talk to *you*," he answered.

"Will you go first? Please? Tell me about you."

"Today was the most amazing day of my whole life. It started with you. Everything I felt when I left here this morning was so foreign to me. But as soon as I left, there was also something terrible. A young family was murdered last night. As best we can tell three wolves snuck in and killed them for no reason... They killed a little girl, no older than three. We can't find her body. It's not anywhere in the Wood."

"Oh..." Sophie put her hands over her mouth.

"Yeah," he exhaled raggedly. "I'll come back to that... I like to be alone. I helped to organize everyone who would be on guard tonight, and then I went off by myself. The Heart spoke to me and gave me my birthright. I didn't even know I had a birthright until today..." His black eyes slid out of focus as he talked. "I never knew my parents. I have these memories of them, memories of how they died. All dryads have these. Most of them are of the day the *shadow* sand was brought into the Wood. You know about Shi and Ler, right?"

She nodded. "Yes, I know the story."

"My mother died that day, but my father was executed a day or two before. He was an elder."

"I'm so sorry," she said quietly.

He shook his head. "He deserved it... Anyway, I just learned a few hours ago that my mother was the historian. And now so am I. The Heart gave me the archives. Eons of dryad history is now written inside me."

"That's incredible. You're *the* historian, as in the only one?"

"I'm it. Look." He held out his hands to her so she could see the words.

She looked down at it, a smile spreading her beautiful lips, then she looked up into his face. "I don't understand the words. I don't know the language. So..." Her smile turned mischievous. "You're like a serious book nerd now."

"I'm still a warrior," he argued.

She chuckled. "Don't be offended. You're a sexy

nerd."

"I'll take that sass but only from you."

She snickered. "So what have you learned from the history?"

"This..." He closed his eyes and exhaled, wooden vambraces appearing on his forearms.

Her eyebrows rose and she touched the armor gently with her fingertips. "Wow... It's made of wood."

"Of course, I've got wood for you all day."

A giggle escaped her lips before she could stifle it. She looked up at him, her expression a mixture of amusement, exasperation, and mild disgust. "Really?"

He blinked a few times, giving her an innocent look. "What?" He demanded in mock confusion.

She didn't answer. She just scowled.

Overdramatic realization filled his expression, his eyes going wide. "*I'm a dryad*. You know, a tree person. Trees are made of wood... You have a dirty mind. I didn't mean that at all."

She laughed. She tried not to but she couldn't help herself. "Oh, of course. You didn't mean anything. It's all me."

"Just so long as you can admit it."

She continued to chuckle for a few moments. "Thank you." Her voice held the deepest sincerity.

"For what?"

"Making me laugh. It feels so good. You made me laugh this morning, too. Before that, I can hardly remember the last time I laughed."

He reached forward and took her hands, his eyes going serious. "Tell me what kind of trouble you're in. Maybe I can help."

"It's horrid. I will tell you, just not in here. His name cannot be said here. I need this place to exist separate from him. A world he cannot touch."

"Alright, let's go outside."

She followed him out of the cave, onto the ledge. He turned on her abruptly, reaching for her, placing one hand on her neck, and leaning his face close to hers. "I know what you're about to tell me is going to change things. Before that happens... May I kiss you?" He whispered.

She didn't give him passive approval. She stretched up on her toes, reached around his neck, and pulled his mouth down to hers. She knew what it would be like this time. The taste. The feel of him. His hands gripped her waist just above the flare of her hips, holding her captive against him. It was crazy the way they kissed each other. In sync, total comprehension, unbridled, stolen... There were no questions in this kiss, for either of them. It was only the second time, but he was right, every moment with them would be stolen. So they kissed each other in the knowledge that it might be the last time.

He could have taken her, she wouldn't have tried to stop him. But when desire pushed them right up to the point of no return, they both pulled away simultaneously. Breathless, they held hands and waited for their breathing to return to normal.

"Are you ready?" He asked.

"Yes... And never."

He glanced over at the rocks that jutted out of the ground next to the mouth of the cave and tugged lightly on her hand. "Come with me."

She followed. "Where are we going?"

"Just up here. Ladies first. Just in case you fall, I'll catch you."

She began to climb the natural ladder. "Don't pretend to be a gentleman. You just want to stare at my ass."

"Well yeah, obviously. But I will catch you if you fall."

She giggled again as she reached the top. The night

wind chilled the silky fabric of her dress. She rubbed her arms, shivering. He came up beside her. For a moment they looked out over the top of the Wood. She glanced over her shoulder at the mountain behind them. She belonged in the mountain, he belonged in the forest, and yet here they were. In between. In the sweet, fleeting, stolen in between.

She leaned into him. He rubbed her arms and shoulders to chase the cold away, but she still shivered. He looked around and then took her hand and pulled her gently toward a thick of trees. She leaned against the largest trunk, letting it block the wind for her.

Eli got down on his hands and knees. She gasped as he pressed his hands to the ground, green light sliding out from his hands into the soil. Vines sprouted from the ground, clinging and climbing up the tree trunk, connecting to more sprouting vines on the next tree. They wove together making a wall. He smiled up at her as she gaped at him. More light went out from his hands. In a minute, they were inside a living structure. Four walls of vines held out the wind.

"What's your favorite color, Sophie?"

"Purple, the color of my mother's eyes."

Magenta light spread from his hands this time and the ground erupted in purple flowers. They pushed under her bare feet, soft and thick as a blanket. He lay on his back looking up at the sky through the branches, his hands laced behind his head.

"Come on, lay down with me. I won't do anything. This is a safe place for you. You can say anything and when it's over, the plants will vanish. Tell me all *of* it and then you never have to see or be in this place again."

She lay down next to him and rested her head on his arm. "What if I want to come back? This is amazing, Eli. And I thought I was the artist."

He chuckled. "I'm not an artist. I can make things grow. Doesn't mean I made them. And if you like this, I can do it again for you anytime."

"Hmm...you might regret saying that."

They lay there in silence for a while. He just waited for her to speak. The words swirled in her mind and Sophie felt like she might cry. Then she did. It was quiet. She didn't sob loudly. "You're a fantasy, Eli. I don't want to tell you because I know I'll never see you again if I say it."

"Don't judge my heart, Sophie. Not yet."

"I'm sorry. I'm so sorry...Damnit. I have to..."

He stroked the side of her face with his fingertip. "You promised. This morning. Remember?"

She pinched her eyes shut. "I'm pregnant."

She braced for him to yell or just get up and storm away. He was very still, then he sighed. She chanced looking at him from the side of her eye.

"Yeah. I thought you might be. I hoped you weren't, but I knew. The baby painting...well all of your paintings actually. I knew."

She sat up and glanced down at him. "You knew?! And you still desired me? What kind of a man are you?"

"Hmm...a real jerk I guess, based your tone and expression. What kind of a woman are you? Pregnant with another man's child and yet you're out here with me."

Confused she buried her face in her hands and cried again. His hands grasped her shoulders.

"Sophie...what right do I have to judge you for anything? This is the first real conversation we've ever had. I believed what you told me this morning when you were threatening to kill yourself. You said you were raped. Is that not the truth? Did you want this child?"

She shook her head. "I told you the truth. But why would you...what you said there back in the cave about wanting me, that you would have a fling with me if I offered. I don't understand that."

He blew out a breath. "Okay, yeah. I can see that now. I honestly wasn't thinking about you being pregnant when I said that. I was just feeling the heat between you and me." He put his finger under her chin and tipped her face up. He leaned in and kissed the tears on her cheeks before kissing her lips softly. She kissed him back.

"I want you," he breathed next to her ear. "Why shouldn't I? Should I act like you're diseased for being in a state you didn't choose?"

She pushed lightly on his shoulders so he moved back from her enough that she could kiss his mouth. He eased her down into a laying position again. The flowers under her were so soft as he pressed himself against her. He moved off of her quickly, rolling to his back again.

"Tell me what's going on. I know it's not just an unwanted pregnancy."

She exhaled and told him about the night Tristan raped her and his threat to Jorgie. She trembled as she described the shrine and how many years he'd actually obsessed over her. Eli didn't interrupt. She felt his muscles tense at times and his breathing would go ragged but he didn't interrupt. When she could think of nothing else to say he sat up, his head in his hands.

"I know Tristan," he said. "I hate him. Even before what you've told me. I've hated him since I met him. I knew he was an asshole...I didn't know he was psychotic."

"He's doing something. Skulking around. He wants to overthrow my mother. He wants to be pack leader."

His head whipped around. "Your mother? You're Sabra's daughter?"

"Yeah…" she said slowly.

He swore.

"I thought you knew that."

"I…I should have guessed, you just never said it directly. You said other things, I should have caught it."

"What does it matter?" she asked.

He sighed. "It doesn't."

"Do you think you can help me?"

His hands shook. He clenched them together. "I want to. I'll kill him the next time I see him. I'm stuck, you know. I can only go so far away from my tree. If he comes into the compass of my tether again, he will die, painfully. I promise you. I'd kill him right now if I could."

"If something bad happens, can I come to you? Can I bring Jorgie to you? Will you protect my brother if I sent him?"

"Yes, Sophie. Of course."

She leaned her head on his shoulder. "Thank you."

"If things were different..." his voice trailed away.

"What?"

"If we just met in a normal way, if you weren't trapped in a sick relationship—"

"And if I wasn't pregnant?" she added.

"Yeah...if I came up to you, hit on you, what do you think you would do?"

She smiled. "What would you say?"

"Oh, something lame and off-color about climbing trees."

She laughed too loud and had to cover her mouth. "Would you?"

"Probably."

"I like climbing trees, by the way."

He chuckled and took her hand, bringing it to his lips. Then he pressed it against his forehead and closed his eyes. "There's some bad shit happening between dryads and wolves right now. You know that don't you?"

"I know Ansel was killed, but I don't believe Tristan's account of what happened."

He told her about that night and what had really

happened to Ansel. In turn, she told him everything she could remember Tristan saying about it.

"I figured it was like that. Your mom came here to talk to Shi and Ler about it. I don't know much else. I wasn't part of that conversation."

"You've met my mom?"

"Just briefly. She was polite, but she's seriously fierce. I could see that behind her eyes. I thought she was pretty hot, too. You know, in an older woman, totally off limits kinda way."

"You just have a she-wolf fetish, don't you?" she teased.

"Hmm...Not sure if there's any help for me. Are there meetings I can attend?"

Sophie covered her mouth again as she laughed. "Okay. I spilled my guts. I'm done with all the darkness for now. I'm just here with you. I'm free for a few more hours. I can just be me."

He lay back down and she lay beside him. "I'm glad we decided to get to know each other." He said.

"Me too. It's a start."

"Yeah? How do the odds look from your end?"

"Odds for what?" she asked.

"That there could be something real between us?"

She reached over, placed her hand on his cheek and with the slightest pressure turned his head toward hers. They stared openly into one another.

"Is this not real? Forbidden, problematic, secret, and yes, stolen. But still real?"

His eyes burned. "This is dangerous. I want you. Right here, right now. I don't care about anything else. I want to see my reflection in your eyes when they cloud over and you cry out."

She blew out a breath. "Damn...Just like that, huh?"

"Yes. I told you I'd tell you the truth. I could elaborate, but I think I've said enough."

She tore her eyes from his and gazed back at the sky, trying to force her pulse to slow off the gallop his words had caused. "Yes. Don't say any more about it just now."

"Do you think tonight is all we have?"

"I don't know..." she hesitated. "No," she said sharply. "When I leave, I don't know when I'll be back, but I will. Will you come to me again?"

"Yes," he breathed. And he would. She could tell there was nothing but truth in his answer.

"What about my baby? Even if you kill Tristan, I'm still carrying his child. I've already decided I'm keeping it. I love my baby. Will that stop you from wanting me?"

She watched his profile. He seemed to mull it over. "I would prefer the baby's father was someone else."

"So would I." Her voice was emphatic.

He sighed. "You interrupted me."

"Sorry."

"Let's say you and I fell in love and it was real and unavoidable. I couldn't give you a child, even if I wanted to. Dryads can only reproduce with other dryads. If you want to experience motherhood, I could understand. I wouldn't begrudge you that."

She gaped at him. "You can't really mean that."

"I was speaking in the hypothetical but I do mean it... What?"

"I have a hard time believing you're so selfless. It's not personal. I couldn't believe that of anyone."

He shrugged. "I don't want kids. I like them, but I really have no desire for my own. The pressure is serious in my culture. I am a part of the first dryad generation in ten thousand years. Growing the population has been hammered into all of us since childhood. It's considered a duty. Non-negotiable."

"Wow. You're a real rebel, Eli. You don't want children, refuse even, and I can see how it could be like that, being gen one."

He nodded. "Yep. I'm a traitor. I warned the Heart, but it still gave me the history. I don't want to be a traitor." He looked at her again. "But the truth is I've never seen anything I want as much as you."

"It might fade."

"It might," he shrugged again. "Time will tell. If you'll give me time."

"I'd stay right here until you grew bored of me if I could..." she placed her hands on her stomach again. "I don't want children either. I would never have them if this one...*wasn't*. I told you I don't like crowds, but it's more than that. I feel other people...it's like their emotions snag and stick to me. It's overwhelming and exhausting...and painful. Even just being pregnant, the love I feel already is just so much. I think about this little child running around, they will get hurt, just falling and scraping their knees..." she shuddered. "A person who carries my heart and soul around with them...It will be like being murdered every day for me. I don't think I'm strong enough for it. I'm not built for it...but it's happening to me."

He pulled her close and kissed her forehead. "You might surprise yourself."

"I hope so...this is lovely, this space, but I'm still a little cold."

"Let's go back to the cave. The wind can't reach us in there."

As they walked away she glanced back. All the vines and beautiful flowers shrank back and vanished under the ground. The cave was cool but it did protect them from the wind. He grabbed her cloak off the wall and draped it over her shoulders before wrapping her in his arms. She pressed her face to his chest and inhaled deeply. *Just here. I'm safe.*

"I love the way you smell," she confessed. "Life after the rain."

"I love the way you smell, too. Feral and still soft, almost floral. Wild animal and flowers, that's you."

She tilted her head back, her gaze grabbing his. "What happens now?" she whispered.

"What do you want to happen?"

Her cheeks heated as her pulse sped again. Defiant, reckless desire flashed through her like fire. "I want to know what you want. All of it."

"You want me to tell you?"

"No. Show me."

His grip on her tightened and it was his eyes that turned feral. "Some of it only. Not everything."

"Scared?" she challenged.

"Yes," he admitted. "Scared you'll break to pieces in my hands and then vanish, only to exist in my dreams forever after."

Her breath feathered across his neck. "You're a thief, remember?"

He moved on her, making her vision cloud until she couldn't see at all. It wasn't everything. He didn't enter her, but he showed her the dark heat he had for her. They played the edge of fulfillment with their hands and lips until they were raw and half-crazed.

Tristan didn't know how to touch a woman... Eli almost killed her with just his hands.

"I can't take anymore." She pleaded.

He backed away, breathless. "Sorry, you did ask for it, though."

"What did you do to me? What was that?" she rasped.

"A promise..."

They stared at each other, but it wasn't just looking, teasing, tempting, or anything else that usually goes between two people's eye contact. This was the inevitable staring both of them in the face. He blinked and shook himself.

"Let's cool off a bit now."

She nodded emphatically in agreement. He reached for her hand. They walked to the mouth of the cave and looked out. He wrapped his arm around her shoulders.

"I don't want you to go back there. To him. I wish you could just stay here with me. How am I supposed to just let go of you and watch you walk away, back into a sick trap?"

"Because you have no choice. Unless you would be just like him. Holding me against my will. Locking me up."

"Low blow."

She shrugged, unapologetic. Then she yawned. He noticed.

"Are you leaving me now?"

"No way. Not yet. I don't have to worry about being back at the Lair until morning. I planned to leave at dawn. Are you leaving?"

He smiled, his dimple peeking out. "Not until you tell me to."

"I'm tired. Will you sleep with me?"

"What do you think?" he chuckled.

They went back into the cave. She looked around, but all of it was going to be really uncomfortable. He moved to the back of the cave to the dark opening she hadn't had the guts to go through yet. The shadows swallowed him as he went in.

"Come here," he said.

Green light began pouring from the dark space. She moved forward and looked in. There was dirt on the floor. Eli had his hands in it, light flowing out from his fingers. Sweet, fragrant moss sprang up and spread out. Light surged out from him three times, building layers of the moss each time.

"This is really soft." He assured her, stretching out on it the way he had outside.

She got down on the ground beside him, resting her head on his shoulder. He pulled her close and closed his arms around her. She exhaled, her eyes fluttering shut.

"I'm in some strange dream and I don't want to wake," she murmured. "This is my favorite place."

"The cave?"

"Your arms."

"Sleep, beautiful artist. You're safe with me," he whispered.

She drifted off before he finished saying it.

Fifteen

Eli! Wake up!

He jolted awake, the Heart shouting inside his head.

"What is it?" He said quietly, trying to not wake Sophie.

Leave her. You are needed. There is fighting happening right now on the boundary. Be careful. The monsters brought shadow sand. Go now.

He gazed down at her. "Sophie." He shook her gently.

She gave a little moan and blinked a few times. Then she gasped and sat up.

He braced his hands on her shoulders. "Calm. You didn't oversleep. No one has discovered us. You're still safe. But I have to go. The Heart called me. There is fighting."

"Oh gosh... Be careful."

He kissed her hard, allowing himself only three seconds, then he pulled back and got to his feet. She gazed up at him desperately.

"When you come back, so will I." It was all he had time to say. He turned and left.

Eli had never run so fast. He heard it first, the scuffling, the snarling, the tearing, the death. Armor covered his skin as he ran, and an axe manifested in each hand. Had Lex given everyone the words? He was still too far away to tell. As he drew near and could finally see what was happening he didn't have time to do anything other than react.

A few dryads were dead on the ground, but there were also a few werewolves that had been killed. He saw Lex fighting one in beast form, and another beast was coming his way. Eli ran up behind the monsters, sinking both of his axes, one for each, into the backs of their heads.

"Where the hell have you been?" Lex demanded as Eli pulled his axes out of the dead beasts.

He wouldn't have told him the truth, even if he had the time, which he didn't. "Where's the sand?" He shouted.

"Like I can tell in the dark!" Lex shouted back as two more beasts came forward and engaged them.

The hulking, elongated monster in front of him bared its fangs and claws. Eli smiled. This would be no problem. The beast swung at him, raking the air with its talons. Eli ducked, almost lazily, sinking his right axe blade into its stomach. Curious at the effect his new ability would have in real life, he dropped his other axe, his poison-coated talons elongating. He sank his claws into the thick skin of the beast and dragged them down its chest. Eli had never moved so fast.

The beast dropped to its knees screaming in pain. Eli stepped back and watched as it grabbed his axe and pulled it from its stomach. The monster didn't get a chance to turn the weapon against Eli. It was *Eli's* weapon, manifested by him, and it vanished in the beast's hands. The claw marks on its chest began to smoke and hiss. The eyes in its ugly face rolled back in its head. Eli moved forward, placing his hands on both sides of its face. The neurotoxin was already working and the beast was tripping. He stabbed the end of his index finger into the thing's temple, forcing the talon to grow as he did until it stretched into its brain.

He jerked his hands back as the monster fell dead to the ground. Most of the sounds of fighting had died down, almost finished before he got there. Eli exhaled as he glanced around. It was over. Whatever the hell it had been. They had suffered losses but they had won, at least for the moment.

All of those that had been fighting now drew close to each other.

"Where is the sand?" Eli demanded again.

"It's over there," Sen said pointing. "There's not much, thank goodness. It's on the arrows."

He grimaced as he approached. Their attackers had tied small bags of sand to the arrowheads, so they would break open when they hit. Two arrows had hit dryad trunks, killing those inside. Two other arrows were sunk into the ground. He held his arm out, blocking Lex coming up behind him.

"Watch your step. None of us can touch it. How are we supposed to deal with this contamination?"

The rest of those who had been fighting came up behind him, crowding to see.

"Well, you're the historian, right?" Lex said. "You tell us."

He sighed and pushed his hair back from his face. "Give me some space, sheesh. Let me think...Go see to the dead and make sure there aren't any more arrows anywhere...Someone go find Ler, too."

All those around him complied as if he was their leader. Except for Lex, who backed up a bit but remained. Eli took a careful step closer to the poisoned area. He exhaled and began searching through the knowledge inside him for some answer of how to deal with this. Nothing came.

Bright red flames erupted on the ground and engulfed the trees and bodies of those who had been killed by the shadow sand.

I will not tolerate this! The Heart screeched in his head. *Never again! I will not allow anyone to bring that accursed sand into my presence and kill my children!*

Eli backed up from the flames as they surged and looked at Lex. "Did you hear that?"

Lex's eyes bugged and he nodded. "If you mean the Heart screaming in rage just now, yeah it was in my head, too."

The entire Wood roused. Every dryad came out of their trees and drew near the Heart, expressions of fear and alarm on their faces.

"What do you want us to do?" Eli asked the Heart under his breath.

Its voice came back into his head, but it wasn't screaming now. *It doesn't matter what you do. I am taking the decision out of your hands entirely. All of your hands. I cannot be idle with this level of threat. I will protect the Wood in the way I see fit. I lived through genocide before. I will not stomach even the hint of it again.*

Before he could ask what that meant the flames in front of him sank back into the ground. He jumped and turned as the ground on the boundary broke open, vicious, thorn-covered vines sprang up forming a wall around the entire Wood. It was so dense you could barely see through it. Then white fire ignited on the wall of thorns. They burned, unharmed. The Heart had encased all of them in a formidable and frightening barrier.

He exchanged a look with Lex, who smirked. "Well, that will keep them out at least."

"Yeah, but does it keep us in?"

You can come and go in your corporal forms, but no one of another race will I allow inside...for now. Don't worry. I know your real tree is outside of this wall and you must be able to access it. And I know you desire to see her. I do not condemn you for it. The Heart whispered to him alone.

"Thank you," he breathed, too quiet for Lex to hear.

You carry a heavier burden as my chosen historian. I will allow you a few liberties...Now come to me. Join your people at the manifestation. I must talk to all of you.

Tristan and Callen looked down from the ridge at the fighting. He squinted, trying to make out what was happening in the dark, but it was difficult from this vantage point. He backed up as three of the wolves Callen had recruited came back his way. He could smell the blood on them.

"So?" he demanded.

One was limping and all of them were bloodied and out of breath.

"The sand worked as you said, but something has changed the dryads. They have armor and weapons. We weren't ready for that. Even in beast form, they were too fast, too strong. They are a real threat now. They killed all the others."

Tristan crossed his arms. "Hmm…So we lost six, and killed how many?"

"Not sure. Four maybe."

Tristan glanced at Callen and smiled. "Perfect."

He snapped his fingers and Satran came out of the shadows, sword in hand, and quickly killed the three who had just come back from fighting.

"Hide the bodies, but not well. Plant the letters on them," Tristan ordered.

Callen pulled out the forged letters with Sabra's seal from his pocket. "This is a little too obvious, Tristan. Too easily refuted. How many wolves do you think will actually believe Sabra ordered this?"

He smirked. "Not that many, but enough. The point is the talk. Everyone loves a juicy rumor. Do you have any idea how many people, the *right* people I've conditioned over the last two years for just this moment? They will side with me instantly when the shit hits the fan. Lies are so easy, Callen. And those who love Sabra will transition to me easier with Sophie at my side. They will see it as only a small shift in leadership. Everything still in the family."

"Do you really have Sophie? Is she in total submission? If not, you're going to wind up dead sooner rather than later...me as well."

"I have her," he snarled.

"I hope so." Callen walked away to help Satran plant the letters on the dead bodies.

The two of them finished and left Tristan. He stood alone in the dark, thinking. Callen's words twisted around in his mind. He looked up at the sky. A few hours and the sun would rise. He was on the edge. This next day had to go perfectly for everything else to fall into place. Nothing could deviate from his plan. Nothing.

Sophie was his. She was! She had given him her heart. She was happy about the baby and their mating ceremony. He had to push that up. They needed to mate as quickly as possible to remove all suspicion from him. The people needed to see that.

Light caught his attention. He looked over the ridge again. The hell? The edges of the Wood was on fire. As high as he was, he could see the whole thing. The boundary burned high in a perfectly controlled line. There were no breaks in the line. It was a perfect circle.

"Tristan..." a whisper moved through the darkness.

He started and looked around. Movement, and shadows slunk unnaturally toward him.

"Who's there?"

"Ready to die, lover?" they hissed.

He pulled his dagger out and faced the person coming his way, then they vanished, their shape jolting to the side. He turned in a circle.

"Come out. Show yourself."

She laughed...it sounded like Sophie. Fury mixed with fear.

"Sophie?"

"Mother has nothing to do with this...and everything, at the same time."

The voice bounced through the darkness. He couldn't tell where it came from. His heart began thundering as it slid from the trees in front of him and he got a good look at it. Green eyes glowed in the female silhouette as it sauntered toward him. Its black hands stretched, the fingers growing into sharp points.

"Too bad you're so vile. You are beautiful." Sophie's voice whispered from it sensually. "I've been waiting for this moment and yet...I feel unprepared. I'm not sure exactly *how* I want you to die."

I'm hallucinating, he thought. She vanished again. He backed up, his head whipping from side to side. He froze. It felt like warm oil was being poured over his back. A strangled cry escaped his mouth before the oil coated his throat. He choked, clawing at his neck, and everywhere he could feel it. It rose up his nose and into his brain.

"You're so scared now," she said. "I think I'll rape you before I kill you. So you have an idea what it's like to be violated."

The feeling retracted, sliding off of him like water running down his body. He staggered forward, gasping as it released him completely. Laughter echoed all around him again.

"Tristan…"

He jumped again and turned. She was standing right behind him.

"Run, wolf."

He did. Cold dread coating him as he ran toward the Lair as fast as he could. He didn't take the time to glance back until he reached the suburbs. He couldn't see anything behind him. Panting, he swallowed once and kept running until he was inside the mountain and locked in his apartment.

Sophie came out of the cave and stood on the ledge, worried for Eli's safety. She blinked a few times as the white flames surrounding the Wood, so bright in the dark, burned her eyes. What had happened? Was he alright? She had no way of knowing. Why was the Wood engulfed in white flames? She stared at it. It was the Heart doing this. Was that comforting or not? She wasn't sure. Was Eli trapped behind the fire? If he was even still alive.

She had to go down there. She had to know. Tears began to threaten. She couldn't go. She would have to live with the uncertainty for now. She had to go home before the dawn broke. Before it was too late. She left the same way she'd come, with a shifted face, and her hood up.

She didn't rush. She walked slowly and silently through the forest to the Lair. Realization of the level of risk she had taken by going to her cave became clearer with every step she took. Leaving the mountain was one thing, getting back in was something else. Would the guards stop her? She didn't know. She usually came and went and she pleased, but those were times when she wasn't trying to hide her identity. Everyone knew who she was. They all recognized her. She was Princess-Wolf.

But she couldn't be that right now. She didn't know who was in Tristan's pocket. Maybe those on guard right now were safe, but she had no way of knowing.

She approached the main entrance and hung back in the shadows. The dawn was turning the sky a pale gray. She watched the two guards at the entrance closely. This was the end of their shift and they were obviously very tired. Perhaps it was the perfect time. Just a simple, easy lie. Not too many details. That was all she needed. Finding her courage, she moved out from the shadow and approached the entrance.

"Hey girl," the guard to her right said. "Show me your face."

She tipped her hood back and gave him a flirtatious smile. Some of the sleepiness left his eyes and he smiled back at her.

"Why are you coming in at such an hour? Where have you been?" he asked in an easy tone.

Relief poured through her at his relaxed demeanor. She glanced at the guard on her left. His head was slumped forward and he looked on the verge of dozing off.

"I've been with my boyfriend," she said conspiratorially. "My parents don't really approve of him. I need to sneak back in before they realize I've been gone all night."

He smirked at her. "Alright, get back where you belong. And when you decide to dump the loser, I'm single. Just saying."

She smiled and put her hood back up. "I'll bear that in mind."

She moved away quickly so he didn't try to keep her there and flirt some more. The halls were dark and empty. Her frantic pulse calmed a little as she climbed the stairs, but now she faced the real problem, the guards outside her family home. She couldn't get in unless she showed them her real face, and if either of them were loyal to Tristan, he would know she had been out. She cursed herself as she climbed for not thinking of this before and the weight of the risk she'd taken fell into her stomach. She shouldn't have gone out. All she could do now was hope that this would not get back to Tristan.

Please. Please. Please. She begged the guards in her head as she approached the double doors. *Please be loyal to my family and not Tristan.*

She pushed her hood off her head and let her face slide back into its natural appearance. Both guards looked at her.

"Sophie," they both mumbled in acknowledgment.

She walked past them and pushed the doors open. She exhaled as she closed them behind her and bolted them, still begging them to be loyal silently in her mind. She made a beeline for her room. Sophie took off her cloak and put it away before moving over to her bed. A familiar lump was right in the middle under her blanket. She smiled as she crawled into bed, pulling Jorgie into her side and kissing the top of his head.

Exhaustion crashed over her. She closed her eyes and fell into a miserable, worried sleep. She hoped with her whole heart that Eli was okay... And that she could see him again soon. Somehow.

Groggy and aching, Sophie dragged her eyelids open as morning sunlight spilled into her room. She was alone in bed. Adrenaline jolted her. What time was it? Was she late for Tristan? He told her to be there for breakfast. He hadn't told her an exact time. If he was angry, she would remind him of that. He hadn't said the hour she had to be there.

Regardless if she was late or not, she needed to hustle. She sat up and rubbed her eyes then ice poured into her veins. She heard Tristan talking. He was there, talking to her mother. She held her breath and tried to hear what they were saying. Then there were more voices. Lacey, Jorgie, and also Callen. She listened closer. If her father was there he wasn't speaking. She got out of bed and dressed quickly, wishing she could shower, but she didn't have the time.

Sophie came down the stairs and into the living room. All of them were at the table, eating breakfast. All of them except her father. Where had he gone?

Tristan looked up from his plate and smiled at her, but there was something very wrong in his eyes. His gaze sent terror down her spine. She returned his smile, crossed the room, stood behind where he was sitting and wrapped her arms around his neck. She leaned down and kissed him.

"Sheesh, I slept so hard. I didn't know you were coming to breakfast," she said sweetly.

"Well, I waited for you, but when you didn't show, what choice did I have but to come find you?"

"Sorry. I didn't mean to cause you worry." She looked around and took a seat. "Morning," she mumbled to everyone at the table.

She fought to eat slowly, but she was starving. There was a lot to choose from on the table, but she stuck to mild things as her stomach was squirming. Polite conversation went around the table but Sophie didn't say anything, she didn't even hear what was actually said. She felt his eyes on her and her fear ratcheted up. What did she do? Did she ignore the hostile vibes he was giving off?

She set her fork down and met his gaze evenly. It was wrong to play dumb. She gave him an intense look and jerked her head toward the stairs that led to her bedroom before excusing herself from the table. She didn't look back but she heard his chair scrape across the floor and his footsteps follow her. She had only a split second to decide how she was going to behave before turning and facing him as he entered her room.

"What's the matter?" she asked.

He pulled her against him roughly, his fingers digging into both of her wrists. She winced.

"What have you been doing? What kind of power have you hidden for me?"

"What are you talking about? I haven't hidden anything from you. I love you."

His fingers dug in harder and she whimpered, acting weaker than she really was. "Why don't I believe you? It's your grandfather, isn't it? He gave you some kind of aberrant ability, didn't he?"

She gazed at him desperately, tears filling her eyes. "No. I don't have any special power. Why do you think that? What happened?"

He narrowed his eyes, his gaze searching hers, and then he let go. He exhaled and put his head in his hands. She moved forward trying to hug him. He held still for a moment then he embraced her softly.

"I'm sorry. I don't... Maybe it was just a nightmare. I can't explain it. You'll think I'm crazy."

We crossed that bridge a long time ago, baby. She thought acidly. "Of course I won't think you're crazy. Tell me what happened. Tell me what you dreamed."

"She was like you... Sort of. A shadow with your voice. She stalked me out in the forest. She said she would kill me." He shuddered. "She touched me."

"How horrible. I'm sorry you dreamed such a thing. I wonder why you would. Do you doubt how much I love you? Is that it?"

He pressed his lips to her neck. "Maybe I am insecure. I've dreamed of you for so long. There's a lot going on and I'm stressed out." He lifted both of her wrists up to his face and kissed them in turn. His gaze jumped back to hers then, harsh, accusatory. "Where's your cuff?"

"It's on top of my dresser. I took it off before bed. I didn't want anything to happen to it. I didn't want it to slip off while I slept. I thought I might accidentally roll over it and break it in my sleep." She walked to her dresser, snatched up the cuff, and put it back on her wrist.

The hard edge in his eyes softened. He bought it. "I know we haven't talked about actual dates yet for our ceremony. I know three months is customary but I want it to happen no longer than two weeks from today. One week would be just about right."

"Why so soon?"

"I have my reasons. You don't need to worry about them. But I don't see why this should bother you. You should be happy about this. If we wait, your pregnancy will be showing. I know you don't want that. You said it would upset your parents that you are pregnant before our ceremony. We don't want to shame them now do we?"

"No, we don't. You're right." she kept her voice modulated but screaming erupted in her head.

She wouldn't go through with this. She couldn't stomach it. He'd pushed her far enough. One week. So that was her deadline. She had one week to figure out who she needed to kill aside from Tristan to remove the threat over her brother.

"I think it would be nice to have a double ceremony. Callen and Lacey, you and me. We can all do it at the same time. It will be a huge celebration. The people will love it. And then no one will speculate that you must be pregnant and that's why we're rushing. You can tell anyone who asks, that you just wanted to do it with your sister."

She smiled and kissed him on the mouth. "That's perfect. I'll talk to her about it today. We'll get it all set up."

"Okay sweetheart. I have to take off for a little while. Check on a few things. Meet me back home at noon."

She dipped her head in submission. "Yes, sir."

He kissed her again briefly and then left the room. She stood still and listened to him bid her family farewell and that he would see them again later. Only when she heard the double doors closed behind him did she exhale and clinch her shaking hands into fists. She flopped back onto her bed grinding her teeth together. Stupid, useless, shadowy version of herself. Her dark creation had been unsuccessful in killing Tristan. All she had done was threaten him and opened her up to exposure. He could never know about her art. Her resolve on that had not changed nor would it. She wished he had told her more details about what had happened. Maybe her dark creation was incapable of real violence.

She lay there and listened to the voices still at the table. In a few minutes, Callen left as well. She repeated the lies that must be truth over and over in her head. *I'm happy. I'm in love. I want to mate with Tristan as soon as possible. I love Tristan. I love Tristan.*

She got up and went back into the main living area. She needed to get this over with and push it if there was any resistance.

"Hey, I just had an amazing idea! What if we had a double ceremony? Don't you think that would be beautiful?" She said exuberantly looking between her sister and her mother.

Both of them just blinked at her for a minute.

"I don't think it sounds amazing," Jorgie said petulantly. "I think it sounds weird."

She gave her little brother a direct look. "Okay. Go get ready for school. I have to talk to mom and Lacey privately. Grown-up talk."

He heaved an impressive sigh, rolled his eyes, and left the room, slamming his bedroom door behind him. She pinched her eyes shut for a moment. *You can do this. You don't have a choice. They'll know soon enough, it might as well be now.*

"You only just announced your engagement a day ago, and now you want to crash your sister's ceremony? Why wouldn't you want your own?" Her mom demanded.

"I'm sorry." She sank down onto the couch.

Sabra and Lacey got up from the table and came and sat next to her, female intuition directing them. They sat on either side of her and grabbed her hands in theirs simultaneously.

"I'm pregnant."

Her mom pulled her into a hug. "Well... That explains the rush. What do you think, Lacey? How does a double ceremony sound to you?"

Her sister pressed against her back, so she was sandwiched in between them. "It sounds extravagant. You know how I love extravagance. Let's do it."

"How far along are you?" Her mom asked.

"Not very, but it won't take long before it's visible. I'm so sorry. I don't want everyone to know. Can we have the ceremony soon? Please? I'm so ashamed already." At least some of her words were true.

Sabra chuckled somewhat darkly. "Well, this will be one of those times I will cash in on the perks of being pack leader. Everything will be set and done elegantly. No one will suspect a thing. And all you girls have to do is choose your dresses."

Honest tears did come to Sophie then, and she clung to her mom and her sister. "Thank you so much."

"I'm glad your father's not here," Sabra said. "Let me tell him in my way. Both of you being engaged has been tough on him anyway lately. Callen doesn't bother him too much, but he doesn't have any great *love* for Tristan. You being pregnant already is not going to heighten his opinion of him."

Sabra took Jorgie off to school. Lacey and Sophie sat on the couch together looking over pictures of possible dresses they could wear for the ceremony.

"This is the one I had picked out for myself," Lacey said, showing her the picture. "So obviously you can't wear the same one or the same style."

Sophie chuckled. "Obviously," she agreed. "This style wouldn't work for me anyway. That particular cut only looks good on flat-chested women like you."

Lacey pinched her forearm, making Sophie howl in pain. "Don't start shit with me, skank. I'm doing you a favor. Don't forget that. So mind your manners."

"You're right. And I love you for it," Sophie said. "You're still an ironing board."

Lacey rested her head on Sophie's shoulder. She absorbed the love and mercy her sister showed her. If things were different, sitting there as they were, pouring over dresses would have been fun. She tried to detach her brain and her heart as she imagined having to walk down an aisle toward Tristan, in the great hall, in front of so many people. She allowed her thoughts to haze as her eyes skimmed over the pictures. She imagined walking toward someone else, someone with long, dark blonde hair and black iridescent eyes. What dress would she want to wear for him?

With that thought in her mind, she chose her dress.

They passed the hours quickly, just looking at pictures, and discussing details. But Sophie paid close attention to the time. A few minutes before noon, she hugged Lacey goodbye and left through the double doors.

Tristan opened the door when she knocked. He moved aside, letting her in, his face set in anger. What now? He shut the door and locked it before facing her. She was about to ask him what was wrong, but she didn't get the chance. He slapped her face.

She staggered and placed her palm to her cheek. He grabbed her by the arms and shook her.

"Where did you go last night?" he snarled.

"Nowhere. Let go of me."

"Nowhere, slut? Really? How come I was just informed by Rolph that you came in early this morning right around dawn?"

She swore internally but Tristan had just slipped up. He told her the name of the guard who was an informant. Rolph had worked for her family for years, on guard at their home a few days every week. He was there that morning when she came in. Was he the threat to her brother, or just one of the threats?

She looked Tristan in the eyes. "Is that right?" her tone was snide. "That pervert has come on to me so many times in the last year. Propositioned all kinds of nasty things. All I've ever done is reject him. Why would you trust him to tell the truth? Especially now we're engaged. He knows he's got no chance. He's pissed. Of course, he'd say something like that."

He flinched and then scowled. He stared at her, searching her face. Then he blinked and let go of her. "He's come on to you?" his tone was easier.

"Yes."

"I've got too much going on right now. I can't handle this type of thing as well. Damnit, Sophie, I want to trust you."

"You should. I got everything set for our ceremony. I told my mother and sister about the baby. Preparation will begin tonight. Mom is pulling out all the stops for it. It will be as grand as you can possibly imagine."

He sighed and gave her a weak smile. "Good. Although I doubt it will be as grand as I imagine. Nothing ever lives up to the hype I have in my head."

He pulled her to him again and kissed her neck, his hands running possessively over her body. She jolted, not quite ready for this just yet. She better go numb and fast. He was hot and ready in seconds. He picked her up and carried her to the bedroom.

"I need you so bad. I missed you last night."

"I missed you, too," she managed as he laid her down.

Someone pounded on the front door just as he began to undress her. He swore through clenched teeth and pulled away from her. She exhaled in relief, even though the relief would be momentary. She could prepare herself for sex. At least it would be short, she thought smugly. She bet Eli had quite a bit more stamina than Tristan. She listened to the voices coming from under the door, but she couldn't make out the words, only the tones. Tristan was stressed.

He came back a minute later, closing the door, and sat on the bed next to her. He took her hand in his.

"We are together, Sophie. Nothing can change that. You are with me. Not your family. *Me.*"

"Okay..." she said slowly. "Wha—"

"I told you things were going to start happening.

Well, they are starting today. The effects will not be known for a few days but they are coming. And if something doesn't work out the way I want, I need to know you are with me."

"You know I am."

"I have many people on my side. Many people. I don't want to have to kill your family, but I will if I have to. When it comes down to it, the decision whether they live or die will rest with you. Understand?" his eyes bore into hers. "I need your family alive, but after we are mated, they are disposable. Once we are mated, I will take over as pack leader. You will not fight this in any way. You will stand by my side. We will be a united front to the pack. Your smiles will not falter for even one second. Your public answers will only ever be what I tell you they will be. Or else, I will have them all killed. Your mother. Your father. Your brother and sister. And even then, you will still be mine."

Her breath shuddered out. "I...please...please don't hurt my family, Tristan. I'll do everything you want. I promise."

He raised her hand to his lips. "Of course you will. I'm sorry for having to scare you. Everything will be fine. You just have to do as you're told...I love you. That is the same as it has always been and always will be."

She nodded quickly. "I'll be good."

"I know. I have to go now and see to some things. I'll be back in a few hours. Stay here. Don't leave. When I get back, we can pick up where we left off."

She nodded again. He stood and left the room. The

lock on the bedroom door slid home. She was trapped.

Shreve knocked on Forest and Syrus' front door.

Syrus opened up and smiled, beckoning Shreve in with a little jerk of his head. He came in and sat on the couch.

"What's up? You want a drink? Kinda look like you need one."

Shreve sighed and gave Syrus a grateful look. "Thanks."

Syrus left the room and was back a moment later, two glasses of bourbon in his hands. He gave one to Shreve and sat down next to him.

"I hate Sophie's fiancé. I *hate* him."

Syrus chuckled. "I see. So that's your problem."

"He's so smooth. Like a salesman." He took a drink and hissed. "I swear he's a villain. Maybe I'm wrong. Maybe I'm just paranoid. I thought you'd understand. You hated X at first and he turned out alright."

Syrus took a drink, too and sighed. "X did turn out alright. But it's true, I did hate him. I never thought he was really bad, though. I just didn't like the way he looked and touched my baby. I knew what he wanted from her, even if he did want a committed forever to go along with it."

"I don't see any good in Tristan. I think he loves Sophie, but everything with him puts me on edge. He's *so* not good enough for my daughter." He pinned Syrus with an intense look. "You felt that way about X, right?"

Syrus laughed. "Hell, I still feel that way." He clinked his glass to Shreve's in a toast. "Here's to having girls."

They both knocked back the rest of their drinks in one gulp.

SIXTEEN

She wasn't sleepwalking, and she wasn't lucid. Melina's rich brown eyes constricted down until her pupils were spiked, star-shaped pinpricks. Her mouth hung partially open, the sea breeze blowing strands of her hair between her lips. She moved forward at a steady pace without her conscious consent. She was a doll on strings, some force outside of herself compelling her.

Mist lifted off the waves by the wind and licked her bare skin with cold. She shivered but did not rouse from her trance. The very edges of the pink waves kissed the tips of her toes as she faced the water. Melina saw outlines only of what was really in front of her. On top of reality, fell a screen.

In this vision, she stood on a floor of warm glass. Liquid, the color of milk, lapped at the underside of the floor. She was inside a vast hall, the walls and ceilings were white, sleek and seamless. Her body was heavy in the overbearing dry heat of the space.

Smooth white sarcophagi lined the room in three perfect rows, each one propped high into the air on stilts. The stilts came straight out of the bottoms of the sarcophagi tapering down from the top into stiletto points on the glass floor. They towered over her. She walked beneath them, in between the stilts. Each one had the same symbol on the bottom, a black circle.

White noise like a mixture of ocean waves and static filled her ears. She shook her head. The sound burrowed into her brain attempting to silence her thoughts. It was almost painful like a budding headache not yet blossomed. She sighed, wishing she could sleep, it was so warm. There was something she needed here...What could that possibly be? Where the hell was she anyway?

Melina stopped walking and looked up. She blinked and narrowed her eyes. Every sarcophagus was the same except the one directly above her. Smooth and white like all the rest, but with one tiny variation. The circle on the bottom was broken. The shape didn't connect. One tiny place, no wider than her fingerprint, was open, so the circle was incomplete. This was not only irksome to her mild OCD, just looking at it gave her a jolt. This was why she was here. She needed to get up there. How did she do that?

Melina blinked, her eyelids sliding slowly down and back up like a lifting curtain.

"Mel? Melina?! Hey!" hands gripped her shoulders, shaking her.

She jumped in alarm and yelled as the vision broke apart. Panting like she'd been running, Melina blinked a few times and looked into the worried face of Erin. She jumped again as a wave licked her bare feet.

"Oh my gosh! I'm sorry...I don't know what I was...I don't know where I was..." she stammered.

Erin grasped her shoulders again and looked closely into her face. "I came to find you cause you didn't show up, and you didn't answer my messages. We were supposed to go shopping, remember? What just happened? Are you alright?"

Melina scrubbed her hands over her face. "I was...sleepwalking, I think."

"Um...no. That's not it. Your eyes were open and your pupils were tiny. You looked like you were in a trance or something like that. Is this something you do often?"

Her breath came out in a whoosh. "Shit. No, not often. Once before, but it was totally different. More like I really was sleepwalking because it was the middle of the night. And what I saw was nothing like this time. I came back to myself, or woke up, in my room the first time."

Erin looked worried. "Have you told anyone about this?"

"No. Do you think I should? Who would I tell anyway?"

Erin frowned for a minute. "If it was me, I'd go tell Rahaxeris first and see what he thought. If he can't help you, then I'd ask Tesla to look you over, map you or whatever the heck it is she does. You need to do something. You looked really freaky just now."

Melina gazed at her desperately, the details of her vision still strong in her mind. They weren't fading as dreams often do once you wake. "I'm scared. Will you go with me?"

Erin hugged her tight. "Of course. Come on. Go get dressed. We'll go to Kyhael together." She looked up at the small house high on the cliff behind them. "Are you going to tell your parents?"

Melina frowned and shook her head. "No. Not until I have to. I don't want them to worry. I'll tell them if it turns out to actually be something."

Erin kept her arm supportively around Melina's waist as they walked up the snaking path chiseled in the cliff face up to her folk's house. Mel tensed as they reached the top. It was mid-morning. She didn't remember leaving the house, no idea how long she'd actually been standing down on the beach in her t-shirt and boy shorts underwear. It must have been before they woke up.

"Don't say anything, Erin. I've got an excuse for them."

"Okay."

Merick and Netriet were sitting at the small round table in the kitchen, talking quietly, the smell of coffee and toast in the air.

"Mel?" her mom said questioningly as they came in. "I thought you were still in bed."

Merick got up first, coming over to his daughter and taking stock of her. "You're shivering." He rubbed his hands on her arms and shoulders to warm her. "What were you doing outside in your p.js?"

Mel chuckled easily. "I wanted to watch the sunrise. I know I only just moved out three days ago, but I missed the view I have here. I wasn't paying attention to how cold I was getting." She snuggled into her father's chest for a moment and then pulled away. "I'm going to get dressed and head out. Erin and I have some serious shopping to do today."

"Of course you do," he said sarcastically before turning his attention to Erin. "Good morning, Erin."

She smiled. "Sir."

"Won't be a minute," Melina promised Erin before rushing into her room and closing the door.

"Yeah sure," Erin said more to herself. "I know you better than that. I might as well make myself comfortable since I know you're going to take forever."

"Would you like something to eat, Erin?" Netriet asked.

"No thank you. I'm good. Sorry for disrupting your quiet morning."

Netriet waved her apology away. The next moment, Melina came out, fully dressed, shocking Erin. Even rushing, throwing on whatever clothes she grabbed first, putting her hair in a ponytail, and wearing no make-up, Mel just managed to look sexy and fashionable.

"I'm ready to go."

Erin chuckled. "Okay. I guess you can get ready quickly when you choose to. Let's go."

"Don't spend too much," Merick scolded. "You're not loaded like your friend here."

"Don't worry, I'm fully aware how un-loaded I am...I'll be home for dinner."

They left the house, walked a few feet away, and Erin touched the medallion on her wrist, opening a portal for them to Kyhael right into the antechamber of the old *Rune-dy* headquarters, where Rahaxeris lived.

"Hello," Erin called out. "Rahaxeris..." she hesitated a moment. "Grandfather? It's Erin and Melina."

Mel glanced at Erin and smirked. "I bet that's weird.

Calling him 'grandfather'?"

"I'm trying to force it until it just comes out. He told me to. Otherwise, I never would assume it would be okay. Calling Forest 'mom' is still a struggle, but I'm getting there."

"You're lucky. I wish I was a part of their family like that."

"You are family to them, Mel. And to me. Don't you know that?"

She nodded. "Yeah, it just doesn't have the weight your connection carries…I want a destined life mate of my own. I'm so jealous of you and Maddox." She looked down and shook her head. "I'm sorry. I've felt so guilty about feeling like that. I thought maybe I should confess. I'm a bad friend."

Erin moved forward and hugged her. "You are not! You're my *best* friend. I understand. If you were jealous in a different way, like wanting my man in your bed, then we'd have words, and there might be blood."

Mel laughed and squeezed her. "M? In *my* bed?" she gave a mock shudder and made a loud gagging sound. "Gross. I don't know how you suffer through it."

Erin laughed so hard she snorted. "Oh, yeah. It's terrible being mated to that gorgeous, sex god who adores me. Just terrible."

"It must be," her voice was heavy on the sympathy. She let go of Erin, her stress coming back, and she began pacing. "Maybe Rahaxeris isn't here."

"Maybe Rahaxeris isn't where?" he asked coming around the corner, an open book in his hands. He looked up from the page he was reading and smiled thinly at them. "Erin. Melina. What can I do for you?"

"I'm sorry for intruding…We don't want to bother you…Umm…if it's a bad time, I mean…" Mel said.

He blinked at her a few times. "What's wrong? I've watched you grow since infancy, Melina. Never seen you falter over your words before."

"It's…" she blew out a breath, her cheeks heating. "It's probably nothing. Just dreams. Sleepwalking."

"Didn't look that way to me," Erin interjected.

"Sleepwalking, eh? When did it start?" Rahaxeris asked.

"A week or two ago. It's only happened twice."

"Notice any physical change?"

"I don't think so. I feel fine."

He narrowed his red eyes at her. "Except you're scared. That's out of character. Follow me."

He led both of them into the center of *Rune-dy*

headquarters, to the library. He began pulling huge, ancient looking books down and placing them on the table in the center of the room. He opened one and began thumbing to the center when he suddenly inhaled abruptly, lifting his head and closing his eyes. Then he shot Melina a piercing look and shut the book.

She raised her eyebrows as he walked slowly up to her, a calculating look on his sharp features. He lifted his long hands.

"Can I touch you?" he asked.

She nodded, her eyes wide. He walked around her, gazing intently at her neck. He twisted the end of her ponytail around his finger and lifted it up, running his other hand over the back of her neck. Then he let her hair drop.

"Hmm..."

Melina shivered as he ran his finger along the edge of her ear, looking closely behind each of her ears in turn. "No. It's not there," he muttered to himself. He grasped her shoulders and turned her to face him, looking her straight on.

"What are you looking for?" Mel asked.

"I'm not totally sure. It was just an idea I had based on my knowledge of your parents."

"What? I'm a full-blooded vampire. Nothing more,"

she said simply.

"Both your parents are vampires, yes, however..." his eyes drilled into hers. "Ah, yes. I see it now."

"What? You see what?"

"The eye inside your eye."

"Excuse me?"

He looked over at Erin. "Do you have a mirror?"

She nodded, reached into her purse pulling out a compact and handing it to him.

"Look closely," he told Mel. "Deep in your right pupil."

Her hand shook as she held the mirror up to her face, looking deep into her own eyes. She didn't see anything. Then Rahaxeris turned off the light forcing her pupils to expand. She brought the mirror closer until it touched the tip of her nose. She looked into her eye like staring down a dark tunnel. Her pulse sped up, and she gasped. An eye, the color of smoke, deep inside her pupil stared back at her. No face, no eyelid, just the perfect circle of an iris. She jumped and dropped the mirror.

"I'm possessed!" she screamed. *"Get it out of me!"*

Rahaxeris grabbed her and gave her a little shake.

"Melina!" his voice commanded her to quiet. "Calm down. It's alright. You're not possessed. I promise."

"What is it?! How did it get there?! Can you remove it?" She was hysterical.

He placed his palm on the top of her head and exhaled slowly. A wave of calm flowed down over her from his hand and she quieted. She blinked slowly, her eyelids heavy. He steered her into a chair and she slumped into it as though drunk. Erin came close and took her hand supportively.

"What is it?" Melina asked again. "How did it get there?"

"It's just another level of sight. You were born with it...You're not just a vampire. A small part of you is Polyhedron."

She sat up straighter, shaking off some of the calm he'd put on her. "The world my mother's arm came from?"

"Yes. That arm isn't just robotic, it's alive, and it's a part of your mom. It grafted into her DNA when it was attached. I'm sure she didn't think of that when she decided to get pregnant. Or perhaps she did and just didn't care. She wanted you so badly, Melina."

Melina shuddered. Her body felt foreign to her suddenly as though his words had changed it, but of course, that wasn't true.

"What does this mean? I'm not really alive? I'm some kind of robot?"

He smiled as warmly as he could manage and shook his head. "Not at all. This is only a very small part of you. You are as alive as you have always been. You're not a doll or a golem. The people of Polyhedron are alive. Machines, yes, in a way. Androids. They live and die."

Melina gazed at him desperately. "I think I'm going to be sick."

He left the room and came back a minute later with a glass of water. She took it gratefully and drank.

"Why is there an eye in my eye? What else of me is wrong? What does it really mean?"

"I doubt there is anything else to you that is different. The eye means you are a seer."

Erin squeezed her hand. "Hey, that's cool, Mel! It's a gift. Stop looking so freaked. Now you can get as rich as you like, you just need to start gambling."

Melina frowned. "Would that work?" she asked Rahaxeris.

He shrugged. "Maybe. But I doubt it."

"Figures," she complained. "it's just going to be some crap that gives me weird dreams that mean nothing to me, or have no bearing on real life. And if anyone finds out I'll become a sideshow and people will drive me crazy thinking I'm a fortuneteller."

Rahaxeris chuckled and crossed the room, taking down another book and bringing it back to her. "Here. You can learn about Polyhedron."

She gave him a dirty look. "Okay. That's really long. Can't you be any more helpful? Or are you just stuck being all cryptic cause you're Rahaxeris, the scary, all-knowing *Rune-dy*, and you'll show me the path but it's up to me to take it bullshit? Is that it?"

He blinked at her and then laughed loudly. "Goodness. There's the Melina I know. Alright. I'll explain but I still think you should research this part of your heritage on your own."

She grabbed the book and laid it in her lap. "Fine," she said tersely. "I'll read. Now tell me why I'm sleepwalking."

"I don't know the extent of your sight, but I can tell you it's probably a hundred percent personal. Based on my knowledge of Polyhedron, the way they access knowledge and navigate their lives, you are having future memories."

She looked down, fear pooling in her stomach again.

SEVENTEEN

Trapped alone in Tristan's shrine with nothing to do, Sophie dozed a little. Under the stress and terror, she was tired from staying up so much of the night. Her mind shifted back and forth. Every word Tristan had said was chiseled into her memory. He'd told her too much. Enough for her to mess up his plans at least. Her family was important to him but only up till she mated with him. And Rolph was a traitor. She'd kill him at the first opportunity. That was all she knew for sure at the moment. She was close. So close to feeling it was time to raise the alarm on him. There was just one thing. She had to be sure she'd taken out the threat to Jorgie before that happened.

She closed her eyes to shut out the pictures on the wall and rolled away from them. She inhaled deeply, a frown creasing her brow. What was that smell? It was familiar and yet she knew she had no idea what it was. She breathed deeply again, holding the smell in her lungs as long as she could. Eli…it wasn't his scent, and yet there was part of it she recognized from him. A tickle of dread climbed up her back like a spider. She sat up, all tiredness vanishing behind a surge of adrenaline, her eyes focusing on the trunk against the wall. More spider legs crawled up her, and she gritted her teeth. Oh gosh, there was something in there. Something terrible. She knew it.

Her fingers clenched as she stood. She didn't want to know, but she had no choice. She knelt in front of the trunk, placed her hands on the lid, breathing hard, her pulse hammering painfully. She blew out a breath. *Okay. Do it. You have to. Open the lid.*

She did.

Sophie clasped both hands over her mouth to silence the scream in her throat. Tears instantly flooded her eyes, blurring her vision. She thought she knew heartbreak. She was wrong. Like porcelain thrown to the floor, Sophie's heart crashed, shattering into shards and dust.

The part of her that was already a mother screamed out fury and a promise of retribution.

She reached into the trunk and carefully lifted the little girl out, cradling her to her chest as if she was still alive, only sleeping. She rocked the corpse, her tears falling onto her lifeless face. "Sweet girl. It's okay. I've got you. I'll take you far away from here. I promise. You won't be in the dark anymore," she whispered. "I'll take you home, baby. I'll take you to the Heart."

Sophie laid the girl on the bed and swaddled her in a blanket. She sat on the floor next to the bed slowly tracing her fingers down the girl's smooth cheek over and over, a fire of insanity building in her. A fire meant for Tristan alone. When he came back he would face a mother. Mother was pain. Mother was revenge. Mother was death incarnate.

Her eyes tunneled and her mouth slicked over with a

thirst for blood. That was before the pain came. Like a knife thrust into her lower abdomen and twisted around and around. Sophie cried out, curling into herself on the floor. A pull, then a pop and the baby in her womb detached from her. She clenched her hands on her stomach as if she could stop the miscarriage. *No. Don't leave me, sweetheart. I love you.*

Blood ran hot and free from between her legs and her broken heart jolted around the sharp edges. She wept as her baby left her body. *Go on then, my baby. Fly. Go where you'll be safe. One day, I'll see you. When I die, we'll be reunited.*

Everything went blurry as if she was underwater. Her heart lost shape. It had been so fast. The child inside her lived, grew, pulled from the life her body gave to it. Then they were gone. Now she was empty. Hollowed out and dead within. The cold stone floor drank up her tears. She didn't move for two hours.

She blinked as the door opened, feet coming right up to her face. She looked up at Tristan. There were no words in her head, no thoughts, no reality. She was still in shock. He reached down and dragged her up to her feet. Rage and violence iced his eyes and he snarled in her face, digging his fingernails into her shoulders until he drew blood. She didn't react.

"You killed our baby," he hissed through clenched teeth.

Her gaze landed on him then and cleared a little.

"No. You did. You killed that little girl and when I found her I miscarried. It's your fault. A life for a life."

He shoved her back and slapped her face. Her ears rang and the room spun. She lost her footing and fell back onto the floor. He moved over her, stepping on her wrist and began to pummel her with his fists. He broke her ribs and damaged her insides still raw from her baby dying. Her mind drifted, the pain only a haze in the background. Then he punched her face, breaking the bones of her cheek. That woke her. She reared up, smashing him in the face with the top of her head. He stumbled back, dazed.

She grabbed the lamp and smashed it over his head. He fell into the corner, unconscious. She jumped onto his chest about to wrap her hands around his throat and choke him to death. *Wait!* A voice in her head stopped her.

Why? He must die.

What about Jorgie? The other part of her argued. *You don't know who else you need to kill to make sure he's safe. Tristan said if anything happened to him, bad things would happen to Jorgie. Remember?*

Sighing, she backed up and tried to make her head stop spinning. What did she do now? The shock still hadn't fully lifted. She'd lost too much blood, broken and hemorrhaging inside from Tristan's beating. She covered the little girl's head so none of her was visible and picked her up. She had to take her home.

Sophie cradled the child against her chest and left. Her clothes were covered with blood and those she passed who didn't see, could smell it. There were only a few people in the halls as she walked out. Some spoke to her. Again it was as though she was underwater. Their words muffled and she couldn't understand. She just walked forward and out.

The evening was beginning to shoot its colored threads across the sky. Her eyes tunneled. Her mind tunneled. Her heart tunneled.

Eli crossed his arms and sighed, sick of the arguing that had held constant since the Heart encased the Wood in a wall of fire. All the dryads were gathered at the flames of the manifestation. Fear and rage mixed with sorrow was all that existed at the moment. The bodies of the fallen warriors who had been poisoned by the shadow sand had already been put into the flames, their trees now grey, petrified in death.

Eli listened and kept his opinions to himself. The most volatile were still running their mouths louder than anyone else and probably still had a few hours of stamina to flap their lips before they took a break and let someone else talk. The truth was he understood the fear. They were under attack, limited in their ability to strike back, not being able to take the fight to their enemies and unable to put a safe distance between their fighters and the children. He wanted to go off on his own for a while and search the history for possible ideas to their dilemma. The original language had already made them so much stronger. Was there more they could do? Untapped power or potential?

Eli... The Heart whispered in his mind. *Prepare yourself. Sophie approaches the Wood. I'm going to let her in. Don't give yourself and your true feelings away. None of the others can know about you and her. Not right now in the middle of all this fear. I'm going to warn the rest of them now. Be calm.*

Calm?! He thought. How the hell was he to manage that?

The white flames sparked around the top. *Silence.* The Heart said inside all of their minds.

Everyone faced the manifestation and quieted.

Listen to me. A she-wolf is entering the Wood. Sabra's daughter. I've allowed her past the flames. Regardless of your feelings toward the wolves right now, none of you shall harm her. Step aside and let her come to me.

Eli stood straight as a board, his muscles tense, trying to hold still as she came into their midst. His heart burned when he saw her and he began to tremble deep inside. Tears were streaming from her eyes and she was covered in blood. His breath caught and he ground his teeth hard. Her beautiful face was mangled. Her eyes were glazed as she walked a straight line to the Heart. What was she holding?

Everyone backed away from her, murmuring.

Sophie fell to her knees at the crystal trees, sobbing loudly as she uncovered what she was holding. An audible gasp rose up from the dryads close enough to see. She lifted Sam's body up.

"I found her. Sweet little thing. I found her. I've brought her back to you."

Uproar ensued as everyone came close to Sophie and saw she had Sam's body.

"She killed Sam!" someone shouted.

Eli moved forward. Sophie needed his protection. But Shi got to her first, standing in between Sophie and the crowd. Shi gave them all a furious glare. Those approaching with violent intent stopped and scowled, but they stopped and that was the important thing at the moment. He continued to move to her. He couldn't stop himself.

Sophie cried out again, speaking incoherently. She was out of her head and pulled Sam's body back to her chest and wouldn't let go. Shi got down on her knees in front of Sophie and touched her shoulders. Then she moved her hands over Sophie's where they clenched around Sam.

"Here, sweetheart," Shi's voice was so calm and warm. "Let me have her. Okay? I'll take care of her. I promise." She spoke to Sophie as though she was crazy and dangerous. "Remember me? Shi? See, I'm a mother, too. I understand. I'll be careful. Let me have her."

"Don't wake her," Sophie pleaded. "She needs to sleep."

"I won't wake her. I promise. Hand her to me."

Sobbing, Sophie nodded and eased her grip. Shi took the body from her, cradling her as though she was alive and just asleep.

"I'm sorry. I'm sorry…" Sophie's voice trailed away and she fell. Eli caught her before she hit the ground and lifted her up. She hung limply in his arms.

He turned and began walking through everyone. Lex put his hand on his shoulder.

"What are you doing?"

Eli looked at his friend and then down at Sophie. What was he doing?

"I…She's hurt."

"Yeah, obviously. Where are you taking her?" Lex frowned.

"I was just…trying to get her out of the crowd."

He looked around. Everyone was staring at him. Shi and Ler confronted him then, Ler taking Sophie from his arms.

"What are you going to do?" Eli demanded.

Shi gave him a questioning look. "Don't worry about it. I'm going to see to her wounds privately. You need to join with everyone else in the song of death as Sam is given back to the Heart."

He was frozen in place as he watched them carry Sophie away, assailed with the wrongness of it. It should be him taking care of her, but no one could know that. It had to remain a secret. At that moment he experienced the weight this secret carried. It should be him taking care of her.

Many were still looking at him quizzically as if his actions had been ridiculous or bizarre. He focused on his breathing and acting normal, and moved back toward the flames as everyone began to sing for Sam. It was a serious effort to focus as they committed her little body to the manifestation. Eli forced himself to relax. Shi would take care of Sophie as if she were her own daughter.

When the song finished and the memorial was complete, everyone dispersed. Quietness settled over the Wood. Unrest and the desire for revenge moved from shouts and arguments into whispers and murmuring. Many dryads just simply retired to their trees, worn out from all the emotional turmoil.

Eli stayed with his friends and they moved out toward the fringe. The white wall of fire was visible through the trees this close to the boundary.

"What do you think about that bitch coming here like that, with Sam's body?" Sen asked.

"I wonder what happened to her. She was seriously beaten up." Lex said.

"What if it's a ruse?" Ara added. "What if she's a spy?"

"She's not," Eli's voice was flat.

"How would you know?" Ara demanded.

He looked away from her and didn't answer, reminding himself that she had sworn revenge on him for turning her down.

"The whole thing is crazy," Rom said putting his arm around Ara. "It could be a trick, some elaborate plan. It puts me on edge for sure. We're going to have to watch her carefully. I don't think we can let her leave."

"I doubt she can do much of anything," Eli said. "You all saw how messed up she is."

"Yeah, and that's weird, too." Lex began pacing. "I want to hear her story. I want an explanation... Unless some of it was theatrical, I tend to think she just wanted to do the right thing, maybe just discovering Sam, and paid a heavy price for it... I mean with everything going on, her coming here was almost suicidal."

"I won't believe a word she says. They are our enemies now. With what they've done to us, we should get whatever information we can out of her, and then we should just kill her." Sen said.

"Well, that's a fine thing." Eli's voice was aggressive. "She risked her life to come here and you want to repay her sacrifice by killing her."

Sen scowled, crossed his arms, and looked down. "All right, all right. Maybe that's going too far. Regardless, I don't trust her and I don't trust anything about this situation."

All of Eli's friends nodded and voiced their agreement. Eli was so angry he felt like he was going to break out of his skin, but he couldn't show it. He couldn't voice it. But if he stood there talking to them much longer they would probably end up in a fight.

"Whatever, guys. I've listened to enough talking today." Eli walked away, toward his fake tree.

He held still. It was killing him, but he held still. Eli climbed into his fake trunk and waited. In the silence, his emotions rushed on him. He couldn't remember the last time he had cried. He pinched his eyes shut, tears running out, refusing to be kept inside. The memory of Sophie overwhelmed him. The blood on her, the broken bones of her face, and the vacant chill in her eyes.

For the first time in his life, Eli hated what he was. He hated being a dryad. Tristan had done that to her. Tristan had killed Sam. He was begging for a painful death, but he stood just outside of Eli's reach. He couldn't protect Sophie, not the way he wanted to, not the way she needed. Desperate, he turned his mind inward and began searching the history for anything that might help him now. Help came to one part of his problem, but no miracle.

He climbed back out into the open. Darkness had matured overhead, and the pale lights deep in the veins of the leaves illuminated the Wood. His friends were long gone and he encountered no one as he moved toward the manifestation. He'd waited long enough. He would find Sophie now and offer her the only solace he could.

He found her with Shi and a few other dryad women, by the waterfall of Silverlight, laid out on the soft sand of the beach. They had given her new clothes and were working on her wounds. He approached slowly. He stopped a short distance away and just stood still, feeling choked. She was so injured. Aside from being clean, she didn't look any better than when she walked into the Wood that evening.

Shi looked up at him. She got up from the kneeling position next to Sophie and came toward him. Her eyes held question, concern, and a slight tinge of anger. She reached out and touched his arm with her soft hand.

"Why, Eli? What is it? What is your concern for her?"

He gazed at her, a plea in his eyes. "What happened to her? What is the extent of her injuries?"

"There are multiple fractures in the bones of her face. A few broken ribs, some internal injuries. At least the hemorrhaging has stopped. She suffered a miscarriage."

He thought he was going to be sick. His hands began to shake. "The Heart made me the historian, Shi. I can heal her... At least, I think I can. Let me try."

"Okay, you can try." Her soft touch on his arm abruptly turned into a vice grip and her eyes burned. "She is not one of us... If you think you're not being obvious, you're dead wrong. You better do better than this at hiding what you feel. She's not for you."

"No one has the right to say that to me, *especially* you."

"Call me a hypocrite if you like, but I'm one of the only people who could understand. Don't make the same mistake I did."

"*Mistake?* Is that what you and Ler are? Ten thousand years of sacrifice and pain... Love that lasted through all of it... Resurrected and given a second chance... All of that was a mistake?" Eli had never spoken so harshly to Shi.

She eased her grip on his arm and shook her head. "No..." She breathed. "The mistake I speak of was falling so fast and so hard that neither of us could see anything except each other. Seduced by what was forbidden and taking it without reverence, without thought."

"Does anyone really choose when they fall, how

hard, how fast, or with whom?"

Shi smiled at him sadly. "Perhaps not. Forgive me. I'm only trying to look out for you. Tensions are high. I don't want you to put yourself or her in danger... As I said before, work a little harder to hide it."

"Okay. I will. I didn't realize." He glanced back over at Sophie, his mouth pressing into a hard line. "She can't stay here. Some think she's a spy. I've already heard talk that we should just kill her. She's not safe inside the boundary."

She nodded gravely. "She's not well enough to leave. She's not even coherent yet."

"Please, Shi. Leave me with her. Let me do what I can for her, and if she's not well enough, explain to anyone who asks that I am guarding her per your request. If I can heal her, then I will take her out of here, beyond the barrier and somewhere safe... Please."

She worried her bottom lip between her teeth for a moment, mulling it over. "Okay, Eli. I'll give you tonight. I'll make the right excuses at the right time. And if anyone has a problem or questions me, it will be my decision, my call they will have to contend with. You won't be at fault for anything. You will just be who I asked to handle the situation."

He clasped both of her hands in his, leaned down, and pressed a kiss to her forehead. "Thank you, mother."

He waited where he stood while Shi went back to the other women tending to Sophie. She spoke quietly to them and he couldn't hear exactly what she said, but in a few moments all of them left and he was alone on the beach with Sophie.

He hovered over her for a moment before sliding his arms under her back and knees, lifting her up against his chest. "I've got you, Sophie. You're going to be all right. I've got you," he whispered. "You're so brave."

He leaned his head down so his face was right next to hers and closed his eyes. "*Ohhr cranic sana mederrum.*"

She moaned and shifted in his arms. He said the words three times over her. Words of healing and protection in the original Dradhi.

She blinked and looked up at him as though she'd just woken from a long restful sleep, her skin returning to perfect, her bones restored.

"Are you a sorcerer?"

He smiled, his heart expanding in relief and something else he couldn't name. "Naw. Just a book nerd."

"A sexy nerd," she amended.

"That's right..." he lowered his voice. "How do you feel?"

"Great. Never better."

"Good. I need to get you out of here. It's not safe."

He stood and began walking.

"You can put me down. I feel fine. I can walk," she protested lightly.

"Shh...I just want to hold you against me for a moment. Let me."

She smiled and laid her head on his shoulder. "Okay.

I don't feel heavy to you?"

He snorted and continued walking, carrying her as though she barely weighed a thing. He moved quickly through the Wood, hoping no one would come out and ask him anything or try to stop them.

"I don't remember how I got here...Tristan..."

"Not yet, Sophie. Tell me after I get you past the boundary."

The flames loomed. The wall parted and let them pass closing behind them. Eli sighed in relief, but he did feel someone's eyes on them once. He didn't know who because he didn't turn to look. At least he didn't hear anyone following them. The wall of fire wouldn't keep anyone in, just intruders out. He set her on her feet and took her hand instead, leading her toward his real tree.

He stopped right next to his trunk and rested his hand against it. "This is me. No one knows. I've never told any of my friends where my real tree is. Only the Heart knows."

"And now me."

"Yes. I wanted to tell you. I don't want there to be secrets between us."

She gazed up into his branches. "You're kinda short."

He huffed. "That's because I break my branches to disguise myself...I'm the only dryad outside the boundary of the Wood."

Smiling, she moved closer and sat on the ground, leaning back against his trunk. "I like it here...with you. Thank you for showing me where I can find you."

Her easy smile suddenly slipped from her face, the

color in her cheeks draining, and her eyes going wide. "Oh gosh...I remember what happened now." Her whole body began to shake.

He sat next to her and pulled her into his arms as she began to sob. She was too loud for his comfort but he didn't want to tell her to be quiet. "Sophie, hold on. Let's go to the cave. You can cry. You can scream or do whatever you need to, just hold on..."

Her bottom lip trembling, she nodded and got to her feet. She practically ran there. If he wasn't so worried about her emotional state, he'd have been impressed with how quick and agile she scaled the cliff face. The cave swallowed them in its dark embrace. He picked her up again as he had when he'd carried her and sank down against the wall, holding her cradled in his lap. She clung to him and wept.

"Tristan locked me in...I found the little girl. He'd put her in a trunk like a treasure he meant to keep...I don't know what happened to me, Eli. I broke inside." She gasped around the words and tears. "I lost my baby!" she wailed. "I felt its life fly from me." She clutched at her stomach. "I'm so empty now. My womb is an empty coffin. Tristan came back, he was furious. He said I killed our baby. He beat me. My mind just drifted. It's like I wasn't really there. I fought back. I knocked him out. I wanted to kill him. I almost did. I was so close, but then a part of me woke up and stopped my hand. I remembered why I couldn't. I wrapped up the girl and walked out of the mountain. That's all. I can't remember anything else. Then I woke up and you were holding me and all the pain was gone."

For a while they stayed like that, quiet and just holding on. He felt her relax and then a new tension began building in her body. Before he could ask her what she was feeling she spoke.

"I'm sorry...I'm sure you never want to see me again." Her voice had never been so light and cold. Her tone was forced. "It's too dangerous, for both of us. It's not worth the risk. Thank you for all you've done for me. You're a good man, Eli. I don't mean to hurt you."

He stiffened under her and sniffed, anger flashing inside him. "So full of yourself. You couldn't hurt me."

He got up and put her down at arm's length. She flinched.

"I thought you wanted me."

"*Want* you?" he scoffed. "I don't want you!" his voice bounced off the cave walls. He reached forward and grabbed her arms with his hands. "You drive me crazy. You keep coming here, drawing me out, ruining everything that could possibly be ruined. If you're going to dismiss me that easily then I never want to see you again. I wish we'd never met. I hate you. I hate you so much...and...and..." his breath came out in short jerks. "I can't breathe without you."

He let go and backed away from her, looking down. The heat and pull between them surged. A dark smile lifted her lips. She moved forward, invading his space and touched his cheek. His gaze dragged up slowly to hers.

"I hate you, too," she whispered.

"Damn it, Sophie."

"Yes," she pressed her chest against his. "You have damned me...as much as I've damned you."

He wrapped his arms around her and took her mouth as gravity tilted sideways.

"We promised to be honest, Eli. You just slipped up...I guess I did, too. I could hurt you, just as you could hurt me. I don't want it to end yet...I'm sorry. I'm just feeling too much. I'm scared. I can't think..."

He took her hand, led her into the middle of the cave, and then backed away. She looked at him confused.

"Paint, Sophie. Paint it all. Everything you're feeling no matter what it is. Let it out so you can heal."

The way she looked at him then, warm pressure spread through his chest. Had he just claimed her heart? Had she just surrendered it to him?

She closed her eyes and lifted her hands. He watched in awe as colors and images ran from her fingers. All of it was ugly. She was purging. He saw it, the horror, the death, it was all laced into the lines. After a few bruised designs she heaved a heavy sigh and opened her eyes. She walked to the back of the cave to the painting of the baby. Her fingertips ran gently along the edges for a few minutes then she began gathering it. It compressed down until it could fit in the palm of her hand. She lifted it to her chest and pressed it against her skin. The light, the color of tears, cut her as it sank in. She reabsorbed it.

"I think I'm finished now."

He went to her. "Not yet. Just do one more."

"What do you mean?"

He moved behind her, pressing his chest against her back and running his hands down her shoulders. He gripped her hips and kissed the side of her neck. Her breathing turned rough. He moved his hands back to her arms, slowly running them down until he laced his fingers through hers.

"What do you feel right now?" he breathed in her ear. "Show me. Paint what you feel for me."

He let go of her hands as she lifted them up in front of her and wrapped his arms around her waist instead, holding her tightly. He didn't look at what she made, not yet. He closed his eyes and kissed all down her neck slowly. Shivers rolled over her skin. He smiled to himself at her body's response.

"You're a dangerous creature, Eli," she whispered. "I can't...we can't...you healed me, but it's too..."

"It's too soon. I know. I'm not trying to get there right now."

She sighed and rested her head back against his collarbone.

"I've finished. What do you think?"

She moved out of his grasp and around the image floating in the air, facing him from the other side of it. He looked at it and then at her. She met his gaze evenly without blushing. It was a tree. Every leaf was a tongue of fire. The light lines danced as if it really burned. He looked closer. Details, tiny details, almost too small to see were etched into the outlines. Confusion, fear, desperation, lust, and defiance. He could look at this one for a very long time, examining all the subtle nuances in the layers she built into it, and he would take the time...later.

"Thank you."

"You say that too much to me." he smiled.

"I doubt it." She rubbed her arms and looked at the mouth of the cave. "You've given me the strength I need...I have to go back now. I have to finish this. I'm going to break the cage he's put me in."

He wrapped her in his arms and leaned his forehead against hers again. "You have no idea what this has done to me. A rage like madness runs all through me and I can't do anything about it. To be so helpless to rescue you. I want to! It feels like my right and I can't exercise it."

"It's not how you want. It's not the violent, bloody way you want to rescue me, but you still have. Just in another way. Because of you, I feel strong enough to do it myself. You won't hold that against me, will you? It's my right as well, to rescue myself."

He kissed her long and hard until they were both breathless. She put her hands on his face and fell into his midnight eyes.

"This is crazy...you and me... you know that, right?"

He smirked. "Baby, crazy is all we have."

She chuckled and nestled closer to him. "I have to go. I won't come back until I'm free."

"When you do, I'm going to show you, you do like sex."

She snorted. "You remember everything I say, don't you?"

"No, but you throw words like sex around and I'm definitely listening."

Her laugh bounced around the cave. Then she gave him a look caught between interest and annoyance. "Do you have lots of experience?"

"No. Not lots."

"You certainly warmed me up a few times. It seems like you have serious skill. Where did you get it?"

He held his hands out to her, palms up so she could see the words. "Not all the history is...shall we say...*dry* reading."

Her smile warmed her eyes. "Sexy nerd."

"Don't forget it, either."

"You don't seem likely to let me."

His expression sobered. "It's more than that. You know that, right? It's not just lust between us. At least, not for me."

She shook her head. "It's not just that for me either. Not even close to being just that, Eli."

She drew close one last time and he kissed her mouth. All his worry poured into this kiss. Reluctantly she pulled away. "I'll survive. I promise. And I'll come back to you."

He watched her go. The bird thing was on his shoulder, it pulsed and moved slowly down till it rested over his heart. He covered it with his hand, drawing comfort from the feel of it. Sophie was with him. So long as her art lived under his skin, she was with him.

EIGHTEEN

She climbed up the natural ladder to the top and looked down at the Wood, circled by flames. This was her last moment in this reality. Tristan had pushed her too far, taken too much. The face of the little girl she'd found in the trunk was forever branded into her mind. Blood would be paid. Tristan would bleed for the dryad lives he'd taken, but also for her unborn baby that she would never meet in this life.

She began to walk at a steady pace. The mountain towering in front of her. What was she going to do? She was going to end this...but how? What did she have to fight with?

A chill swept up her body and she stopped. Sophie smiled as she heard it coming up behind her. She turned, her gaze cutting through the shadows.

"Come here. Don't be scared."

The shadow she created looked back at her from the darkness with its glowing green eyes. "I'm sorry, mother. I failed to kill him. I want to try again."

Inspiration and pressure filled Sophie to a height she had never experienced. "I said, come here."

"Why?"

"I need you. Come back inside me. We'll kill him together. Together maybe we'll be strong enough."

The silhouette slunk forward. "I am my own. I don't

want to disappear."

"Too bad," Sophie lunged forward catching the art with both hands.

They struggled. It tried to slip from her grasp. She thought it would reabsorb as soon as she touched it. It pulled her down and they rolled on the ground. Sophie pinned it and it quit fighting but it wouldn't sink back into her. Desperate, she leaned down and bit into the oily skin.

It screamed once as Sophie swallowed, feeling the hate and rage slide down her throat. *More.* She needed all of it. Running her hands over the thing, it blurred. The shape, the face, the voice, all discerning elements of a personality hazed until it constricted in on itself into a black pool, cupped in Sophie's hands. She raised them to her lips and drank it all.

The strength of her hate coated her bones and slid into the chambers of her heart. *Monster, artist.* She thought. *I am.* She paced a circuit around and around until the sunrise. This was the day she would change things. The day would not end as it began. Morning light on her shoulders, her stride ate up the ground. *Come get some.*

So much of what she had been afraid of lately all fell away. She didn't care who saw her or what they thought, or if they were in Tristan's pocket. She marched through the suburbs, up to the mouth of the mountain and in without a word to those standing guard. She went to Tristan's apartment. The door frame was broken. Had she done that? She must have. She pushed the door open and went inside.

She found him on the floor in the bedroom, on his hands and knees, crying softly.

"Tristan."

He gasped and looked up at her. He was on his feet the next second, snarling at her. She pointed in his face.

"Don't start with me!" she commanded. "I've taken as much physical abuse from you as I'm willing. Any more and I'll never mate with you."

He blinked, taken aback. Then he sighed and sat on the edge of the bed, his head in his hands. "I guess you were pretty scared when you found that girl. I should have warned you. Oh gosh, Sophie..." he reached for her hand. She gave it easily. "You've been through a lot. But you came back to me."

"Yes. I was angry, but I came back."

He frowned up at her. "Did you tell anyone about the girl? Where did you take her?"

"I told no one. I took her to the Wood, where she belongs."

"*What?* You went to the Wood? How did you get past the fire?"

"I have no idea. I don't remember much. I'd lost a lot of blood and you'd broken my face. I think I was in shock." Her voice remained modulated as if she was discussing the weather.

He stood and cupped her cheek. "You got better very fast. You look perfect."

"The dryads took care of me."

He sniffed derisively and took a step back from her.

"I'm surprised they didn't kill you."

"Some wanted to, but there was this guy. He seemed to like me. He argued I should be let go. He was very flirtatious."

His expression was a mix of fury and disgust. "Just another reason for me to kill all of them. How dare he? You're mine. You're a wolf."

"Half wolf," she amended.

"What was his name?"

She shrugged. He swore and began pacing, muttering to himself. She waited. In a minute he was back in her space grasping her by the arms.

"You forgive me? You're still with me?"

"Yes. I love you."

He sighed and pulled her into a hug. "Alright. Nothing has changed. Not really. Our ceremony will still be on the same day. You will not tell anyone you lost the baby. My threat to your family still stands."

She snuggled into his arms as though she loved him and he spoke only soft words to her and not violence.

"Hello? Sophie?" her sister's voice called from the front door of the apartment.

They both stiffened and left the bedroom. He shut and locked the door behind them. Lacey was standing on the threshold looking in.

"There you are." Lacey smiled. "You know your door is broken?"

"Yes. We know," Tristan said tersely. Then he shifted back into his charming self and smiled at her. "Good morning, Lacey. What are you doing here so early?"

She reached forward and took Sophie's hand. "Mom sent me." She bounced once on the balls of her feet grinning excitedly. "The dressmaker is coming up. You have to come so we can have our fittings. Tristan you come, too. Callen's there already."

"Mom wants us to come now?"

"Yes! Come on!"

Sophie gazed at Tristan, he nodded and they followed Lacey out. As they approached the double doors, Sophie's eyes landed on Rolph, standing stoically on guard. *I see you. I know what you are. The clock is ticking for you.*

Jorgie ran to her as they came in and wrapped his arms around her waist. She leaned down and kissed the top of his head, whispering, "Remember your promise."

His grip tightened for a second in response and he scampered away. She looked through everything she could see, calculating the possibilities. Her father wasn't there. That nagged in the back of her mind.

Two dress forms stood in the center of the living room, the beginnings of gowns already draped on them, covered in chalk lines and pins. The dressmaker, a stern looking, middle-aged woman, ordered Lacey and Sophie to change into the new dresses so she could get started.

Even in its initial stages, Sophie's gown was gorgeous. Gold embroidered vines and flowers cascaded from the bodice down the skirt. Standing on a platform, she closed her eyes for a moment, collecting herself. She wasn't screaming inside because she knew she wouldn't ever wear this dress once it was completed. She looked down at the dressmaker, hunched over by her feet, pinning the hem to the right length and then out over the whole room.

Lacey was next to the full mirror that had been set up, playing with how she might want her hair for the ceremony, her mom was at the kitchen table, pouring over papers, Tristan was watching Sophie closely...then she looked at Callen and her sight sharpened.

He was talking to Jorgie, trying to play with him. Trying to make him laugh, only there wasn't anything innocent about it. He was keeping Jorgie close to him on purpose. He touched him too much. It looked casual. It wasn't. Her stomach hardened. There. She saw it. Violence mixed with perversion deep in Callen's gaze as he looked at Jorgie. Callen was the threat.

She exhaled, her fingers picking at the gold thread on the skirt of her dress. She pulled the color off the thread and rolled it between her thumb and fingers. Then she swallowed and stepped off the platform. The dressmaker protested, but she ignored her, moving forward. She looked at her sister.

"I'm sorry, Lacey. I have to."

Before Lacey could ask her what she meant, Sophie caught Jorgie's eye. *Run.* She mouthed the word. He obeyed instantly. She grabbed the color on her fingers with her other hand, pulling it out, stretching it into a long, sharp point. She strode up to Callen and stabbed the gold dagger through his neck.

His blood sprayed over her as he fell. Lacey screamed and ran to him. Tristan knocked her off balance from behind and then threw her to the ground. He straddled her, his hands on her throat, choking her. Gasping for air, Sophie reached up and put her thumbs on his face. He screamed and let go as she smeared his eyes like paint on a canvas.

Sabra rushed up behind him, grabbed the back of his collar, and yanked him off her daughter. He continued to scream and claw at his face. She'd blinded him and his face now looked like abstract art. Rolph burst into the room, sword raised and came at Sabra. A knife came around Rolph's throat from behind and slashed it open. He fell, choking to death in a pool of his own blood. Her father stood over him wiping the blood off his knife.

"Nice little bunch of traitors," Shreve said. "I've been on to you for a while, Tristan."

Tristan was subdued on his knees in front of her mom, still crying and clawing at his mangled face. "Don't kill me! I surrender. Please! It's not what you think! It was all Callen. Everything was his idea. I was going to come to you privately, Shreve. I swear. I was going to tell you all about his plans today. Please don't kill me. You can't. It's not lawful."

Sophie got to her feet, holding her abused neck, and coughing a few times.

"Don't listen to him," she croaked. "He's a monster, a rapist, and a murderer. Kill him and be done with it. Or let me."

Tristan whimpered. "I love you, Sophie. I've always loved you."

"Yeah, I know. Sorry, it's just not my flavor. It's not you, it's me." Everything seemed to break loose inside her then and came pouring out in loud, wild laughter. "No...No, it's you. Oh, and just so you know, I've been cheating on you with a dryad."

He roared in rage and began calling her dirty names. She came forward, ready, anxious to end his wretched life. Her dad stepped in front of her, blocking her way. "He will die, but not right now. Hell, if you still want to, I'll let you play executioner when the time comes. But he did surrender. The laws have to be followed. He's under arrest."

Outrage burned her face. Her dad pulled her into a tight hug. "Trust me, Sweetheart," he whispered quietly in her ear.

Tristan's hands were bound and Shreve personally took him to the underground. Sophie went to Lacey and pulled her away from Callen's body. Sobbing, she clung to her sister.

"I'm sorry, Lacey," she said again. "He was false. He was a part of a plan to kill you, Jorgie, and mom and dad. Once I knew for sure, I had to take him out."

Time didn't hold its usual pace as Rolph and Callen were cleaned up from the floor. The dressmaker left in a hurry swearing she would never come back. And after a while Sophie found herself sitting on the couch huddled in the middle of her mother, sister, and brother. She had Jorgie tucked into her side and she didn't feel inclined to let him go anytime soon. Finally, the adrenaline crash came, leaving her lethargic. She told them everything, leaving out the details too adult for her brother's ears. And finally, *finally,* she showed them her gift.

The art she made was a simple heart shape but it was all she had the energy for and it adequately demonstrated her ability.

They didn't move from the couch until dinner time when her father came back.

"He's being guarded by only those I trust. And I don't intend to leave him there for long. I will go at different intervals through the night and make sure Tristan doesn't go anywhere. All of us need to be on our guard right now. If more is going to happen, we need to be looking for it and for betrayal in those around us."

"How did you know?" Sophie asked.

"Oh, being pack leader comes with regular assassination attempts, and political bullshit," Sabra said. "Tristan was more cunning than most. We're not sure how deep his web goes yet."

"Go clean up, Sophie. You're still covered in blood."

She went to her room and slipped out of the ruined, macabre gown, placing it reverently on her bed before heading to the shower. At dinner, all of them ate as though starved, except Lacey. She picked at her food, her eyes hollow. Lacey would be alright. She was tough.

Was she really free? She'd never have to go back to the shrine. She'd never again have to hold still in the center of Tristan's psychosis. But she didn't feel easy. She wouldn't until he was dead. She wanted to go to Eli. She wanted the problems and bad blood Tristan had created between the dryads and wolves to go away so they could be together and not have to hide.

She put Jorgie to bed. Taking her time, reading him a story and making all the character voices. She pulled his blanket up to his chin when his eyes finally closed. Her parents were talking quietly on the couch and she went to her room to change. She was going to the Wood.

Lacey came into her room as she slipped the bloodied gown back on.

"What are you doing?" she asked sitting on Sophie's bed. "Why are you putting that back on?"

"It's going to sound sick, but this blood is a gift. I want him to see it."

"Are you really seeing a dryad?" Lacey asked.

"Yeah. It's a long story. I'll tell you later. His name is Eli."

Some of the light came back into her sister's eyes. She looked more like herself and she grinned a little. "What does he look like?"

"Hot. He's strong. He has long, dirty blonde hair, black dryad eyes, oh, and a dimple in one cheek when he smiles. My head spins when he kisses me. Gravity goes all sideways when he puts his hands on me...he sees me in a way no one else ever has."

Lacey looked down. "Wow. That sounds nice. After what you've been through...I'm glad you've got him. Even if he's nothing but a distraction for now."

She sat next to her and pulled her against her side. "I love you. I'm so sorry for what I had to do today. I know your heart must be broken."

She sniffed and leaned her head on Sophie's shoulder. "It is broken, but not like it would have been if Callen would have had his way. I can't believe I fell for all of it. All his lies. He didn't love me."

"No, sweetie. He didn't. You'll get over him."

Lacey sighed and slumped. Sophie moved and let her lay down on her bed. She kissed her cheek and tucked her in as if she was a child. She turned the light out and left the room.

"I haven't lost my mind," she said as she faced her parents, sitting on the couch. "I have a valid reason for wearing this again...but it's kind of personal."

They both gazed at her with raised eyebrows.

"I'm going to see Eli. I need to be with him. I need to tell him everything that happened today."

Shreve scowled. "Who's Eli?"

"He's a dryad warrior. We've been spending time together, secretly. I'm going to see him. I'll be back in the morning. We need to make amends with the dryads. They need to know we aren't their enemies."

"That was my plan," Sabra said. "I am going to the Wood in the morning. I hope the Heart will let me in."

They both stood and hugged her tightly. "Helluva day," her dad said.

"Yeah. Helluva day." She agreed.

They released her. "Be careful, Sophie."

"I will."

NINETEEN

Ever since Sophie left him the night before, Eli was so distraught, so worried, he decided to lock himself away from the world until she came back. If she ever did. He climbed into his real tree and forced himself into a half-lucid trance, using words in the original language to make himself stoned. He drifted through the hours in a haze.

The bird thing over his heart began to throb. An image flashed in his mind. Sophie running through the forest. His heart clenched. Moonlight slid over her, illuminating her long hair, and flashing in her eyes. He woke on a gasp and climbed out of his trunk. It was night. The aquamarine moonlight shot down through the branches in sharp lines just as it had in his vision a moment ago. He held his breath and turned toward the mountain.

In the distance, he saw her. The full skirt of the white gown she wore rustled softly around her legs as she ran. She wasn't running away, she was running to. To him. He'd never seen anything as beautiful in his life, even covered in blood, like a princess in a dark fairy tale. She said she wouldn't come back until she was free. Even if she hadn't said that he would know. Stress, worry, heartache clung to her since the first time he saw her. All of it was lifted now.

She bounded up to him and jumped into his arms, wrapping her legs around his waist. She kissed him. "It's over," she kissed him again. "Everything is going to be fine now." She kissed him again.

"I never thought blood stains could look so sexy," he chuckled. "I want you to tell me everything, but we should get out of the open. The wall still burns. My people are still on edge. If someone saw us together, it could mean real trouble."

"Okay. Should we go to the cave?"

He looked up into his branches then back at her, smiling. "Why not just go up? You said you liked climbing trees."

She pointed. "Up? In your branches?"

"Yes. I've fantasized about you up there. It should be concealed enough so long as we are quiet."

Her smile widened and she shrugged. "Alright."

She bent over and tore some of the front of her skirt so it wouldn't hinder her climbing. She faced his trunk and hesitated then she turned back to him. "Is this a joke? You really want me to climb you?"

"You can do it. Grab my wood."

She rolled her eyes, shaking her head. "Still going there, huh?"

He blinked innocently at her. "I don't know what you mean."

She snorted and had to cover her mouth. "You're terrible," she said affectionately.

"Up, woman."

She grabbed the lowest branch and began pulling

herself up. He had been on the ground next to her but the next second he was above her, offering her his hand. She took it and he lifted her up into his arms at the top of his canopy. She smiled, looking around at everything. The faint glow in the leaves was so beautiful and soothing. She understood now how he had noticed her the day they met when she stood on the edge in front of the cave. The cliff face was right there in easy view.

"You've fantasized about having me here?"

"Yes. Quite a few times. Reality is better than I imagined." He kissed her slowly until she relaxed all the way, leaning into him. "Tell me everything."

The branches crossing under her feet began moving. She gasped and gave a little jump but he held her tightly.

"It's okay. I'm just shifting. I just want you to be comfortable."

His canopy changed around them. He eased her down until she was lounging, supported perfectly and amazingly comfortable. It continued to morph around her until she was sure no one would be able to see them even if they were standing directly under, looking up.

She smiled at him stretching out next to her. "Oh, I like this. It's a little bizarre but wonderful too."

"Comfortable?"

"Totally. This actually even feels better than my bed at home."

"Good. You can spend the night then."

"Spend the night? Are you asking me to go steady?"

He smirked. "At least. It's not safe to go public yet, but I'd like to get there."

"I'm glad I was able to break my cage, so we can have a chance to see where this might go."

He kissed her again and then pulled back. "I was afraid when you came back things would be different between us. Like we might lose what we felt once your life wasn't in such danger."

"I wondered that as well. Do you feel different?"

"Hmm...I do, but nothing has been lost." He touched the edge of the wing of her art on his collarbone. "I still have this. Your longing just under my skin. What I feel is stronger...there is still danger for us. We have to be careful. Do *you* feel different?"

She closed her eyes and exhaled. "As soon as I knew my family was safe, all I could think, all I wanted was to come to you. It's problematic. I doubt that's going to change. I don't care." She moved closer and he wrapped his arms around her. "I stand by what I said before...in your arms is my favorite place."

"Tell me what happened."

She sighed and recounted everything from the moment she left the cave to when she came back. "I guess it was silly to wear this, it just felt right. It feels awesome actually."

"You weaponized your art. That's fantastic...I don't like that Tristan is still alive."

"Me neither, trust me. But I see the point. My father said he'd let me kill him when the time came."

He raised his eyebrows. "Do you think you will?"

"I don't know. Maybe knowing he's dead will be enough for me and I won't feel the need to do the actual killing." She shivered. "I killed Callen. I actually killed someone."

"Does that scare you?"

"No. I didn't get off on it. Although the fact I put this dress back on might suggest otherwise. I really just wanted you to see it. I wanted to prove to you I was strong enough. I wanted you to be proud of me."

"I am. Believe me...Will you stay the night?"

"Yes."

He held her but he didn't move to take things to a new level. It felt wrong at the moment. Having her there with him like that was more than enough and it felt right to be still. To just be. To have her breathe easily against him. Exhaustion seemed to crash over her and she fell asleep.

Long into the night, he just stared at her. The oddity of them was real. He knew it. Why it was her, he couldn't understand. A shifter-wolf. Tormented artist. Giving, tender, beautiful monster. So odd. So different from him. Yet, it was her. That was his truth. She was for him.

What did he have to offer her in return? How could he be to her what she was to him? How did he convince her the trouble of being together was worth it? He'd do his damnedest to convince her every day. Finally, he fell asleep, too.

Tristan rubbed his face, over and over and over. All day and into the night, he gently tried to reshape his features. It wasn't his doing at all, but through the hours, his face did slowly morph back to normal, his sight returning as his eyelids began to work again.

He blinked in the dingy torchlight of his cell in the underground. The faint whooshing sound of the fire as it burned on the torch and a slow dripping sound of water was all he could hear. He had no idea what time it was or how long he would have to wait.

His love for Sophie twisted around and around inside him. How had she done what she did to his face? How had she blinded him? She was gifted. The bitch had hidden that from him. He remembered the thing that stalked him in the forest and spoke with Sophie's voice. Somehow she had made that. Or it was an extension of her.

He would make her beg for mercy. He would show her his real heart, how it was hers and always would be...then he'd kill her.

He straightened his clothes and combed his fingers through his hair, doing his best to look presentable and unruffled. He waited. Listening. He didn't have to wait long.

They were quiet, but still, he heard them coming. Shreve's guards rolled down the stairs and landed in a bloody mess in front of his cell. Seven of his followers came in, dressed in black, their faces covered. Satran leaned over one of the dead guards, grabbing the keys off his belt, and opening the cell door.

Tristan clapped him on the shoulder. "How many?"

"All of them. Sixty-eight. They are all ready to do your bidding."

"We take the top of the mountain first. Kill Sabra and her family. Except Sophie. I will kill her in my own time and way."

Satran looked away.

"What?" Tristan demanded.

"Umm…Sophie's gone."

Tristan growled and rolled his eyes back in his head, beginning to pace. "She went to the Wood?"

"Yes."

He sighed. "Okay. Change of plan. Get everyone ready to fight. Get all the shadow sand we've accumulated. We're going to the Wood first. I need Sophie for everything to work."

"Why?"

"Trust me. This will be two birds with one stone. We get Sophie back and we annihilate the entire dryad race. Not one is to be left. We kill them all. The sand will go back into the Wood as it was in the past when the wolves owned it. We all know the stories. Philippe understood the importance of controlling the Heart. Of claiming it. I will be a leader like him. I will restore his legacy. At dawn, we strike."

"How do we get through the fire wall?"

"We cut it down, and if that doesn't work, the sand will draw them out. We'll use archers again. The arrows will go over the top. If we can't get in at first, they will come out to meet us."

Twenty

Sophie smiled before she opened her eyes. The dawn was only moments away. She leaned forward and pressed her lips to his. He sighed and opened his eyes.

"I like waking that way."

"I think I need to sneak away now. We can't be discovered yet. The dawn is about to break."

He nodded. "When will you come back?"

"I don't know. Soon. As soon as I can. I'll try to be at our cave by dusk. Can you meet me then?"

"Not at dusk. I'll have to socialize in the evening. But I'll be there as soon as I can get away without it looking like I'm trying to get away."

"Okay. I'll think about you all day."

He smiled and took her mouth softly. "And I you."

Eli dropped to the ground and caught her as she jumped down. There was no more time. He kissed her again and let her go, his heart attaching itself to her as she left. He watched her go until the remaining shadows ate her up. He sighed, missing her already and longing for the day they didn't have to hide as he slid into his trunk.

He needed to be a part of everything today. He hadn't seen or talked to anyone since he snuck Sophie out after she'd brought Sam. He remembered talking to his friends, their unrest and speculations about Sophie. He needed to start preparing them. He needed to tell Lex everything first in confidence otherwise it would be a violation of their friendship. He would make them understand. In time, they would accept her. For one moment he was calm, resigned for what he had to do, then the wings under his skin jolted. The pulse of the bird thing began to race. Sophie…

He climbed out of his trunk and heard her muffled scream, a struggle, and then running feet. He ran toward the sound, an axe materializing in each hand. He couldn't see her, or who had attacked her. The direction of the running cut a sharp left and headed toward the wall of fire. He ran faster. Still muffled, he heard Sophie scream again, this time in pain. Whoever had her had dragged her through the wall.

He jumped through the flames and continued chasing them through the shadows of the end of the night. They were taking her to the Heart. He skidded to a halt in shock as the manifestation loomed before him.

Ara had Sophie next to the flames, her hands tied behind her back, her mouth gagged. Lex, Sen, and Rom stood in a line between him and where Ara held Sophie, facing him down.

"Let her go," he said through clenched teeth.

"You're a traitor." Rom smiled nastily.

"Okay. You're right. Deal with me then. Let her go."

Lex took a step forward, hurt mixed with the anger in his eyes. "Your lies astound me. My whole life, I thought you were my friend. But come to discover, none of us even knew where your tree really was. And now as we stand on the brink of war with the wolves, you start an affair with one! I don't even know who you are."

"I'm the same person I've always been. I *am* your friend. So, I have some secrets. So what? I bet you have a few of your own. You're mad. I get it. But what do you plan to do?"

"She's a spy," Sen snarled. "She's seduced you just to infiltrate us. You've been duped, Eli."

"Even if that were true, what's your end game here?" Eli demanded.

"She has to be dealt with, and since she's turned you, so do you," Rom said.

Eli charged at them. Lex met him first. Eli dropped his axes. He wasn't going to kill his friends. Beat the shit out of them, yes. Knock the stupid from their heads, but not kill them. He grabbed Lex by the front of his shirt, shoved him up against the nearest trunk, lifting him a few inches off his feet.

"I love her!" he shouted in Lex's face.

"Eli!" Ara yelled.

They all turned. Ara smiled at him and stabbed Sophie in the chest with a long knife. His breath seized in his chest as time slowed, barely moving. His eyes held Sophie's. They rounded, the light of her life darkening like lengthening shadows. Her blood rushed from her body. He moved forward but there was nothing he could do. That was a mortal wound.

He cried out. The agony of his voice echoed through

the entire Wood as Ara pushed Sophie into the flames of the manifestation. He had no time for retribution, he charged into the flames after her.

He fell to his knees in the rushing white fire, Sophie's body clasped to his chest. She wasn't breathing.

"Bring her back!" he begged the Heart. "Please! I'll do anything. Just bring her back."

I cannot. Most of her soul has flown. Not much remains. The Heart said sadly. *You only have a few seconds to decide, Eli. My chosen historian. If you would sacrifice yourself for her, then speak the most powerful words in the original Dradhi. The most powerful words in any language, if you know them.*

The art of her longing lifted off his chest, its wings beating slowly. He wrapped his hand around it, bringing it to her chest, and pressed it against her open wound. "*Ce narra phera ceroe,*" he whispered.

The art climbed into her body. *Please.* He thought. Let it be enough of her spirit to save her life. Let it be enough. Were his words wrong? Were they not the most powerful?

How did he sacrifice himself for her? He put his face on hers. "*Ce narra phera ceroe,*" he said again pushing his lifeforce into his hands, making it slide into her the same way he used to put himself into his faux tree. Only now he didn't hold anything back. She could have it all. He'd give his life for hers.

In the blinding white light, darkness began to take over his vision.

Stop, Eli. Stop now. Peace. Feel it. She lives.

He blinked, looking into her lifeless eyes. A tremor began deep inside her. The wound closed. Like an image behind a screen, something rose up through her body coming clearer as it neared the surface. She closed her eyes, took one breath, and opened them as though she was waking from a peaceful sleep. But as she opened her eyes her appearance changed. Her eyes were green, her skin a half shade warmer and her dark brown hair turned a light blond just in the front.

He shook himself, amazed, sure he had died. Sure they were both dead. She was more beautiful than before. She was like some feral angel in his arms, gazing up at him. As the seconds passed he grew aware neither of them was dead. He took the gag off her mouth.

"Say that again," she breathed.

"*Ce narra phera ceroe.* It means,"

"I know." She cut him off. "I love you. It means I love you."

"You look different, Sophie...better."

"Different?"

He lifted the ends of her blonde hair in front of her face.

"Are my eyes green?" she asked.

"Yes."

She smiled. "How about that? It's my true face."

"But...I don't feel...Dryads don't have destined life mates. How can I see your true face?"

By choice. The Heart said. *You are not destined life mates. But you have both chosen each other over any other possible future. She chose the moment death*

324

began to claim her. You chose the moment you were willing to die to bring her back. A choice that final, that strong and sure, carries its own ties. Neither of you has chosen an easy path. Your life together will be rife with trials given to none before you. But you will also have joys no one else has ever experienced. Just as you both are unique, so is your love...

She reached around his neck and he stood, holding her against his chest, where he could feel her heart beat next to his. She was his future. That was not in question now. In a moment the rage would return. But for this moment there was only them, wrapped in white flames. They would come out of the manifestation and confront those who opposed them. Justice would be dealt.

Leave Ara to me. The others were only hurt by your deception and did not truly mean Sophie any harm. Perhaps with time, your friendships might heal. They will answer for the part they played, but I am willing to forgive Rom, Sen, and Lex. If you forgive them or not is up to you. Ara will die, however.

Screaming and violent shaking filled the Heart. Eli and Sophie pulled together, cringing away from the sound.

"What's happening?" Eli asked the Heart.

Fighting. The wolves brought the sand back. I feel the poison. It seeps into the ground. Your people are facing them just outside the wall. I will not lower it. I will not let them in. Go, Eli. You too, Sophie. Make deadly weapons of your art. Spill their blood.

They both had to blink as they came out of the

Heart. The sounds of battle filled the Wood but none of it had come inside the wall. Ara, Rom, Sen, and Lex were still there. All three of his former friends were shouting at Ara. They all gasped as Eli and Sophie came out.

The manifestation bent and grabbed Ara. She screamed as it pulled her inside it.

No one will use my power for their own vice as Ara did. No one!

A terrible ripping sound came from the flames and Ara's screams stopped.

Eli held Sophie's hand and faced his friends defiantly. "She is with me. She's not a spy and you will never lay a hand to her again. You will not speak to her, or even look in her direction unless she speaks or looks at you."

"I'm sorry, Eli," Lex said. "None of us knew what Ara planned to do. We weren't going to hurt her."

"I believe you only because the Heart told me just that. We will deal with each other later. Now we have to fight together. The wolves have brought the sand back. We can be enemies after we kill them, until then I have your back. Do you have mine?" Eli demanded.

"Yes," they all said.

"Fine. Let's go."

He moved forward but Sophie held back. He turned and looked at her. She held one shaking hand up next to the flames.

"Let me have some of you, please," Sophie said quietly.

Sparks snapped off the Heart at her request. She put

her hand back into the flames, grabbing a handful and pulling it back out. White fire engulfed her hand. Excited light lit her eyes as she pulled the flame into a long sword.

Eli smiled as his friends gasped.

"What is she?" Lex asked.

"Mine." Eli's voice was absolute.

Sophie held the white sword with both hands and swung it, bringing the tip directly under Lex's chin. He held his hands up and she smirked. "I'm an artist. Nothing more. Let's go. I want Tristan."

They all ran together toward the boundary. "Stay beside me," Eli told Sophie. "You look for Tristan. If he's here, I'll get you close to him. Cover you. He's your kill. Unless you need my help."

"I love you said that," she called without breaking stride. "I've never been so hot for you. You better satisfy me later."

He chuckled. "Let's just survive. Your satisfaction will be my next order of business."

They reached the fire wall. The dryads jumped through as though it was nothing, Sophie cut a line in the fire with her sword and it parted for her. She stepped through and was instantly splattered with blood.

She blinked, trying to orient herself in the chaos. The air was heavy with death, clanging blades, talons tearing flesh, growls, cries, and the smell of blood. Bodies littered the ground, dryad, and wolf. She'd never been in a battle. Whether she was ready or not, it was before her.

Everything that came toward her, Eli hacked down. She gripped the sword and walked forward slowly, her eyes cutting through it all, searching for Tristan. Would she be able to know it was him? Half of the wolves were in beast-form, the other half came at them in man form with blades. Arrows flew around them, sinking into the ground, shadow sand spraying up into the air as they did.

Eli roared in rage. She glanced over. One of his friends was hit in the shoulder with an arrow, the sand entering his blood. She didn't know his name. He bent over and grabbed his head with his hands. His veins popped up purple. He fell, his body jerked once and then was still.

Her heart clenched. That's what would happen to Eli if the sand touched him. He'd be poisoned and die within seconds. Damned if she was going to let that happen.

Across the distance, she saw his eyes, those terrible beautiful, psychotic, blue eyes. Tristan stood away from the fighting, just watching, behind two beasts protecting him.

"Tristan!" her shout was louder than the fighting.

His gaze fixed on her and his jaw tightened. He said something to those guarding him and they both started toward her. She braced herself and moved forward to meet them, Eli firmly at her side.

The hulking monster coming her way was too strong for her, too fast. She only had a second to decide. She grabbed the sword and pulled the fluid blade, lengthening it into a spear instead, and threw it. The power of the Heart gave it speed and the end sank into the beast's stomach. He went down on his knees, trying to pull it from him. The spear lost shape and engulfed him in flames. He screamed once and died, burned down to the bones.

Eli faced off with the other one. She couldn't help. He didn't need her help, he moved so fast, so precise. Both of his axes sank into the top of the monster's skull. She looked back for Tristan. He was still in the same place. He pointed at her.

"You're still mine," his mouth formed the words and he drew a sword.

More wolves came at Eli. She needed a new weapon. Sophie grabbed the blood off her dress, mixing the color with her hatred and pulled it out into another sword. She swallowed. It would end now…

Only it didn't.

Just as she was about to move forward something stopped her. Tristan looked as well, his eyes burning, his mouth falling open, and he lowered his sword. It looked as if all the breath had been snatched from his lungs.

TWENTY ONE

Melina rose up from her bed, her pupils constricted again into tiny star shapes and began walking. She moved with no sound. No one saw her. No one heard her. Her eyelids blinked laboriously, but they didn't clear her eyes to the here and now.

He's out there. I will find him. My love. My destiny. I will find him.

She walked many miles, leaving a trail of blood, as the ground sliced into her bare feet. The morning chill on the breeze brought her body temperature low and her lips lost their color. She felt nothing. Only the pull, directing her forward into the forest.

Nothing startled her. Not even the battle around her. She glided through the fighting, none of it touched her. Screaming, hacking, blood, and bodies. She moved through it as though it weren't real, or she wasn't.

Melina gasped, her trance dissipating like steam, and her eyes clearing one second before they connected to his. He lowered his weapon as transfixed on her as she was on him. Light and fire and soul connected them across the distance. Hands, lungs, hearts, and souls tied together with the immortal cords of destined life mates.

They had never met before. And now she felt his heart inside hers. She knew his name...

Tristan...

He held still as she came to him. Unable to resist the pull, Melina wrapped her arms around his neck and kissed his mouth.

All I've ever wanted...she thought.

His soul tangled with hers. She felt it all. She knew it all. Everything he was coiled inside her. He was her destiny. She gave herself over to the light and heat of the soul bridge between them. Her hands ran down his arms and she took the sword from his hand. He let go.

She took a small step back and gazed at him. He was so beautiful. She committed his appearance to her memory before stepping forward again and thrusting the sword into his heart.

No, no, no, no...her heart cried out in agony as he fell. She felt the blade in her own heart.

Her scream ripped through the forest and tore the sky. Those remaining in the battle stopped fighting and looked at her.

She straddled him, pulling the sword from his chest. His eyes held hers, and in the last moment of his life, he reached up and caressed her cheek. "I love you," his voice rasped as he exhaled for the last time.

Tears burned her eyes and her voice cut through everyone as she cried out stabbing him again. The sound of her agony was jolted with moments of insane laughter as she continued to stab him over and over.

She cried, growled, laughed, screamed, cursed, and cried again.

His blood covered her skin, burning her like acid. She

didn't know what was happening around her. People approached her but she could barely perceive them. All of them were blurry as though underwater, their voices muffled.

She screamed at them when they tried to touch her. No one could touch her. And she wouldn't let anyone touch him. He was hers. His body grew cold next to her.

Melina had done something no other person in all of Regia had ever done. She killed her destined life mate. She became a shell. She'd committed suicide of the soul. Some piece of her clung to him just as some of him tainted her, like a bloody handprint on a wall. A stain she couldn't remove.

If only she could rewind...just to feel him touch her again. Just to look in his eyes.

Even if she had the chance, she'd kill him again. His soul was disgusting and made of bloodstained shadows. She wouldn't live tied to him. She wouldn't love him. And yet, against her will, she already did. She loved and despised him in equal measures. What had she done to deserve this?

Melina laid her head on Tristan's shoulder, a seed of madness germinating in her mind. She would find Destiny, no matter what she had to endure to get there, no matter the cost or the pain. She would find Destiny and make her answer for what she'd done to her.

 THE END

TENAYA JAYNE

DON'T MISS

FORSAKEN,

THE EXPLOSIVE CONCLUSION TO THE SHADOWS OF REGIA TRILOGY!

COMING SOON!

ABOUT THE AUTHOR

Reading my bio, huh?
Real life sucks. I bet you feel like that sometimes,
maybe even right now. That's why I write fantasy. I
need to escape depression, bitterness, bills,
illness...I could go on, but you get it. In the pages of
fiction, I can slay the dragons, triumph over the bad
guys, be immortal, and never struggle with love
handles. For a short time, I can let it all go, and be
everything I can't be in real life. Maybe you're
hurting right now. Maybe you're in the waiting
room of the hospital, or just stuck in traffic. I've
brought a portal. Come with me...Let's ditch this
crappy popsicle stand and go somewhere great,
where we can forget all this, at least for a while.

That's why I write. I'm not an author, I'm an escape
artist.

If you want to come play with me, visit
www.tenayajayne.com

Made in the USA
Columbia, SC
22 April 2018